STOLEN JEWEL

HOSTAGES

BOOK SIX

ALEXIS ABBOTT

PATHFORGERS PUBLISHING

Contents

CHAPTER 1

STEFAN

Hot drops of blood spatter my face.

No pain follows.

That's good. Must not be mine.

Vlad's.

My comrade for the evening.

I blink the red out of my eyes as lines crack across the windshield like a spiderweb.

I grab my gun on instinct. My reflexes are faster than Vlad's on a good day, let alone when he's wounded. I thrust the weapon into his lap, because we need cover. Immediately.

"*Gavno,*" he curses through his teeth in pain. He clutches the bullet hole in his shoulder. It's not his dominant arm, thankfully. He stubbornly pushes my offered gun away, grabbing his own weapon from its holster.

At least the adrenaline is flowing now.

Three shots split the otherwise quiet night.

We're on the outskirts of a sleepy upstate suburb, so no doubt some little housewife is furiously dialing the cops.

The bullets echo eerily out here.

There's no ricochet.

Vlad gives me a look of disgust as he pulls his arm back inside the speeding car.

"Who the fuck is this? Did someone get a tip off?!" he shouts as I veer the vehicle in a sharp right turn. His blood-damp hand wraps around the handle to keep upright.

We skid onto the exit ramp at a dangerous speed. I'm heading us toward the winding, lonely roads through the dark forest. If these people are looking for a bloodbath, we need a better battleground. We can't have a firefight in the middle of town.

"We're carrying four hundred grand in cash," I growl at Vlad. "It could be a cop for all we know. I told you this wouldn't go smoothly."

"Shut the fuck up," he snarls before pushing his arm out the window to fire off two more blind rounds. His shots are answered with a rapid pop of bullets from the enemy.

"Shit!" Vlad recoils in the passenger seat. This time they got his dominant hand.

Great.

The gun clatters to the floor between his legs and he clutches his injured fingers. Blood pours down his wrist and forearm, and his face has a disgusting pallor in the tailing car's headlights.

Before I can say anything, our pursuers shatter Vlad's rear-view mirror. Vlad flinches away from the open window to avoid the falling shards.

"Were we fucking set up? It shouldn't be like this!"

Vlad isn't the smartest comrade. I knew that within

moments of meeting the man. This time, however, we're of the same mind. There's a reason they've assigned me to more dangerous missions lately, such as this current bloody disaster in progress.

But there's no saying no when the Bratva gives you an assignment.

I snatch up my gun in my right hand and quickly aim it using the left rear-view mirror. Once my eagle eyes have narrowed in on the spots of light coming from the vehicle tailing us, I fire off a couple shots. The power of the gun jolts through my muscles as I pull my arm inside and glance back to see the carnage. One bullet grazes the top of the car and disappears into the darkened woods, but the other goes straight through the back window. There's a shout, and luckily, it's not Vlad this time.

The pursuers aren't slowing down, though.

"Take the wheel with your good hand." My voice is level but commanding. Basic training back in Russia has long been my default setting in crisis. "Now!"

Vlad seizes the wheel as I try to aim another shot through the mirror, stabilizing my arm on the side of the car. Sparks from a ricocheting bullet hit my door. I have to look away, and I lose the shot.

Vlad curses in Russian.

They're closing in on us, and a bullet grazes past my cheek. No time to aim. We need to build in some distance. I shoot low, and the bullet disappears under their vehicle before sparking beneath it. They veer, but I don't ease off. Another bullet finds their tire, and they're forced to hit the brakes to avoid hitting a tree.

I toss my gun to Vlad and take the wheel again.

"Reload for me."

My heart races as a faint smile curls my lips. My foot presses down on the gas, steadily picking up speed, and the wind tousles my hair. Everything's gone to shit, but I can't say I don't love this part.

Adrenaline pumps through my body, and I feel alive for the first time in months.

The roads are quiet, but I'm not counting on that lasting. We need to get away, and we're far from the route I'd planned to take. The cops my people bribed to keep the path clear won't be around to help us if some cowboy of a patrol officer catches us in a fire-fight.

Our pursuers don't share my caution.

They've recovered from the tailspin I put them in. Guess I only nicked their rim.

Fuck.

"You took us on a straight fucking road, Stefan!"

I grip the wheel tight to fight the urge to smack him. I swerve back and forth to evade the volley of bullets, but it's only a matter of time before they get lucky.

"If this happens anywhere near town, we're dead men. Gun. Now."

He fumbles to get the bullets into my gun, his fingers trembling. Not good. When he hands me the weapon, he goes back to clutching his wounds, and I know I'm in this by myself before long.

"You heard the boss. This has to be kept quiet."

His glare is scathing, and his helplessness is making him petulant.

"How the fuck are we going to lose them then?!" he snaps. He wraps his jacket around his injured hand to staunch the bleeding.

"We aren't."

I lean back in the seat, holding onto the wheel with one hand. In a quick motion, I put on the brakes and fire.

A blast fills the air, and I grin triumphantly.

Unable to offset the ruined balance of the blown tire, the pursuing car spins out. Tires and metal squeal on the rough asphalt. I grab the handbrake and whip around, screeching to a halt.

Vlad cries out and ducks down as our pursuers careen past us, anticipating fire.

They're still spinning as I throw the driver's side door open and leap out.

"Stay down, you're hurt!"

I dash over the hood of the company car for cover, taking aim at the pursuant vehicle as it finally comes to a stop.

"Fuck that!" Vlad barks back in defiance.

Whatever. It's his life to lose.

I have to focus on my target.

These men are out for blood. They will not get mine.

Vlad opens fire, shouting obscenities while his injured hand bleeds on his shirt. He's too amped up, and he's not even providing me suppression fire. He's going to be out of bullets in three, two…

My initial shot drops the first man getting out of the backseat with a weapon. The other two thugs are smarter, and they keep low as they exit. The driver mirrors me, taking cover behind the hood, but not before firing a shot at Vlad.

When I don't hear a grunt of pain from him, I know what has happened before his body even thumps to the ground a moment later.

No use going to check.

He's dead.

Idiot.

My jaw clenches tightly. Like most of the ill-tempered men I get saddled with on jobs, Vlad was an impatient hothead, likely to get himself killed out of careless bravado. I caught onto that within minutes of meeting the guy.

Still, I hate being right.

Few will mourn him, and I don't have time to be one of them.

I drop to my stomach, old reflexes as sharp as ever. Closing a dark eye, I stare down the sight of the gun and fire off two precise shots. Practice tempers the violent recoil in my wrist, and the hiss of their punctured tires is my reward. I compromised their cover.

Good.

They shout curses as they leap to their feet and try to run.

"Not so fast."

My next shot shatters the ankles of the passenger, dropping him to the ground with a bellow of agony. He rolls on the dirty asphalt with his knee pulled to his gut, moaning.

Springing back up to my feet, I take aim over the trunk of the car before the driver even knows where I've moved to. The man on the ground spots me, our eyes locking as he glares at me with gritted teeth. He raises his good arm to take a blind hip shot at me.

Unfortunately for him, I am faster.

Shooting him dead would have been quick and easy, but I take out his firing hand instead. He cries in pain, and his gun skitters down the road. I'm not sparing him out of mercy. I only need one goon to question.

The other gunman darts out, and he takes his eyes off of me for a split second. It's all I need. A single, precise shot to his head. It fires clean through, leaving a perfect, smoking hole in its wake.

He drops as quickly as Vlad did, like a heap of potatoes.

The victory goes uncelebrated.

I can't let my guard down yet.

My gun is raised at the ready as I stand up and cross the short distance between our cars toward the last wounded man.

Shit. He doesn't have long to live.

He's crawled a few feet, a trail of blood glittering on the asphalt.

Maybe he's dead already. He isn't moving.

My black steel toe boot nudges his side. He scowls at me, spitting up blood just before my heel presses into his throat.

I point my gun at his stomach as I look him in the eye.

"Who paid you to get yourself killed tonight?" I ask him in my gruff English that still carries a faint accent.

"Fuck you," he hisses, clutching his bleeding wrist and glaring up at me.

"No use protecting your boss now. You're a dead man. You don't owe anyone anything anymore."

"Could say the same for you, *kozyol.*"

Been a while since I heard that insult.

Wrenching all of his remaining strength, he whips a blade from his pocket. I sweep back away from the knife that comes arcing up toward me in a single, smooth motion.

I'm finished with him.

One gunshot is all it takes to put him down for good.

His arm drops flat at his side.

The unsettling silence after a fight sinks in as the ringing in my ears fades. I rub my jaw, the tension still coiled there, and Vlad's blood coats my fingers.

The natural sounds of the forest are diminished, the animals scared off by the gunshots.

It is not a peaceful silence.

It's an ugly one, and I still don't feel at ease when I put my weapon away and survey the scene.

I step over the dead bodies, cautious not to get blood on my boots. Once this is done, there will be no sign of me.

The assassin's car holds no leads. Just guns and blood and unanswered questions. No ID. No helpful business cards with their boss' name and address and hours of business. They got unlucky coming after the likes of me, but they weren't stupid enough to leave a trail.

"That would've been nice for once." My voice sounds strange in the uncomfortable silence.

A familiar, deep sense of loneliness haunts me like a shadow.

Fuck off.

I shrug off the unsettling sensation. I still have a mission to complete, and cleaning up the scene is almost therapeutic. The tire tracks might be a giveaway that Vlad wasn't the driver. That doesn't bother me. I'm betting whoever gets the call at the police station will be eager to wrap it up neatly without investigating too deep.

This is already a shit show, so I don't call my boss. Not yet.

For all I know, this was a fucking trap. If Brusilov had anything to do with this, I will not expose myself to another hit. Your enemies might kill you, but your friends? Just a matter of time. Never let someone get close enough to make me forget that a soft heart leads to a rotting corpse.

That's what life is as a made man in the Bratva. Constant paranoia. Violent nights. Days full of vice and loneliness. Not a terrible trade off. Most people are lonely without the vices to numb those away.

These three men?

Scum.

Little comfort, I know. I'm not proud of what I've had to do tonight, but we all have our crosses to bear.

Both vehicles are totaled, so once I've finished wiping down my fingerprints from the surfaces, I grab the duffel back from the back of the car.

I sling the heavy sack of cash over my shoulder.

The scene is still bloody, but it's devoid of evidence of me. A gift for the cops, a straightforward case to use as P.R. about cleaning up the city, or to get more funding.

I stalk down the road into the night. It's easy to forget just how dark the world can be outside the cities. I grew up in a concrete hell, but once in a while, during a blackout, I'd stare up at the stars and dream.

What did I used to dream about?

No time for memories.

Nothing pleasant to reminisce about anyway. Gotta bring my mind back to the present. If need be, I'll hitchhike. It's difficult getting a ride at my size, but my duffle bag will probably mark me as an innocent backpacker who got lost in the woods, if I'm lucky.

No lonely housewife called the cops after all, I guess. There are no sirens. Hell, even as the forest stirs again, it's subdued. I hate it. Leaves me with my thoughts. It's far better to drown those all out.

It's too quiet.

Damn it, what I wouldn't give for the din of the slums again. The smog of the factories blotting out the sky, poisoning everything it touched. All we had was each other, but those moments of kindness were always stolen away too soon.

My entire life has been nothing but piss and blood. What did they expect would happen to us in that place? A million people piled on top of each other, begging and stealing for scraps.

We had to get hard.

I had to be hard.

Individualism.

That's what the state wanted. That's what it got.

Selfish, cruel, lonely individualism.

And now, I don't know any other life but the one I have with the *bratva*. They're just as corrupt as the cops selling kids back home after the fall. Rich old men who care nothing for the people who secured their wealth; who pay for it with their own blood.

A bag of money for human lives is a steep price, regardless of how contemptible the humans are.

But there's always a worse assignment.

If I'm a marked man like I think I am, it's gonna find me soon.

Maybe it already has.

They have another job for me. Kidnapping this time. A young woman.

It's a new low for them. Rather, it's a new low they're pushing me towards. I've always had a code, and they've always respected it, begrudgingly. I would not fuck with kids, and I would not hurt a woman.

But this is the *bratva*. There's no way out except for a bullet.

Their foot is on my neck, and their gun is aimed at my head.

If I want out, I can't refuse.

My shadow appears in front of me. A car. They must have passed by the scene. There's not been any other on ramps since. I clutch the duffle bag's strap tight on my shoulder as my other hand goes to my gun.

CHAPTER 2

JEWEL

I stand with my back pressed up against the slightly slimy wall across from the busy bar counter, blinking into the darkness.

The dimly-lit cavern of the nightclub feels like an explosion of pure chaos all around me. Writhing bodies, drunken laughter, and rowdy conversations everywhere I turn.

Men high-fiving over the heads of giggly, tipsy young women.

Gaggles of sorority sisters mingle with droves of frat guys in their fuckboy finest.

There's a lot of people talking and dancing close, but I have a feeling there's little real connection going on here. This place activates my flight-or-fight response, and right now, I'm definitely leaning toward flight.

I want nothing more than to just get *out* of here as fast as I can, but unfortunately that's the one thing I'm not able to do. Obligations led me to this place, but my shyness keeps me tethered to the sidelines. I realize, with a sigh, that I'm a literal wallflower.

I feel my heart pounding in my throat as the harsh, throbbing music of the club fills not just my head but my very bones, making me twinge in discomfort every few seconds.

The pounding bass excites the crowd around me even more, buzzing under my feet like the earth is about to split open. I clutch my barely-touched vodka tonic and hope the tectonic plates aren't about to open up and swallow me whole.

Not that anyone would notice. Between the grim lighting, the strobes pulsing colored shafts of light around the room, and the clouds of smoke, I can barely breathe, much less see in a place like this.

It's safe to say this not my scene.

Not at all.

My head is already pounding even though I've only had a couple of typically watered-down mixed drinks. But I know it has nothing to do with the alcohol. I can hold my booze, but I'm less equipped for a pulsating crowd of horny strangers.

I have no idea where Gina, my roommate and so-called best friend, is hiding. This is supposed to be a night of celebration, a chance to blow off steam after nonstop studying, but the party feels even more stressful than the law exams I just took.

I'm supposed to be relaxing and unwinding, which for me would usually involve some nicely-scented candles, soft mood music, a good book, and a bubble bath. Maybe a glass of champagne if I'm feeling frisky.

But instead, I let myself get dragged out for celebratory

drinks. This is not the vision I had in mind for how my first year in law school would end. Then again, nothing about law school has really lived up to my hopes so far.

"Jewel!" I hear shouted at me through the dense crowd, and when I look around wildly, I realize just how disoriented I am. Every turn of my head feels delayed, like my brain is sloshing around in pickling juices inside my skull. Before I can make heads or tails of the situation, a sweaty hand grabs my arm and I yelp in terror, sending a splash of my drink spilling to the sticky club floor. My shoulders relax ever so slightly as I recognize Gina standing in front of me.

"I'm so sorry," I say abruptly, apologizing to her by reflex even though she's the one who surprised me into spilling my drink.

She barely seems to clock my words.

"Girl where have you *been?!*" she asks with a big, drunken smile on her face.

"Trying not to get trampled," I reply with a nervous laugh.

I rein in my composure in a matter of seconds, bringing me back from anxious to cool. It's one of the many unofficial skills competing with my fellow law students has taught me so far. Like withstanding cutthroat criticism or recognizing when someone's playing devil's advocate just to mess with my head. Law school is a challenge in and of itself.

"It's getting kind of crazy in here, isn't it?" I add, hoping she'll catch the hint that I'd like to get some air. Preferably air not contaminated with beer burps and vape clouds.

"What?" she says with a laugh as the music gets even

louder, drowning out my voice. She cups her hand around her ear like a cartoon character and I lean in closer.

"Want to step outside?" I shout insistently over the music, a hint of hope in my tone. I pull back to clock her response, hoping she'll take pity on me.

Oh no, there's the eye-roll. No such luck.

"We just got here!" she protests, which is just plain wrong. We got here easily two hours ago; I've been keeping track and counting down the minutes until it's a socially acceptable time to hightail it out of this chaos dungeon.

"I think I need a breather," I insist.

Rather than giving me a real answer, she merely smirks and takes me by the arm. I let her guide me toward what I think is an exit, for one hopeful moment.

Until we get closer and I realize it's just a cordoned-off outdoor area of the bar packed with just as many people and a circular fire pit glowing in the center. Still, at least there isn't a claustrophobic beveled metal veiling over my head or music blaring in my ears. I feel a touch of relief as I breathe in the cool night air and tuck an unruly lock of chocolate-brown hair behind my ear. Gina guides me easily through the crowd to an unoccupied standing table, which I seize upon with gratitude, like a drowning sailor clinging to a life raft in the raging sea. I prop up my elbows and lean in, idly swirling the tiny black straw in my drink.

"Here, if you don't want to celebrate our exams like a normal person," Gina begins in a lightly teasing tone that still very much comes across as a subtle jab. "Let's take a break out here and finish these drinks before another round, huh?"

The idea of downing another drink is the last thing on my mind right now, but if that's the going exchange for a much-needed breather, so be it.

"And hey, for real," she says, leaning forward in a softer tone and smiling at me as she takes my hand across the table. It's sweaty, very sweaty, yet sincere. "Relax, Jewel. We just made it through our first year of *law school,* girl! You ought to chill and let that sink in!"

Her words are a little slurred, but damn, maybe Gina isn't as drunk as I suspected.

"I-I know, I'm sorry," I reply quickly.

"Don't apologize," she interrupts, and I nod. She tips back her drink.

Working up my fortitude, I remind her, "I told you this just isn't my kind of thing before we left." I force a feeble smile after a big gulp of my drink, welcoming the burn of liquid courage down my throat. But my twisted nerves don't subside, not even with the vodka flooding my system.

"I don't know if getting tipsy is helping," I add.

"Okay, how about this to cheer you up," she says with a mischievous smirk. She squeezes my hand and raises it up to prop our elbows on the table and interlace our fingers together. There's a conspiratorial look on her pretty face.

She moves in close and lowers her voice to say, "We've been standing here being all cute and shit for like, less than a minute, and there are no less than three people checking us out I've counted so far."

"Oh. Wait. Th-that is not *good* news, Gina," I stammer, my heart dropping.

She just grins back at me, pleased with herself. I glance

over her shoulder around at the scattered crowd as subtly as I can, which isn't very. Sure enough, out of the sea of college frat guys and other rich kid students in the bar, some eyes seem to be drawn our way.

I sense Gina is being modest, or at least experiencing the closest thing to modesty she can manage. I don't hold it against her-- she's a young, hot, flirty woman with nothing to hide. And her salmon-pink bodycon dress certainly doesn't hide a thing. There's more than enough of her curvy body on display for me to be sure she's the one turning heads. Compared to my own flouncy baby-pink dress and powder-blue cardigan, especially.

I smile politely and sip more of my drink.

"Do any of them look like they're about to come over here?" I ask. I force myself to sound playful, but I'm trying to find out if I should brace myself for Gina to make eye contact with one of them long enough.

"I don't know, but that tall guy by the fire pit in the black sweater sure isn't looking at *me*," she says meaningfully. She flits her eyes in the direction of the low decorative fireplace in the middle of the square, urging me to check him out, too.

I take a breath and finish my drink before trying to look in that direction without being too obvious. But the guy she must have been pointing out stands out so easily, I've already noticed him out of the corner of my eye without realizing that his piercing gaze was fixed on me.

I tear my eyes away and glance back to my empty glass with blushing pink cheeks and a pounding heart. I don't know if it's because of his startling good looks or the sheer intensity of those dark eyes, but it's a feeling unlike any I've felt before. In a way that actually scares me a little bit.

As though I'm stricken by the intensity of my own feelings.

Even as I stare down into my drink, his image is frozen in my mind's eye like a crystal-clear photograph. My fingers itch to run through his thick, cropped black hair. His eyes are a vivid, powerful dark brown, wide and expressive under a strong brow. While everyone around us is bouncy with levity, he sticks out like a dark shadow. The light doesn't find him; it resists him. Something about the way he's dressed and the way he sits makes me think he isn't American, maybe some kind of European, but I don't want to assume.

Wait, why do I even care?

"Are you *okay*?" comes Gina's laughing voice, snapping out of my trance. "Jesus, girl."

"What?" I reply, wide-eyed. "What happened?"

"Are you *thirsty*?" she says in the same tone through a giggle, and my face goes redder.

"Oh my god, hush! He'll hear," I whisper urgently.

"You're totally crushing!" she squeals.

"No," I lie, "he just had this, like, really intense stare, and--"

She cuts me off with laughter, to the point that I can't help but resign to a halfhearted laugh myself as I let my face sink into my palm. I can't deny it. She's right. I was definitely zoning out on that fine-ass probable-European. But that's so unlike me. I need to splash some cold water on my face or something. Anything to get me out of this predicament.

"I need to go to the bathroom," I say, shaking my head. "Do you want to--?"

"I'll get our drinks, this one's on me," she says with a wink.

She gives me a nudge on my shoulder and flounces off to the bar counter, abandoning me at the standing table. I give a feeble laugh as I adjust my purse and look around, avoiding the direction of the guy whose eyes I can still feel piercing me from behind. A chill goes up my spine...but it's not the worst feeling in the world. Far from it, in fact. Without sharing a single word, this mysterious man seems to have hacked into my emotions. I feel a flash of something dangerously close to desire. I almost want to break my own rules. I almost want to give in.

Maybe I've had enough to drink.

With some more looks around, I put together that the women's bathroom in the outdoor area is right next to an exit through the stone wall enclosure to the parking lot where Gina's car is. Neither of us should drive tonight, and I can foresee a chaotic cab ride crammed with the students from our group who came out to party in my near future.

The bathroom is crowded, but it's at least a comforting crowd of harmless tipsy girls reapplying their makeup, gossiping, and taking mirror selfies. On my way to the mirror, I hear three to four compliments slur my way that I take gratefully before taking a long, deep breath in front of the sink and closing my eyes for a second or two to pray for my composure back.

No such luck. That same ticklish feeling along my spine remains. That same hungry flicker of desire. Longing to get closer, to fold into that man's strong arms...

I should be able to have a good time and relax, I tell myself. The night's still fairly young and, if Gina is any indication, anyone else I came here with isn't interested in leaving yet. I need to learn to do this kind of crap and be adaptable. Forget my worries for once and just enjoy myself like everybody else here seems to be doing.

My phone buzzes.

While a couple of girls loudly and enthusiastically complement each other's hair in the open stall behind me, I read a puzzling text from Gina.

> fuck my card fell out in the car!! can u get it?

I confiscated Gina's keys several drinks ago, and rather than feeling annoyed by her request, I actually feel a little relief. Finally, an excuse to get some air away from the bar. I reply quickly that I'll get it to her ASAP. I put my phone away and hurry out of the bathroom and around the corner, thankful for an excuse to flee.

The low heels of my boots click on the asphalt as I weave my way through the cars. It's quiet and fairly empty of human beings. Most of the lot is full and the hour is still too early for people to be thinking about leaving yet.

It's the most pleasant sense I've felt all night, I realize with a twinge of regret.

What is the matter with me?

Why can't I just relax and have a good time like my supposed friends? Am I really so boring and studious that I can't hang?

Gina's compact white car's lights flicker as I use the remote key to unlock it, and I open the passenger's side to hop in and start searching the floorboards for her lost debit card. My fingers brush over the fibers of the carpet when I feel the hairs on the back of my neck stand on end.

I turn my head toward the back seat almost at the same time that I feel a strong hand lurch out and grab me by the back of the head.

I have no time to let out a scream before he shoves a cloth up against my face that smells strongly of chemicals.

Panic floods my veins.

I put my hands on his arms to dig my nails into his sleeves, feeling rock-hard muscle underneath. But my resistance is futile; he is infinitely stronger than me.

The world goes dark and my body feels fuzzy all over.

Finally, my eyes roll back in my head and my knees buckle beneath me, my body going limp in his hands.

Chapter 3

Stefan

You would be amazed to find how easy it is to get away with certain crimes.

Well, the majority of crimes, in my experience.

For example, breaking and entering is child's play.

You would be surprised how many people simply leave their doors and windows unlocked at night. I can't fathom it, the idea of living without paranoia. Without the expectation of adversaries lurking around every corner just waiting for a lapse in vigilance to attack.

But optimism is a luxury I've never been able to afford.

I can't let my guard down that way. A life spent looking over my shoulder and double-bolting doors has taught me that. For me, there's always going to be another nemesis, another battle. So, I've had to learn the tricks of the trade.

Picking a pocket in a crowd, slipping through a cracked window or jiggly side door under cover of night, sneaking up behind an unsuspecting enemy to press my blade to his throat before he even realizes I'm there: these are all skills I had to develop from a young age.

Just part of the life I was thrust into.

Youth is supposed to be a time of freedom, adventure, measured risks with ample rewards.

Pushing the boundaries of the little world you grew up in, but still enveloped by the safety of that world.

With parents, teachers, and community all conspiring happily together to keep you safe from harm. Protected from any true hardship. True conditioning.

It always struck me, as a young man, to think about that Other Life. The one never offered to me, the one I could never fully grasp because it felt so alien to my own. Around the world, there were teenage boys throwing parties, landing a first kiss, and learning about biology or math or how to read a poem properly. But my experience could not have been more different back then.

The skills I picked up aren't the type you learn in any school I've heard of. The people who brought me up did so with discipline, not love.

And the outcome of all that cold, loveless training is evident in me, in every decision I make and step I take.

Confidence is integral to my ability to stay alive. I can't hesitate when a target steps into my crosshairs. It may be my only shot, and it's kill or be killed. I can't lie awake at night, agonizing over the horrors I've seen and the violence I've caused. My days are hard, and I need every wink of sleep I can get. But at the same time, I have to sleep with one eye open, at least metaphorically. I trust no one, and no one fully trusts me. It's the only way I've ever known.

Perhaps this is not the life I would have chosen for

myself. But as I sit in this stolen car with my hands perfectly relaxed on the steering wheel, driving deep into the woods with a human life as cargo, I have to wonder what it says about me that these nefarious skills come so naturally. I imagine most people would feel some remorse, at least some discomfort about the dark things I've been asked to do. The truth is, I can usually push away those nagging questions about whether or not I'm doing the right thing. I just assume I'm not. It's easier that way. I do bad things for bad people, and usually I can accept that.

Still, this mission is...different.

Getting into the car and lying in wait to ensnare my human prey in her clacky heels and pretty dress was easier than most such ambushes I've had to perform. But usually, my target is a man with blood on his hands. Some lackey who wouldn't think twice about killing me. I've never had to go after a civilian like this, especially not a woman. I've kept my hands clean of what I consider the *bratva*'s dirtiest work by proving myself skilled enough to stay among the hardened men who would stab me in the back without a moment's hesitation. But over time, the bosses have figured out my only weakness: I don't like this kind of dirty work. In their eyes, that's a problem. Weakness must be forced out by whatever means necessary.

That's why they assigned me to kidnap this girl.

The only reason I accepted is because if I were to pass it up, the bratva would only assign someone far less gentle than me for the job. I don't trust these men enough for that; so much so that I choose to work alone. I don't need backup, anyway. More men means more bodies, more potential for betrayal.

The fewer people who know where we are, the better.

Right now, that's just me. It's a liberating realization, that for a brief window of time, I'm almost free. Almost. But obligation ties me to the cargo in my trunk.

I see the silhouette of a deer bound across the road far up ahead, and I'm starting to see more stars in the clear night's sky, telling me I'm getting farther and farther away from civilization. It will be a shock for her.

I do my homework before a job, especially a high-profile one like this. I know more about this girl than she would like. Jewel Albany, the young woman bound up in the trunk, seems to have lived a very comfortable life so far. Her father is an ICE agent on the take, and I have a feeling that *bratva* bribes probably helped pay for that fancy law degree she's working on. Law school is no picnic in the park, so she's most likely a hard worker, and I have no plans to underestimate her tenacity or intelligence. I can imagine that her beauty distracts from how smart she probably is. But that doesn't mean this brat won't be a pain in the ass at best, or a liability at worst. All my research still can't fully prepare me for her personality. Her reactions to being captured and held against her will. Nobody takes well to those circumstances, but whether she'll be a puddle of tears or a wildcat with claws is yet to be seen. I'll know more when she awakens.

It's deep into the night when I turn the engine off in front of the safehouse far in the woods. I don't know how long this will be my home base, but it's stocked for months, and I know how to lie low. This place has long been abandoned and partly overgrown on the exterior, not that much of it is even visible this close in the darkness. It's nothing much to look at in the light, either. Every sorry inch of the place is familiar to me.

It's perfect.

And with my recent renovations, there will be no chance for Miss Albany to escape. That's the most important part. For me, this is a temporary home, but for her it's more of a cage. I calmly take the binding ropes out from the back seat to prepare to do what needs to be done. As I walk around back to the trunk, I wonder how my new, unwilling housemate will fare.

I loop the rope over my muscular forearm and reach for the key to pop the trunk. I never asked for her, but she's mine now. But I remind myself that if she weren't, she'd be in the hands of someone far, far worse.

THE REMAINDER of the night passes slowly. I usually sleep well, but for some reason, I toss and turn. Still, I rise before dawn. The sun has just begun to carry light into the kitchen to find me bent over a stove, moving scrambled eggs and chopped maple sausage around in the frying pan. I hear the toaster pop behind me, two perfect slices of wheat toast steaming and fragrant. I smear a generous amount of butter on the hot toast and tip the eggs onto two plates. Some of this high-protein breakfast is for me, but some of it is for my new guest.

Jewel will wake up soon, and it's time to make introductions.

Of course, I'm under orders to keep her starved for the first day so that she's 'easier to work with,' but she doesn't need to know that, and my bosses don't need to know that I'm forgoing their instructions. I'm feeding her because hungry people do foolish things, and a cooperative one is easier to keep secret. I have no wild expectations of building a real connection with her. She's still my captive, my assignment. But I don't want her to get the idea in her head that braving the wilderness is safer than staying with me. Not only would her escape be trouble for me, but there's no way a girl like her would survive long in the deep woods. So, it's in everyone's best interests to approach her with some softness. She will respond better to friendliness than fear.

Leaving my own plate in the microwave for now, I carry Jewel's plate of sausage, eggs, and toast down the rickety stairs to the old basement. I wait at the door, holding my breath while I close off all other senses and simply listen. I hear the distant chirp of birds outside, the rustle of wind through the tree branches. Through the basement door, I can only detect the faint, rhythmic pull and sigh of Jewel's breath as she sleeps. My shoulders relax a little. I'm careful to avoid any jangling as I slowly fit the key into the basement lock and give it a turn. There's a soft click, and the door parts open just enough for me to peek inside.

The sight before me sucks all the air from my lungs. The girl is lying across the rudimentary bed with one leg pulled up and the other stretched out. Her free arm is tucked underneath the single pillow, while the other is handcuffed to the metal headboard. I can see the dried tracks of tears on her cheeks. She must have woken from her drugged haze last night, semi-conscious just long enough to be frightened before she cried herself back to sleep. My heart, typically buried under a permafrost of unfeeling cold, twinges a little.

The safehouse is built into a slight hill, so that the basement room has one very narrow window near the ceiling. Strands of sunrise spill through the tiny window and cast across the bed, drenching Jewel in golden light. Her breasts rise and fall with her soft breathing. Her flimsy pastel dress exposes her long, shapely legs and a peek of her panties. I can't look away. Her rich brown hair glistens in a messy halo around her head on the pillow. My eyes follow the curve of her cheekbones and the swell of those plush, full lips. Her long lashes flutter gently as her eyes move behind her eyelids. I wonder what she's dreaming about. Is she in a warmer, kinder place right now? Would it be unduly cruel to wake her up to her harsh new reality?

I stop and remind myself of who her father is, and that the apple likely does not fall far from the tree. Freddie Albany is a terrible man, and I would do well to assume his progeny is just as awful. Even if she does look like a delicate angel sprawled across the bed with her own tears barely dry on her cherubic face. As I step into the room, she slowly starts to stir. I harden myself against her. She's not my guest, she's my captive, and I have to treat her accordingly.

When she first opens her eyes, she looks confused. Her hands move up to her head and she winces with pain. There's a split second of trying to figure out where she is before her expressive green eyes land on me. They go wide and her mouth falls open in a silent scream. Still weak from her rough night and handcuffed to the bed, she scrambles to scoot as far from me as possible. She presses herself against the headboard and pulls her knees up to her chest, making herself small. She tries to lift her arms to shield herself, but she realizes her wrist is still cuffed, which causes her even more distress. Jewel looks over at me with pure terror in her eyes. She's starting to hyper-ventilate as I step closer with the plate of food.

"St-stay away from me! Leave me alone!" she cries out bitterly.

I don't say a word but walk closer. With every step she shrinks back more, until she's basically climbing the head-board to get away from me. I keep my expression cold and unreadable as I set her plate down at the end of the bed.

"Eat. You'll be here a while," I tell her gruffly.

"Where am I? Who are you?" she asks in a trembling voice. "Why am I here?"

"You can blame your father, the ICE agent," I reply pointedly.

Her lower lip quivers. "What did he do?" she asks.

"He arrested one of my colleagues. More than arrested him-- your daddy took him to a very, very bad place," I go on.

Jewel shakes her head. "I don't know anything about that, I promise!" she insists.

I wave my hand dismissively. "Doesn't matter. You don't have to know a thing. All I need for you to do is be a good girl for me. That, and hope your father is willing to negotiate."

"Please, just let me go. I won't tell anyone about you. I won't even tell my dad," Jewel pleads with me.

Her big green eyes are captivating, and it's almost diffi-cult to resist her. But if I can shoot a man dead without blinking an eye, I can definitely handle one beautiful, fragile young woman. I have to scare her enough to keep her at arm's length. She needs the fear of death in her soul to deter her from doing anything stupid.

"You think it's that simple?" I smirk. "You think I can

just let you go after everything your father has done? No. Someone has to pay for his crimes, and if you don't behave, that someone will be you."

I stare at her a moment, letting the darkness of my threat sink in. I can see tears welling up in her beautiful eyes. I harden myself against her. I won't let my heart be swayed.

"In the meantime, you will do exactly as I say. Get comfortable with this room, because it's now your home. I will not tolerate disobedience or insolence. Make no mistake-- this is not a five-star hotel. This is a holding cell. However, I won't starve you, and I won't hurt you...unless you leave me no other choice. Do not push me to that point," I warn her.

She gulps.

I continue on, gesturing vaguely toward the outside world.

"Out there, you may be a spoiled princess. Daddy's little girl. But in here, you belong to me only. You are my prisoner, and you will abide by my rules," I command.

"Please," she begs. "I'm not who you think I am. I'm nothing like my father, I swear."

"I know quite a lot about you, actually," I reply, sauntering along the side of the bed.

With every step I take closer to the headboard, she pulls back. She's straining away from me, her cuffed arm sticking straight out. A tear rolls down her cheek as she tilts her face up to look at me. I feel the strangest urge to cup her cheek, to caress her impossibly smooth skin. But instead, I stand taller and loom over her, using my formidable size to intimidate the girl.

"I've done my homework on you, Jewel Albany," I

growl. "And have you been doing *your* homework? How did you like your classes this semester? What about your teachers? Did you cover a situation like this in your law exams this week, little attorney?"

She's stunned into silence as I reveal just how closely I've been monitoring her.

"You're a good student. A fast learner, I bet. So, I'm hoping you'll catch on quickly to the way things go around here," I explain. "I don't leave tracks. Nobody knows where you are. Nobody is coming to save you."

"I'll do whatever you want. Please, anything," she whimpers as a fat tear rolls down her cheek and drops to the pillow in her arms.

"I'm not the one to bargain with," I reply. "Your fate lies in your father's hands."

Somehow, this seems to be the most frightening thing I've said so far. Jewel goes ghostly pale and she starts breathing fast and hard. Her eyes flit around the room, a look of absolute horror on her face as my words sink in. Her mouth twists up and she buries her face in the pillow, her shoulders shaking with sobs.

Watching her dissolve into panicked weeping, I slowly back away out of the room. As I close and lock the basement door, I can still hear her crying. I feel a slight pull of guilt leaving her in tears like this, but it's for her own good. And for the good of the bratva. It's better that she feels afraid and hopeless; it will keep her from trying anything brave. I force myself to wrench away and go back upstairs. I walk into the kitchen and start picking at my breakfast, but suddenly I have very little appetite. Instead, I take out my phone and call my boss to check in.

The line rings three times, and then I hear Brusilov's grimy voice answer, "Stefan."

"I'm here. The deed is done. The girl is secure," I report.

"Good. Very good."

"Have the demands been sent to Freddie yet?" I ask him.

Brusilov gives a grunt of uncertainty and says, "It's in the works."

"What does that mean?" I ask.

"It means you should keep doing what you're doing. Continue with the plan. You stay put, only leave when absolutely necessary. Do not allow this girl even a fraction of freedom or she will take it and run," he says with disgust.

"I can handle her," I retort.

"Good to hear, Stefan. Don't be afraid to be firm with her. Show the girl that we mean business. A little fear never killed anyone. Make her understand that you are in control by whatever means necessary."

Something about his wording makes me grimace.

"She's not going anywhere on my watch," I assure him.

He chuckles grimly. "I know you have a weakness for the fairer sex. Especially one so enticing. But you must show her the same cruelty you reserve for other missions."

His words sting a little, but only because I know he's right. I don't enjoy harming women or any other innocents. That makes me too lenient by the bratva's standards. But I brush it off.

"I'm on it, boss. You can trust me," I assert.

"Good. Prove it," Brusilov says, and promptly hangs up.

I tuck the phone in my pocket and, with one last lingering look toward the stairs to the basement, I stalk off to my own bedroom to clean my arsenal. I spend the day patching up the safehouse, getting it back to full working order after a period of disuse. I keep my hands busy. I don't make another trip down today to see my captive. I want her to take the time alone to really consider the gravity of her position. I want to let that fear percolate and intensify in my absence. But although I keep away from her, I'm unable to keep my mind from wandering down the stairs and into that basement cell. I think about her dark chocolate hair and her emerald eyes. I replay the way the morning light danced across her body. By the time night falls and I retire to my bed for the evening, my head is so filled with thoughts of Jewel that I dream about her.

She's on the other side of a door. I hear her crying. I keep trying to grab the handle to throw the door open and get to her, but my hands won't work. The handle keeps disappearing, and Jewel cries and cries.

The next morning, I'm awoken with a bang from downstairs.

I jump to my feet and grab my gun, rushing down to the basement.

CHAPTER 4

JEWEL

I have never been so afraid in my life.

Ever since I first woke up to find myself hand-cuffed to a rudimentary cot in a place I don't recognize at all, my adrenaline levels have been at peak capacity. Every cell in my body is on high alert, like someone tripped an alarm somewhere in my brain. I'm sitting on the bed, soaked in paranoia.

The walls here seem pretty well-insulated, but still, I keep hearing things. Distant thumps and creaks through the building, the occasional bird call or blustery wind outside.

Every noise makes me jump.

I stare bug-eyed at the door, waiting with mingled dread and anticipation for it to swing open again. I rico-chet between being terrified that my captor will come back, and terrified that he *won't* come back.

I can't figure out which one is worse.

My mind runs wild with frightening potentials. What if

he leaves me to rot in this room? What if he has more nefarious plans for me? What if he's right, and my father is the only one who can save me? If that's the case, I might as well die here. These fears cycle through my head again and again. I roulette from one terrifying idea to the next, all the while desperate to corral my thoughts into something actually useful.

After all, I'm not a fool. I'm a clever, resourceful woman who just survived my cutthroat law exams. I should be figuring out how to get out of here. I should be putting my academic brain to use. But it's hard to take action when everything feels so hopeless. My stomach is churning and won't settle. My hands have been trembling the whole time, especially my right arm latched to the metal headboard of the cot. I reach over and rub comforting circles on my aching, bruised wrist. I wince in pain, having just realized how deep the bruise goes. I must have strained against my bindings in my sleep. Not that there is much sleep to be had down here.

My heart is pounding like it's about to burst out of my chest and fly away. Like a panicked bird fighting to break free of my ribcage. I feel a bit like a bird myself right now, trapped in this musty, decrepit room. There's nothing here to look at, apart from the cot and a toilet just barely close enough to the bed for me to use it. There's a single toilet roll on the back of the commode, and a few cloth napkins folded at the foot of the cot. I imagine I was supposed to use those along with the plate of breakfast my captor brought me, but I hardly touched it. I mean, this guy did use some kind of chemical to knock me out and kidnap me, so I don't exactly trust him not to poison my food.

Still, I know I'll eventually have to eat if he keeps me here long enough. I don't want to think about this as a long-term situation, but maybe I'll have to.

It's difficult to tell exactly how much time has passed since I was so cruelly ripped from my life and dumped here. There's no clock on the four walls of the cell, and I can only assume my charming kidnapper must have confiscated my phone along with everything else in my purse. The only means of measuring time I have is the amount of light coming in through that high-up, narrow window. For a woman who's used to being attached to my cell phone twenty-four-seven, it feels like an even sharper blow to be without it.

I'm the kind of person who repeatedly checks the time, the weather, the news, garnering every bit of helpful information I can gather in the palm of my hand. I'm accustomed to being able to check every time zone, just because I want to. But now, all time feels the same. Without a digital number to go by, minutes feel as long and agonizing as the hours. Shadows move on the walls. Light trickles in and fades away. It's maddening to just sit here while the world turns without me. I have done everything I can think of to keep myself from going totally insane.

I replay the events of the other night at the club. I remember wanting so badly to escape the crowds, the loud music, the obligation to my friends. Now, I feel foolish for longing to be alone. What I wouldn't give for a vapid, mostly one-sided conversation with Gina right now! That feels more like my life, what I expect.

But this?

Being kidnapped and held hostage by a massive, intimidating (but oddly handsome) stranger with a faint Russian accent? This is not my world. This is not what I ever thought could happen to me. Sure, I know my father doesn't have the cleanest hands. He's a man of great power and influence, and I'm not naive enough to think he's above corruption. In fact, he's always made it very clear that the best way to climb the ladder of success is by stepping on the heads of everyone else in your way. But I never imagined he could be involved with something on this level. I wonder what he did to my captor's friends, and if it's a fair trade for whatever is about to happen to me. I wonder if my dad would even feel remorse. Would he change his ways to get me safely home?

The lurch in my stomach tells me… probably not.

I wish I remembered more of how I got here. Maybe then I'd have some idea how far from home I really am. But I recall nothing after being grabbed from behind and forced into darkness. I woke up to find that man standing in the doorway with a plate of food, watching me sleep. A shiver runs down my spine as I sit in the dark and play back that moment again and again. I see his bulging muscles, his enormous height, his cold, dark eyes, and unfeeling expression. I hate that I feel drawn to him as much as I fear him. Is this an early inkling of Stockholm Syndrome? Am I so weak-hearted that one plate of eggs could make me empathize with my own kidnapper?

"No," I murmur aloud.

My voice sounds rough from lack of use. And crying. I glance up toward the narrow window to see the pale first tendrils of dawn peeking through. Morning is coming. And with that, perhaps another visit from my captor. My heart flutters at the thought of him coming back. What if this time, instead of breakfast, he brings a weapon? I have to get out of here before then. I look around the room again, wracking my brain for an answer. With my arm still cuffed to the headboard, I slowly twist myself around and slide off the side of the cot. My toes curl when they touch the cold floor. I lean as hard as I can into the metal frame of the cot.

"Please be quiet," I mutter.

The metal legs scrape on the dusty floorboards and I wince. I hold my breath and listen for any retaliatory sounds. My heart pounds in my ears, but I don't hear any footsteps or voices. I push against the cot again, this time sliding it a couple feet closer to the side wall.

"Almost there," I whisper.

Using all my strength, I shove the headboard flush against the wall. I climb onto the bed and wrap my hands around the metal prongs of the headboard. I take a deep breath and start banging the headboard into the wall as hard as I can. I pound my fist against the wall. I cry out with my face pushed into the dusty wallpaper, begging for some neighbor to overhear me.

"Help! Help me!" I yell, punctuating my words with thumps against the wall.

I know I only have a short window of time to do this before my captor hears me. It's a major risk, but I have to try. I can't stay here a moment longer in limbo. Whatever happens, at least it'll be a change from waiting for nothing in the dark.

"Please! Somebody help!" I cry out, pounding my fist against the wall while I use my cuffed hand to slam the headboard. The wall rattles. I feel blood gathering under my skin as my hands bruise, but I don't stop. Not even when I hear the telltale thump-thump-thump of heavy footsteps coming down the stairs. Adrenaline pumps through my veins. I scream louder.

There's a momentary rattle of keys, and then the door bursts open with a bang. I fall down on the cot and flip around to look as this absolute mountain of a man steps into the room. My heart skips when I see the pure rage in his dark brown eyes, his hands curling into big fists at his sides as he approaches me. I shrink back, but I keep my eyes locked on him. I wear a defiant look on my face even as frightened tears sting in my eyes.

"What the hell are you doing?" my captor bellows.

"What do you think I'm doing? I'm calling for help! And somebody had to hear me out there. Somebody's probably calling the cops on you right now!" I shout back.

"Who? Who is coming to save you?" he growls coldly. "There's nobody around for miles, *malyshka*. No neighbors. No one to hear you scream."

Hot, angry tears burn down my cheeks. "There has to be someone," I choke out.

"The only people you're likely to attract out here with all this racket are people way worse than me," he snaps. "The wrong kind of people."

"Hard to imagine anyone worse than a man who kidnapped me and handcuffed me to a shitty bed," I retort fiercely.

"Then count yourself lucky you haven't encountered them yet," he snarls, taking another aggressive step closer.

"How can I possibly believe you? How can I trust a word you say?" I shoot back.

He heaves a sigh and shakes his head slowly, looming over me. I feel instantly smaller, delicate and diminutive compared to his hulking size and presence. His large, calloused hand reaches out and I flinch away, thinking he's about to hit me. But instead, he wraps his fingers around the metal headboard and yanks it back a few feet. What took me several full-body pushes he's able to undo with one hand. My eyes go wide and my heart stumbles over a beat as I realize, once again, how formidable he is. How much stronger he is than me. If he could move the cot with me on it so easily, what could those powerful hands do to my body? It both terrifies and thrills me to think about.

"I warned you before: my colleagues are not as forgiving as me. When I say this-- all of this-- is for your own good, I mean it. I know you're afraid. You're desperate. You want to fight back, even if it's just to feel like you're doing something," he says in a low voice.

I bite my lip to staunch the tears from falling. I hate that he's right.

He softens his voice and bends down slightly to look me in the eyes.

"Listen to me, Jewel. It will be much easier if you cooperate with me," he asserts.

"Cooperation is a two-way street," I reply, after gathering my courage.

He narrows his dark eyes at me and gestures to the bed, the handcuffs, the holding cell itself. "And what leverage do you have?" he growls.

I hold my head up high and poke out my chin defiantly. It's time to tap into my lawyer mode. I need an argument, even a weak one.

"Well, even if nobody can hear me scream out there,

you can still hear me. If we're stuck here together, that means you can't leave. And that means you have to listen to me scream. I bet that will get old pretty quickly," I threaten.

I see a flicker of something akin to a smile pass over his face, and then he glowers at me like before. "I'm not going to let you go," he says firmly.

"You could at least take off this stupid handcuff," I argue.

He scoffs. "Hell no. I'll put a gag in your mouth before I do that."

"A gag won't stop me. I'll just push the bed and bang on the wall again," I point out.

"Maybe I should handcuff your other arm. Your ankles, too," he warns.

"Well, then, have fun cleaning up after me when I can't reach that toilet," I remind him.

"Something tells me you would be even more uncomfortable with that than I am," he reasons. He folds his arms over his chest and fixes me with a cold stare.

Damn it. He's right. I don't even like to go more than a day without a shower back in my regular life. But I can't give up just because he's backed me into a corner. The longer I keep him here, the more likely he is to listen to me. At least, that's what I tell myself.

"Okay, fine. Handcuffs are non-negotiable for you. Got it," I sigh. "But what about this awful cot? This mattress has to be older than I am. And only one lumpy pillow? Who can sleep like this? I'm going to be up all night, every night, just thinking of ways to escape. You have to fall asleep sometime, you know, and I bet your bed is a lot more conducive to sleep than mine."

"What are you bargaining for, memory foam?" he scoffs.

"I'm just saying, if there really is nobody around to save me, why do you need to keep me down here in the dark? At least give me some scenery to look at," I contend.

"I had a feeling you would be a spoiled brat," he hisses.

I glare at him. "Well, I'm sorry for being a high-maintenance *prisoner*."

He stares at me for a moment, his expression unreadable. His eyes bore into my very soul as he looks me up and down. Sizing me up like a wolf regarding his prey.

"Fine. You want a change of scenery? How about this," he grunts.

In one quick step, he closes the space and grabs one of the cloth napkins at the foot of the bed. I yelp and cower away from him, curling up in a ball. But he easily unravels me. He grabs my free hand and pins it behind me to the headboard, my arm aching with the strain.

"Ow, ow, ow," I mutter as he deftly wraps the napkin around my head, covering my eyes.

My heart sinks. Is he really going to leave me like this? But no sooner has that thought occurred to me than I hear the rustle of keys. I feel him fiddle with the handcuff. There's a soft *clank!* and my arm drops to my side, free at last. I breathe a sigh of relief, but it's short-lived. With my eyes still blindfolded, my captor scoops me to my feet. He wrenches both arms behind my back and prods me along in front of him, forcing my cramping legs to walk across the cold floor. I stumble blindly, but he holds me steady. My heart is racing.

"Where are you taking me?" I ask.

"For a change of scenery and a better mattress," he grunts. "Take the stairs."

With his guidance, I wobble my way up the staircase. I try to use my remaining senses to figure out where I am, but it's impossible to orient myself with my eyes covered and my hands pinned behind me. We walk across creaky floorboards, the air feeling warmer and less stagnant. I swear I can almost feel sunlight on my face as he prods me down what seems to be a long hallway. He stops me and opens a door, then pushes me inside.

"Where am I?" I murmur.

"The bedroom," he replies.

I complain, "Can't I at least see where--"

But he quickly whips off the blindfold. Bright, warm light beams into my eyes as I blink. The world comes slowly into focus as I look around, drinking in my surroundings. It's a very simple room, but compared to the basement, it's a feast for my eyes. There's a queen-sized bed with a thick mattress and a utilitarian wooden frame, a tall amber lamp in the corner, a threadbare rug on the floor, and a dusty mirror hanging on the wall next to a ticking clock. As I look around, I'm surprised to see my captor stalk out of the room, leaving me alone for a split second. I immediately glance at the window, but before I can fully form a coherent thought about escaping some-how, he returns. But he's not empty-handed.

He's pushing a couch through the doorway as easily as though it's a sack of feathers. I look at him sideways, trying to make sense of it.

"What's this about?" I pipe up.

Satisfied with the position of his couch, he strides over

to me and grabs my arm. He all but drags me to the bed and throws me onto it. I bounce a little on the springy, soft mattress as he pulls me to the headboard. He pulls out the handcuffs from his back pocket. My heart sinks as he clinks it around my left arm this time, and connects it to one of the wooden spokes of the headboard. Once it's locked, he tucks the key in his pocket and steps back.

"How do you like your upgrade, madame?" he grumbles.

"Well, the bed's much nicer, but what is the couch for?" I ask.

He raises an eyebrow. "I have to sleep somewhere."

"Wait, so I've gone from having my own room to sharing one with *you*?" I exclaim.

"Would you rather us share the bed, too?" he threatens.

I hate that I feel a little twinge of something deep inside. I shove it down.

"Of course not," I reply sharply. "But what about if I have to, you know, use the bathroom or something?"

"Then I'll take you," he answers.

I wrinkle my nose. "I'm starting to think this upgrade is anything but."

"Well, take it or leave it," he shrugs as he turns to walk out of the bedroom. "Don't try anything stupid, *malyshka*."

"What does that mean?" I mutter under my breath as he disappears through the doorway.

But he doesn't come back, not for several hours, according to the clock on the wall. I spend the time lying around on the bed, taking in every detail of my new digs. It's definitely more to look at, and infinitely more comfortable. It feels more like an actual bedroom than a cold, musty prison cell. However, I'm nervous about the idea of my kidnapper sleeping on that couch. He'll be even closer to me now, able to catch me before I even think of pulling an escape run. What little privacy I had has evaporated along with it.

Still, I can't help feeling like I won a small battle. Only two days into my captivity and I've already managed to barter for a better room. That has to count for something. So, I decide to settle in and catch up on some desperately-needed rest while I'm alone for a while. I lie back on the bed, close my eyes, and let the soft sounds of nature outside lull me to sleep.

I'm in and out of cozy consciousness for the bulk of the day. Every time I drift off, I have wild and vivid dreams. I wake up with a start, my wrist aching from being held in the same position in the handcuff. Each time, the room is a little darker. Every now and then, I can hear my captor walking or tinkering around in the rest of the house. He keeps the bedroom door shut, presumably so I can't figure out the blueprint of the building, but the added privacy is appreciated during my naps. The last thing I want is to wake up and find him watching me sleep again. I still haven't quite recovered from my first brutal awakening here.

By the end of the day, I lie on the bed watching the sunset paint the sky pink and gold through the single window. I watch the trees sway in the evening breeze. I really have to pee, but more than that, I am itching for a shower. My hair feels greasy and knotted around my head, and my body is coated in sweat and grime. I've been wearing nothing but my flimsy dress, and I feel positively grubby. Showers and baths have always been a favorite relaxation tool of mine. I fantasize about standing under hot water in a steamy shower stall and feeling the ick rinse off my body. I know there's a bathroom somewhere around here.

When my captor finally returns to the bedroom at nightfall, I'm damn near excited to see him. I perk up and immediately shuffle to the edge of the bed. He looks just as intimidatingly handsome as always, but there's an exhaustion to his movements. He must have been working on something today. Or maybe keeping me hostage is more taxing than I thought.

Good, I think sourly. If I have to suffer, so does he.

But for now, I give him a big, sheepish smile and he immediately knows I'm about to ask him for something. He sighs.

"What is it?" he prompts.

"Where's the bathroom?" I ask, like he's a hotel concierge and not a dangerous criminal.

"I'll take you to pee, but I'm going to blindfold you first," he says, whipping out the cloth napkin again as he walks over to me.

"Wait!" I blurt out. "I need more than that."

He grimaces and I blush instantly.

"No, not that. I need a *shower*," I emphasize.

"You look fine to me," he reports.

I roll my eyes. "Maybe to you, but I feel gross. I won't be able to sleep tonight if I don't get a shower first," I leverage.

"You know, I have ways of keeping you quiet I haven't used yet," he says ominously.

But I stay strong. "Wouldn't it just be easier to let me

get cleaned up? Come on, it's not like I'm going to escape through the plumbing or whatever," I argue.

"Fine," he grunts. He uncuffs me and wraps the blindfold around my eyes. "But I'm staying in the room with you to stand guard."

"But I'll be *naked* in there!" I balk.

"I won't look," he says.

"Sure you won't," I grumble as he scoops me off the bed and pulls my hands behind my back like before.

He guides me out the door and down a hall to what I assume is the next room over. When he flips on the light and pulls off my blindfold, he closes me in.

"Use the toilet. When you're done, open the door," he commands. "And before you even think about locking it, remember that I have a key for everything."

"Ugh, understood," I sigh. I quickly do my business and push the door open again.

He comes back, now with a green towel and some other linens draped over his arm. He turns the knobs for the shower and steps back, gesturing for me to go ahead.

"Well, turn around or close your eyes or something. I have to take my clothes off," I say.

He begrudgingly turns away while I whip off my dress and hastily hop in the shower. I feel terribly vulnerable and exposed, but as soon as the hot water hits my skin, I'm awash in relief. I tilt my head back and let the water soak my face and hair. I sigh with pleasure and reach for the bar of soap to lather myself up. It feels so damn good, I can almost imagine I'm safe at home. Almost. But there's a marked difference: I don't usually have a gigantic, terrifying Russian man guarding me in the shower. I have to trust that he isn't secretly ogling me every time I close my eyes. After a couple minutes, my curiosity gets the best of me.

Careful not to make a lot of noise, I peel back an inch of the shower curtain and peek out at him. To my surprise, I can see him reflected in the mirror and he's still partially facing away, giving me the privacy I need. I look at him there, standing strong and silent. He's fascinating to look at, with his chiseled jaw and sharp cheekbones. But he seems to sense me watching him, because suddenly his eyes flit to the mirror and he makes eye contact with me in the reflection.

I let out a little gasp of surprise and disappear behind the curtain again. My heart is hammering like crazy. It's hard to sort out all the feelings going haywire in my mind. On the one hand, I feel spooked by his watchful gaze. But at the same time, his constant presence is oddly soothing. Like he's guarding me from the dangers of the world beyond, the so-called "far worse" people he warned me about. Is he protecting me or imprisoning me?

Or both?

After my shower, he hands me the towel without looking. I dry off and step out of the shower, my dark hair fragrant and damp. I get goosebumps when my feet touch the cold tile, and he seems to notice. Instead of giving me back my grimy dress, he hands me an oversized flannel shirt and some plain black boxers that are almost too big to stay up. Still, it's way cozier than what I had before, and I feel considerably more put-together as I curl up in bed, still handcuffed.

The nighttime settles in. Insects hum outside the window. Darkness falls across the bedroom, and my captor takes his place on the couch. I wait for a long time in silence for him to fall asleep, my own brain whirring a mile a minute. I listen to the minutes tick by and turn into hours. I toss and turn, unable to fall asleep myself. Once I'm pretty sure his rhythmic breathing indicates that he's unconscious, I slowly move my free hand down my body. I know it's probably not a smart idea, but there's one sure-fire way I know to help me drift to sleep: touching myself. Over the years, dealing with the stress of my father's expectations and the rigorous schedule of law school, I've counted on this to help me relax. Of course, I wish my captor wasn't in the room. It's certainly not the ideal circumstances for a masturbation sesh, but I'm desperate.

I slide my hand down between my legs, spreading my thighs apart. I suck in a tight breath as my fingertips brush over my mound through the thin fabric of the black boxers. My clit tingles. My body warms up as I slowly stroke myself under the sheets. My toes curl and I close my eyes as the sensation intensifies. I rock against my own hand in the darkness, letting the delicious spirals of plea-sure take over. I work up the courage to slip my hand underneath the waistband of the boxers. My fingers trace soft, warming circles around my sensitive clit. A soft moan escapes my lips as I get closer and closer to coming. But then, I remember with a jolt that I'm supposed to be totally silent. I'm not alone.

I open my eyes and look over at the couch. To my horror, I can see the faintest lick of moonlight reflect from a pair of dark, watchful eyes. I know I should stop. I know I should look away. But I'm so close to release, and I need it so badly.

My fingers keep working on autopilot even as my heart

pounds with adrenaline. He's in the way, but I won't let him take this small comfort away from me, too.

He doesn't move or say a word to stop me. I breathe harder, my pussy slick with desire.

I can't find his eyes in the darkness anymore, and I start to think maybe I'm in the clear.

Until he stands up.

Chapter 5

Stefan

Most of the time, I have very little issue sticking to my guns.

Often, quite literally.

The life the Bratva have carved out for me is not a gentle one. I have been trained for years to restrain myself when needed, and to unleash my full rage and force when the situation calls for it.

I can look into the face of a battered, beaten man with no hesitation, no regrets even as the blood drips down his fearful features. I can interrogate him until he's weeping for mercy at my feet and still have the capacity within myself to hurt him further if the situation calls for it. To pick at his armor and break him down slowly, shattering his willpower piece by painful piece. Bone by broken bone. I have wrung information out of human life, turned a seasoned career criminal into a hapless pile of bones and wasted potential.

To pick up a weapon and wield it without a shred of fear comes naturally to me. When I point a gun at an unlucky target, the weapon might as well just be an extension of my arm. It is just a metal limb with which to dispense death and atrocities. A part of me almost as integral as my calm, steady heart. There isn't much these days that can rattle me. Not betrayal, not physical pain, not even the desolate loneliness of working for the Bratva. For an organization meant to be built around the idea of brotherhood, there is a lot of time spent alone, a lot of hours second-guessing and mistrusting the very men who would be my 'brothers.'

It is a cold, callous way to live. I've stared into the wild eyes of dangerous, unhinged criminals, both within and outside of the brotherhood. I rarely feel even a flicker of fear for my own life. I can swagger into any situation, no matter how grim the circumstances, do my filthy work, and walk back out the same man I went in. A lot of the time, I feel as much disdain for the men assigned to work beside me as I do for the lowlife scum we are commanded to punish. I have learned again and again that no one, not even those closest to me, can be trusted. Every new person is a potential threat, so I have to sleep with one eye open all the time. That kind of constant vigilance can be exhausting. But it's the only way I know how to live, and so I have made a home for myself among the bloodshed. I get as comfortable in the muck as I can get, but never too comfortable as to become complacent. It's imperative that I keep on my toes. I am always waiting for the other shoe to drop, and when it inevitably does, I have to be ready for it. Guns a-blazing, no turning back. The blood on my hands is just part of the job, the lifestyle.

I may not have chosen this path, and in another life perhaps I would happily turn away from the obligations put upon me by Brusilov and every other boss I've worked under all these years. But in this reality, I have no choice but to accept whatever bloody fate assigned to me. Working for a man like Brusilov is not like any other job. I can't quit. I can't take time off. I certainly cannot turn down a mission once it's given to me. To do so would be a breach of the unspoken contract that binds me to this dark underworld, and the Bratva are not kind to traitors. My boss holds not only my payment hostage, but my existence. There is no other option. I carry out my orders dutifully, leaving a trail of destruction in my wake.

So I should have known this assignment was going to be a departure from most of the work I normally do. I expected it to be a somewhat foreign territory for me, a different kind of mission at least on the surface. After all, I have spent my life and career hunting down slimy men, not kidnapping beautiful young women. For a long time, I have regarded women, children, other innocents as off-limits, the one area I refused to touch. The one category of human being I absolutely cannot degrade the way the Bratva asks me to. I evaded this kind of mission by excelling at all other kinds. My tactic has been to make myself indispensable, a master of my trade, in the hopes that it would be enough. But I should have known there would be consequences eventually.

The bosses know about my perspective on harming women. Even without my outright saying so, the ever-present eyes and ears of the brotherhood have collected enough tidbits of information to put it together: I have a weak spot. Victor Brusilov knows that, and it's probably the main reason why he forced this particular mission upon me. If the bratva discovers a chink in your armor, they will poke it with a hot iron. They will draw it out and torture you, immersing you in the very thing you fear or despise most, until finally you are conditioned into obedience. Men like me don't get the luxury of moral superiority. I don't get to say no when my heart tells me something is wrong. If I don't follow orders, if I don't subjugate my target into oblivion, then it's my neck on the chopping block instead. Hunt or be hunted. I've learned to accept that. I silence the storm in my heart and move on to the next target, rarely looking back over my shoulder. After all, there is no un-taking of a life. Hesitation is often the split-second difference between killing my enemy and my enemy killing me.

As horrific as it sounds, that is the world I've grown comfortable in.

Still, nothing could have prepared me for *this*. For Jewel.

In the nearly complete darkness of the bedroom in the safehouse, I have been watching the young woman sleep. Or at least, I thought she's been sleeping. I assumed her soft sighs, the faint rustle of sheets, were signs of her tossing and turning in bed. I imagine the kinds of frightening dreams she must be having. I know perhaps better than anyone how the stress of reality presses its claws into the realm of dreams. You can never escape your own fear, not even when you're unconscious. But Jewel is not asleep. She isn't dreaming some fitful nightmare.

She's touching herself. When I first noticed it, I was too shocked to respond. I never could have seen this coming. I've dealt with my victims sobbing, begging, wasting away under lock and key. I have learned to drown out the suffering, to ignore the pleas for mercy.

But never, in all my years of duty, have I had to contend with my victim's sexual appetite. Never before have I watched a target slowly, seductively caress her own body with her free hand while the other hangs locked and bruised in a handcuff for which only I have the key. The implications of it all consume me as I sit in the darkness. My own body responds in kind, even when I try to quash the feelings. Lust bubbles up inside me. Desire makes everything hazy. Jewel makes my steady heart beat faster in a way nothing has before. Why is it that I can look death in the eye without a hint of palpitation, but a woman touching herself under the sheets is powerful enough to affect me?

Surely, she thinks I've been sleeping. But how does she not sense my eyes on her in the darkness? It occurs to me that maybe she does feel me watching her. That concept is even more enticing. That she would be so brazen as to do it in front of me. There's an erotic edge to our silent stare. Who will move first?

I do.

When the temptation prickles up within me, I have no choice but to walk away. I stand up, no doubt startling the hell out of Jewel. I hear her breath catch and hold, like she's too stunned to breathe. I'm sure she thinks I am about to punish her. Hurt her in some way.

But instead, I simply turn and walk out of the room. I close and lock the bedroom door behind me. It takes all my willpower to walk away from her, especially when every cell in my body is screaming to get closer. But I have to maintain our boundaries. I can't let this gorgeous, clever, stubborn woman get under my skin. Besides, if masturbating brings her comfort in this darkest hour of her life, I can't deny her that. She needs the release. I am happy to leave her to it, let her have this small but powerful thing.

I stroll across the dark, quiet house. I take a coat from the rack and shrug it over my shoulders. It's getting colder outside every day, and at this hour of night, it's downright chilly. I step outside into the brisk night air. My breath forms in puffs in front of my face as I take my cell phone from my pocket and quickly dial a familiar number. While I'm out here, I might as well ask for a status update. I lift the phone to my ear and listen for the rings. One, two, and a click.

"*Privet,*" says the gruff voice on the end of the line.

"Oleg," I greet him. "My apologies for the late hour."

"I don't sleep anyway, Stefan. You know that," he grunts.

"Good. Then perhaps you will have the information I need," I begin. "Has there been any word on the Freddie Albany case?"

"The ICE agent and his unfortunate daughter?" Oleg chuckles cruelly. "No."

I sigh, pinching the bridge of my nose in frustration. "You don't know if we have made contact with Freddie yet?" I push him.

"Not that I know of," he answers. "But Victor keeps us in the dark about these things sometimes. You just have to be patient, *tovarishch*. Wait for further instruction, as they say. The Bratva works at its own pace, and our sworn duty is to follow orders."

"Of course. I am certainly not abandoning my mission for impatience," I reply. "I just want to be kept in the loop."

"*Da, da.* I am sure the bosses will pass down information as soon as it becomes relevant to you," Oleg asserts.

I roll my eyes. It's the kind of typical, canned response I should've expected from him. Oleg is another pawn, like me. Just a bloody-knuckled scrapper who handles dirty work for the brotherhood. But unlike me, he has an unwavering allegiance for our bosses. He's a good soldier, perfect by Bratva standards: recklessly brave and obedient to a fault.

"What is your hurry? Is the woman giving you trouble? *Vozmozhno* you should show her a little discipline, if you know what I mean," he laughs derisively.

His vulgar cackle makes the heat rise in my face, anger burning in my chest. Normally, this brusque way of speaking wouldn't faze me. I work with rough men, and they speak roughly too. But it's somehow different when he's talking about Jewel. I feel protective of her, even possessive in a way. She's not some hardened criminal, she's a law student who got plucked out of her normal life and dumped into a safehouse with the likes of me. She may be my prisoner, but as long as she's in my custody, I have a responsibility to keep her safe.

"You still there, Stefan?" Oleg prompts me.

"Yes. Thank you, Oleg. That's all I needed to know," I answer.

Before he can say anything else that might incense me further, I hang up. I tuck the phone in my pocket and gaze out toward the tree line, deep in thought. All of my calls for updates have been fruitless. Nobody seems to have the information I seek. And for an organization of cruel men who work quickly in the shadows, it's taking an awfully long time to establish contact with the very man at the center of this mission: Freddie Albany. Jewel's father. She's just leverage in this game. Freddie is the true target. With Jewel in my possession, I can see no good reason why the mission must drag on. I've made my move, and every moment longer we spend here at the safehouse brings us closer to danger. A speedy job is a job well done.

So why the delay? If Freddie Albany is such a major mark, why wait any longer to make our next move? Something feels amiss to me. I don't like surprises. I don't like suspense. I want to know what's happening and when it's going down so I can be prepared.

I walk back into the safehouse with a growing suspicion that something isn't right. I stroll through the dark house, back to the hallway where I can see the bedroom door. I pause there, staring at the door and wondering what exactly I will find on the other side. Is she still in there with her dainty hand shoved between her thighs? Is she moaning and writhing in pleasure on the bed where I have slept so many times? I think about her beautiful body, the way it looked in the dim light of the basement. I imagine my own hands, much bigger and rougher than hers, caressing her soft curves. I can almost feel her smooth, milky skin under my calloused fingertips. I picture her full, perky breasts rising and falling with each indecent moan. I see her dark hair spilled out on the pillow, and her pearly teeth biting down on her plush bottom lip to keep from crying out with pleasure.

My cock stiffens at the thought of what I could do to her. It has been a long time since I last enjoyed the company of a beautiful woman, and I'm starting to think there are none on this planet who could compare to Jewel. As much as I resist, there's no denying how my body feels about her. All my pent-up frustration needs an outlet. A release of my own. Being so close to a woman like Jewel only makes my desire more potent. Every hour I spend with her makes me despise this mission even more, because it's becoming impossible to think of her the way I think of most targets. I can't demonize her. I can't degrade her. I don't want to. Even if she is a spoiled, high-maintenance brat, she's not a bad person. I appreciate her courage and intelligence, her stubborn way of standing up to me when so many others fall to their knees.

Quite frankly, she doesn't belong in this world. I want to put her back where she belongs, back in her own life. That way, I can clean my hands of this mission, set her free, and hopefully walk away with a chunk of change from her father, the ICE agent.

I give Jewel a little longer to finish and fall asleep before I silently step back into the bedroom. I'm relieved to find her passed out, her eyes closed and her breaths regular. I resume my place on the couch and wait for dawn.

The next morning, I rise before the sun to start working out. While Jewel is still asleep, I seize the opportunity to run a few long laps around the property, keeping close to the tree line. I go back inside, cook up two high-protein omelets for breakfast, and bring them to the bedroom. As soon as I walk in and the aroma of freshly made food wafts over to Jewel, her green eyes flutter open. She yawns as she watches me approach with the plate. This time, she doesn't shrink away from me.

"Good morning," she says, stretching her legs and her one free arm. "What's this?"

"An omelet. Enjoy," I answer simply.

"You know, this whole breakfast-in-bed situation would be a lot *more* enjoyable if I could use both my arms," she points out.

Still, she reaches for the plate and starts eating, to my satisfaction. Good. The last thing I need is for her to lose strength. Judging by the glacial pace so far, we might be here a while.

I sit on the couch to eat my own omelet. Having both arms at my disposal makes it a quick meal for me. Jewel is still picking at her food as I drop to the floor to continue my workout. She watches me do countless reps of push-ups while she eats.

"Breakfast and a show," she jokes. "Lucky me."

I move on to lifting weights as she sets down her empty plate. I glance over to see her squinting at me thoughtfully, her pretty lips pursed in a pout.

"What's wrong?" I ask between reps.

She shrugs. "It's just not fair, you know. Why do you get to work out and I have to sit in this bed letting my body waste away?" she asks.

"Dramatic," I mutter.

Jewel scoffs. "I'm serious! Back home, I have a whole routine. I do yoga and pilates and stuff to stay in shape and keep myself sane. My body feels awful after sitting around tied to a bed for so long," she points out.

"You're a prisoner," I remind her. "That's how it works."

She raises one perfectly arched eyebrow. "Well, even prisoners get exercise time."

"Does this look like a federal prison to you?" I grunt as I lift the weights over my head.

"No, it looks like somebody's rundown bed and breakfast," she says.

I have to stifle a laugh. She's not wrong.

"Well, you got your bed and you got your breakfast," I remark. "Check."

"And what am I supposed to do with these calories, huh?" she says, taking another bite of omelet. "Just twiddle my thumbs?"

"Last night you seemed to find a way to burn some calories," I mention.

She freezes up, clearly stunned that I would bring it up. Her face flushes a bright, adorable pink. Jewel looks away and bites her lip. The poor girl. I decide to cut her some slack.

"If it will help you sleep better at night, then fine. You can have your little workout. But you're going to do it right here in this room, under my supervision," I tell her.

She looks downright surprised when I set down my weights and walk over to release her handcuff. I grab her arm and fit the key in the lock. It falls open with a clanking sound, and she starts rubbing her sore wrist.

"Thank you," Jewel says. She sounds as surprised to be saying it as I feel hearing it.

"Don't mention it. Now get to work before I change my mind," I command.

She hesitantly slides off the bed, still clad in only the oversized shirt and boxers. Her long, slender legs are exposed as she walks to the center of the room. She wiggles down to the floor and stretches out like a cat. I take my place on the couch and pick up a book on wildlife foraging I found in one of the random closets here in the safehouse. I do my best to get lost in the pages of mushroom identification and poison ivy treatment tips, but the content of this book simply can't compete with the show right in front of me.

Jewel's perfect body is splayed out on the floor. She does several leg lifts, arching her back as she stretches out. She twists from side to side. I watch her get down on her knees out of the corner of my eye. She kneels with her arms flat down on the floor and her taut, juicy ass sticking up in the air. The boxers ride up to show an enticing amount of bare thigh. I'm almost salivating watching this beautiful girl work out the kinks in her body. It's impossible to ignore her. I try to keep my eyes on the page, but my gaze constantly wanders back to Jewel, twisting and contorting her flexible frame just a few feet away. She's almost close enough to touch, and God knows I want to. But I resist.

She sits up and stretches her long legs in front of her. She leans over to touch her toes. I hear her clear her throat-- once, then again. I look up from my book.

"What?" I prompt her.

"I was just wondering...how does this all work?" Jewel asks.

I frown at her. "What are you asking?"

She bites her lip. "How many of you are there? Is it just you running this operation or do you answer to someone else?" she pries.

"Why do you want to know?" I retort.

She shrugs. "I don't know, just making conversation."

"Well, talk about something else," I answer sharply.

Jewel rolls her eyes. "I mean, it's hard to think about

anything besides, you know, being a captive and stuff. It's kind of the pressing issue here."

"You don't need to know. I'll take care of all that," I answer.

She doesn't back down. "I'm just saying something feels off. Not that I have a lot of experience being kidnapped for ransom or whatever, but my dad isn't a hard man to find. He's a public servant," she says.

I snort. "'Public servant' is quite a euphemism for what your father is."

Jewel looks away. I've hit a sore spot.

In a small voice, she says, "I guess I just don't understand what's taking so long. If Dad knows I'm here... why hasn't he acted yet?"

I bristle, getting uncomfortable with this line of questioning. Especially because I don't exactly know the answer myself. Jewel keeps going.

"I'm trying to figure out, you know, how long I have to be here. What's going to happen next? What if my father doesn't-- doesn't come through?" she asks.

She sounds broken. Like she's already considered the answer to her question, and she doesn't like it. The tension in the room grows more and more palpable. I don't know what to tell her, or if I should even tell her anything. She's not in on the plot, after all. She's a pawn.

Before I have to reply, the tension is cut through with a sharp ringing from my pocket. I hastily whip out my phone to check the screen. My stomach turns when I see Brusilov's number.

"I have to take this," I growl.

I leap to my feet and rush out of the room, closing the

bedroom door behind me. I walk down the hallway several feet and answer the call.

"Stefan," Brusilov growls.

"I'm listening, boss," I answer.

"I expect you still have the girl under lock and key," he says.

"Of course. She's secure. I'm awaiting orders," I report.

"Good. That's what I like to hear," Brusilov says. "It's time to move to a new tactic."

"I'm ready to work," I affirm.

"Your next order is to eliminate the prisoner."

Everything goes quiet except for the thump of my heart. Surely, I heard him wrong.

"Sir, did you say 'eliminate'?" I ask for clarification.

"*Da*, Stefan. Kill the girl. I don't care how you do it, but don't leave a big mess. The safehouse must remain a neutral location in case of discovery," he says, like he hasn't dropped a bomb on me.

"What about Freddie? What about the money?" I press.

"It isn't your job to ask questions, *mal'chik*. You do as I tell you. And I am telling you to kill the captive. It's a simple command, Stefan. You've done it before," Brusilov says.

"Not like this. Not with a woman," I hiss.

"There is a first time for everything," he chuckles darkly. "Do as you're told."

Click.

I hear the dial tone. I stare at my phone for a moment, totally numb. I can hear my own blood rushing in my ears. I feel sick in the pit of my stomach. This is the one command I did not prepare for. The one thing I did not want to do. I should have known the bosses wouldn't let me off so easily. I don't know how to bring myself to do it. How can I go from letting her do pilates on the floor to suddenly killing her? How can I put my feelings aside and do my job, when every piece of me is screaming to let her live? To protect her, not hurt her.

I heave a sigh and walk back to the bedroom, still lost in my own dark thoughts. I push open the door, expecting to see her still stretching. But to my surprise, she isn't there. I look at the bed-- it's empty.

"No," I murmur.

My eyes flit up to the window, and my heart sinks. It wasn't locked.

The pane is pushed up, just large enough for a slim, petite body to squeeze through. Fresh air wafts through the open window.

She's gone.

CHAPTER 6

JEWEL

Go. Just go. And don't stop until you can't go anymore.

The words beat ceaselessly in my head like a mantra. In moments like this, fear becomes so palpable it crystallizes. It turns monstrous. A spark of worry explodes into an entire raging inferno that threatens to choke my lungs with smoke until I'm too tired to go on. I felt a flicker of this fear before. Walking into my law exams. Seeing my father's name on the caller ID. Having an absolute hulk of a stranger grab me from behind and force chemicals up my nose. And of course, waking up to find myself chained to a bed, with that same hulking man looming over me. Watching me sleep. The stark realization that my life and everything I thought I knew, everything I had planned out-- it was all gone. Changed in an instant.

And yet, I would trade this moment for any of those. The terror bubbling up inside of me is so potent I could not have stayed in that bedroom even if I wanted to. Even if I hadn't already been looking around for a way out. But I had thought I was getting somewhere. My captor was listening to me. We were finding common ground. He gave me a morsel of freedom, just enough to do some sloppy pilates on the bedroom floor. In that moment, just before arriving at the precipice, I felt almost hopeful, despite everything.

Until I started asking questions, and I didn't get the answers I wanted. That was strike one. But when my captor left the room to take that call, I had no choice but to eavesdrop. I immediately jumped to my feet and rushed to the door. I pressed my ear against the mottled wood to listen in on what he was saying. It was frustrating, only being able to hear my kidnapper's side of the conversation. I was desperate to know who was on the other end of the line. Who was he talking to? Who does he answer to?

And why did they decide to kill me?

My heart is beating so hard, so fast, I'm afraid it might just give out. Like an exhausted bird flown too far over the sea, wings heavy and soul hopeless, ready to drop into the crashing waves forever. The forest is my sea. If I can't keep up, it will open up and swallow me whole. The thought of stumbling to the forest floor in a heap to await my inevitable execution makes me feel nauseated. My stomach lurches. My lungs ache and burn with the panicked breaths coming fast and short from my lips. Faint puffs of fog appear in front of my face, my breath showing in the chill. I look up to the canopy for a moment as I run. The sun is perfectly aligned above me. It must be high noon. The tall white pines and black ash trees rise tall and proud around me. They sway gently in the whirling wind. I would stop and admire the beauty if I wasn't so scared.

Streamers of golden light dapple through the overlapping tree branches. Little spots of sunshine dot the woods around me. It illuminates a fallen tree just off to my right, its trunk decaying and returning to the earth that grew it. I realize with a jolt that I have more in common with that dead tree than ever before. We are both victims of our environment, and I, too, might end up falling to pieces on the leafy ground. My brain flashes an image of my captor looking at me with those black, hawklike eyes. Sizing me up. Ready to rip me to shreds. He could be right behind me, close on my trail.

Keep moving. Don't look back. For the love of God, don't turn back.

I swallow hard and bite the inside of my cheek to stem the hot tears that sting in my eyes. I can't afford to let my emotions take control. I can't allow my fear to consume me and make me still, when I literally need to run for my life.

All around me, the forest is a singing, living, almost breathing thing. Birds call and tweet from their branches, hopping from one to the next in their autumnal fly about. They flit around in the canopy and flutter along the narrow passageways between the dense trees. When they hear me coming, they take to the sky in a frantic flapping of wings. Little flocks of them bound from their perches, calling out a warning to their brothers and sisters. In the bushes, tiny furry creatures rustle and bound away, abandoning their hidey holes to flee.

I am definitely more of a city girl than a woodsy type, but even I can tell the animals are frightened to see me running. They must wonder what it is that could so thoroughly terrify a creature of my size. If I'm afraid, they must be petrified, too. Any beast that would hunt me is one to hide from. They probably picture a big bad wolf. A bear with his shiny black coat and his great gnashing jaws.

I almost wish I was running from an animal. At least then I could take the bludgeoning without my heart breaking, too. Because as much as I detest being held prisoner and denied basic rights, I can't pretend like there weren't feelings developing between us. At least, from my end of things. I wanted to hate him from the moment I woke up to find him watching me in that dark, dank basement. But I couldn't. Our short time together brought me closer to him, made me think of my captor as a real person instead of just some random soulless criminal.

I was a fool to let myself feel that way about him. How could I have felt anything but revulsion for the man responsible for ruining my life, and probably about to end my life if I don't keep moving fast enough? How could I sit handcuffed to that bed and look at him and think warmly of him? What is wrong with me that it took only so long to make me almost trust him? I wish I could go back in time and tell myself to curb my enthusiasm. To never let my guard down even for a second. God, if I survive this, I'll never trust a living soul again.

I push myself on and on, fleeing almost blindly through the trees. Over and over again, I very nearly collide with a tree, it's so densely packed out here. Each time, I barely evade collision. The rough bark breaks off in contact with my shoulder. It rains down my arm and prickles my arm as it falls. Twigs and leaves break off, fall into my hair, and tangle there. I'm sure I would look like an absolute wilderness witch if someone saw me now, but I can't stop to untangle myself. If I slow down, I face almost certain death.

My bare legs sting like crazy. The underbrush here is prickly and dense. Every bounding step I take is harried by the long tendrils of thorn bushes. Their spines poke and tear my skin. I can feel drops of blood beading cold on my calves and shins, but I don't dare look down. My bare feet pound into the cold clay mud and slide across the slippery dead leaves. They're so scratched up by now, my feet feel like two raw, screaming wounds at the ends of my aching legs.

It's far colder out here than I would've expected for early autumn. Back in the city, the temperature has been in the sixties, the perfect climate for a cozy stroll down Harvard's winding walkways. But here in the unforgiving forest, under the thick canopy that blocks out most of the sun, even noon feels as bitter as dusk. My toes and fingers are starting to go numb now. My feet aren't as sure of their steps as when I first bolted for the tree line.

But what else could I do? Where else could I run to?

It had been the perfect storm. I was alone on that bedroom floor, holding my toes and straining my body back to life. I'm grateful now for that, at least. A little pilates warm-up comes in handy when you have to run for your life a few moments later. I see it so clearly in my mind: my captor watching me out of the corner of his eye. He didn't want to look at me that way, but he couldn't help it. I was intriguing to him. Irresistible in some small, curious way. It was his interest that gave me the courage to ask questions. Now, I wish I hadn't. Maybe I pushed him too far. Maybe I proved myself not worth the challenge of keeping me hidden. All I know is that I heard him say he was going to *eliminate* me. Sure, he probably got the order from his superior, but he's shown me mercy before.

Not this time. I couldn't stick around to risk it. I saw the opportunity: he was out of the room, I was no longer cuffed to the bed, and I had been eyeing that window ever since he took off my blindfold. My heart raced as I slid the pane up, fighting the rusted hinges and the pine sap sticking it to the sill. It took a feat of strength to open it, and an act of reckless courage to clamber out the narrow opening. I know I'm turning the tables; I am causing extra trouble. If I wasn't walking down to the gallows before, I am definitely on my way there now.

But it's not just my captor's fault. In fact, the thought that aches even deeper inside my soul, the realization that makes my eyes sting with hot tears is that my own father isn't going to save me. Not from what I heard.

I can hear my captor's voice clear in my head, asking, "What about Freddie? What about the money?" My heart fell when he said those words. More proof that my dad isn't coming to my rescue. In fact, I should have seen that coming all along. He's never considered me a real priority, much less a beloved daughter to protect.

That stings.

I wish I could be surprised, but if I look deep down, I've always known this truth. He doesn't care about me any more than he cares for the long, varied lineup of wives and mistresses who he's marched in and out of my life. Human beings are more like collectibles. Or pawns in a long, cruel game. That's how my father sees the world, and now I see it, too.

Looking back, it's always been this way. Growing up, he was never there for me. Not physically present, and barely reachable by phone either. So many times I watched him get on a plane and disappear into the sky, one of many nannies holding my hand while my true guardian abandons me yet again. He is less of a father figure and more of a constant specter haunting my life. Whispering under his breath about how I disappoint him. Shouting obscenities over the phone in his locked, off-limits office. In my braver moments as a child, I would listen at the door in an attempt to discern anything of value. Anything that would tell me more about the mysterious, cold man who claimed to be my father, but in title only. He was always cavalier about the lives he impacted through his work, but I knew there was more. I knew he was keeping secrets from me, even when I was little. I could hear the lie in his voice when he spoke to me. I could see the way his cruel smile never reached his beady eyes.

I don't remember ever seeing him exhibit anything close to remorse, sympathy, or even just base-level compassion. Not for the victims of his work, not for his colleagues, and certainly not for his soft, yielding daughter who disgusts him. That's what I am in his eyes- disgusting. Worthless. He tried so hard to turn me into the smaller, female version of him. He did his best to teach me what was important to him: apathy over empathy, fear over love. He wanted me to be strong the way he was, but I never measured up. I simply couldn't be as cruel as he wanted. I've always cared too much. He didn't approve of anything I did, anything I was. Dad doesn't even like my personality. I've overheard him telling people that I'm too soft. I care too much about justice and doing what's right.

In his eyes, that means I'll never amount to anything worthwhile.

The only way forward is bulldozing everything in his path, but I couldn't do it. It was a lonely upbringing, and I'm thankful for the nannies and teachers who held my hand when Dad wouldn't do it. But I didn't escape my childhood unscathed. I grew up thinking so low of myself, desperate to make a difference in the world. I wanted to help people. I still do, deep down.

When I decided to become a lawyer, he laughed in my face. Then, he yelled. What use was I if all I wanted was to help other people rather than myself? My loyalty made me foolish, and my softness made me weak. His unkind words have left a lasting impression on my soul.

I always feared him. More than anything. More even than my captor. At least... that was the case until I heard him say he would *eliminate* me.

I'm so tired now. Every muscle in my body is screaming to slow down. But then, I hear a horrible sound: the snapping of twigs somewhere behind me-- much closer than I expected. I knew he would follow me, but I thought I had a better head start. His footsteps hit the ground hard. And then I hear the eerie echo of his deep voice bellowing through the woods.

"Jewel!" he shouts. "Don't do this!"

My heart breaks. His voice sounds more pained than angry. But I can't let that stop me. I have to keep moving even though my hope for escape is dwindling. I'm simply not prepared for a long chase. My bare feet, legs, and arms make me vulnerable. But my kidnapper is wearing pants, a real shirt, and boots. He's built for this. His footsteps get louder behind me.

He's catching up, and fast.

Through the blur of tears, I see a clearing up ahead, ringed by thick bushes. I summon what tiny shred is left of my energy to make a mad dash. I propel myself through the clearing and dive into a cluster of bushes, scratching the hell out of myself in the process. With my chest heaving, I peer wide-eyed through the foliage as my captor comes careening into the clearing, only a couple feet away from me. He's not even out of breath as he looks around. His dark eyes scan for signs of me. I'm desperately trying to hold my breath and keep still. But when a drop of blood rolls off my chin and splashes onto my arm, I'm so startled by the cold, ticklish sensation I can't help but stumble backward a little. A gasp falls from my lips and several twigs snap underneath me. I freeze for a moment, wide-eyed with panic. My captor turns right toward me, those wolfish eyes locked on me. I've been caught.

No. Not yet, growls the stubborn voice in my head.

I scramble to my feet and immediately go pitching down a leafy slope. My feet are bleeding, my face is bleeding, but I run like hell. I slip and slide all over the place, but my pursuant is nimble on his feet. He leaps over a decaying log and bounds up beside me. I cry out with pure terror and skid to a stop. With so much momentum in his imposing frame hurtling through the forest, he takes a couple more leaping strides and lands steady on his feet. He whirls around to face me. His eyes are narrowed. His massive hands are balled into tight fists. Any *one* of those knuckles could take me out in an instant.

I gulp. My body starts to tremble uncontrollably from head to toe.

There's about six feet between us. He doesn't necessarily know how exhausted I am. He's probably thinking that if he moves one millimeter in my direction, I'll go bounding away again like a startled doe. I'm thinking that I'm so tired, so beaten down, so frightened that if he lunges for me now, I'll be too helpless to save myself. But neither of us wants to make the first move.

We're at a stand-off.

Suddenly, all the pent-up feelings I've had since we first met days ago come bubbling up from a deep well within me. The tears course down my face and mingle with the blood.

"Jewel, don't do anything stupid," he growls at me.

I glare at him, shaking my head.

"Stupid? Running for my life is stupid?" I blurt out. "That's right. I heard your phone call. I heard you say the word 'eliminate.' I know you were talking about me."

"I was too soft on you. I let my personal feelings cloud my judgement," he says.

"What does that mean: 'personal feelings?'" I ask, putting my hands on my hips.

"*Bozhe moy*," he groans, pinching the bridge of his nose. "You ask so many damn questions."

"Because you're withholding information!" I shout.

"You don't need to know these things, Jewel," he sighs.

"I don't even know your name!" I hurl back.

"It's better if you don't," he insists.

My arms fall slack at my sides. My shoulders start to shake. I can hardly see, the tears are so thick in my eyes. I'm so confused. I'm hurting so much inside. I feel betrayed. He stares at me with those cold, unfeeling eyes.

My voice is thin and wracked with sobs when I say, "You have taken *everything* from me. And you won't even give me your first name."

Something changes in his demeanor. He stands a little taller. His dark eyes almost seem to soften when he looks at me. He nods slowly.

"Stefan," he says. "That is my name."

A feeling of inexplicable warmth rolls through my

body. I feel some of the tension in my muscles release. My heart skips a beat, but it's not pounding anymore.

But I have to remember that he-- *Stefan*-- is a threat. He's not Prince Charming. He's come to take me. To kill me. I suck in a deep breath.

"Stefan," I begin softly, "if I go with you, I'm a dead girl."

"If I were to leave you out here by yourself, dressed like that, in these woods with the weather getting colder and the sun going down, I would be leaving you to die," he says. "Not a quick death. Not an easy one. A slow, painful, starving death. Is that what you want?"

He underestimates me. Just like my father. Just like everybody.

I swipe the tears out of my eyes and bitterly retort, "Well, I'd rather die trying to escape than die a prisoner to some criminal!"

There's a split-second flicker of something like hurt in his eyes. And then, in one forceful movement, he lunges at me. I scream and brace for the hit. But instead, he simply sweeps me up into his arms.

I'm in shock as he throws me over his shoulder and starts striding back the way we came. Back to that damn prison cell and my inevitable demise. I have an impulse to kick and scream, but it quickly fades when I realize how outmatched I am. Stefan is carrying me like you'd bring a towel to the bathroom. I might as well weigh nothing. His arm around my waist is nearly the width of my thigh. He towers above the forest floor. From my place over his shoulder, the way down looks to be of dizzying height. All the fight left in me dissipates and I go limp. I'm so exhausted. I'm so heartbroken. I just want it to be over.

The walk back to the safehouse feels so much shorter from this perspective. It takes him no time to climb the steep slopes and crunch over the thorny brush. We emerge from the tree line. The building swims into view. At this point, it's almost a welcome reprieve. It's the closest thing to a home I've had the past couple days. If I'm going to die, it might as well be here.

He carries me up to the house. I'm too tired to take note of the layout of the building. My muddled mind couldn't possibly memorize it right now. And it doesn't matter anyway, because as soon as we walk through a side door into what looks like a kitchen, Stefan sets me down, pulls a black bandana from his coat pocket, and ties it around my head in a blindfold.

"You don't have to do this," I murmur. "I give up. I won't try to escape again."

"We're not staying here," he growls.

I frown under my blindfold. "Where are we going?"

"Somewhere else," he replies simply.

"Whatever," I mutter.

I feel him grab my arm and start leading me across the house. We stop off somewhere-- I'm pretty sure it's the bedroom. I can still smell faint traces of our omelets. He lets go just for a few minutes. I stand blinded and helpless, just waiting. I hear him unzip a bag, stuff something inside, and zip it back up. Then his hand is on my arm again. I hear a familiar metal clink as he closes the hand-cuffs around both of my wrists. He pushes me through the doorway and across the creaky floorboards. He opens another door and a little gust of cool air rushes in. We step out into the crisp autumn afternoon. I hear gravel crunching under my feet, then the sound of a car door clicking open.

"Oh!" I yelp as Stefan links his arm around my waist and hoists me into the vehicle.

He fastens my seatbelt.

"Safety first," he grunts.

"Where are we--"

The door slams shut. I hear Stefan's heavy footsteps go around the vehicle. He opens the front and slides behind the wheel. I must be in the back seat. He fires up the engine and we start rolling backwards. With the blindfold on, I can't orient myself. Everything just looks dark. I could probably reach up and take it off, even with my handcuffed wrists. But what would be the point? Stefan isn't going to just take that sitting down. I realize now how fruitless it is to resist him. He's infinitely stronger than me. He has the upper hand.

"I take it you're not going to tell me anything about where we're going," I grumble.

Silence. Then he switches on the radio. Some old crooner music wafts from the old speakers. I sigh and slump against the seat, my head tilting back. Clearly, he's taking me to the place where I will die, and he's going to punish me with silence on the way. But I'm under no obligation to shut up.

"If it's money you're after, I'm sure I can find a way to get it to you," I say.

Stefan doesn't answer.

"You're really giving me the silent treatment? Really mature," I goad him, hoping I can make him respond. But nothing. He's resolute.

We drive for what feels like hours upon hours. I can't

tell which direction we're going, and I'm not even sure where we started. I simply rest my head and wait. After an eternity on the road, we start slowing down. The vehicle makes a turn and rolls a little further before coming to a stop.

"What's going on?" I ask fearfully.

"Stopping for the night," Stefan replies.

I'm so oddly relieved to hear his voice again. He comes around to let me out. He scoops me out of the backseat and onto the asphalt. I wonder if we're in a driveway or a parking lot.

"Come on. Quickly," he commands.

We walk for a minute or so. He fiddles with a key and a door creaks open. The dense, unmistakable smell of a cheap motel room fills my nose. Mildew, citrus cleaner, smoke.

"Five star," I murmur.

Stefan leads me to a bed and handcuffs me to a wobbly post. He takes off my blindfold. I blink as my eyes adjust to the dim, grayish lighting. It's a typical motel room with two twin sized beds and an en suite bathroom with a perpetually flickering light. I glance at the window. The curtains are drawn, but I can see a sliver of dark blue sky on one edge. It's nighttime. I wonder what time it is. I don't see a clock anywhere.

I drag my eyes back to Stefan and my heart skips a beat when I see him pull off his shirt. He reveals his broad, powerful chest and chiseled abs. My jaw drops, taking in his impressive build. He turns to look at me with those piercing dark eyes and I feel a tingle run down my spine.

"I'm going to take a shower. Don't try anything. I'll be

back in less than five minutes," Stefan instructs me. "Understood?"

I nod. "Got it."

He lopes off into the bathroom and shuts the door three-quarters of the way. I sink back into the pillows. It does feel good to be in a bed, even if I do have to be handcuffed to it. While Stefan's in the shower, I seize the opportunity to look around the room. There's a single nightstand located between his bed and mine. Stefan's simple black cell phone is sitting there. With a burst of inspiration, I extend my free arm as far I can, but it's just out of reach. I'm about to look away when I notice the phone screen light up.

There's a new text message on the screen. I squint to read it.

Is it done?

My heart sinks. His people are asking about it. About me.

That text message is all the confirmation I need. I really am going to die.

CHAPTER 7

STEFAN

I set my wristwatch for four minutes and put it on the counter, then I turn to the shower. The showerhead sputters for a second before the spray comes to full power. The water pressure looks surprisingly decent for a motel that probably houses more rats than people. I turn the knobs and feel the cold spray turn to a welcoming, tempting heat. Peeling back the flimsy curtain, I step into the steaming shower. I tilt my head back and let the hot water pelt my bare chest. It runs in rivulets along my defined abdominal muscles and downward. I can feel the tension in my whole body resisting still to the warmth of the shower. I have my guard up all the time. Moments of true vulnerability don't come along very often, and that's by design. But it does get tiring, living in the world of life-or-death decisions every night and day. Constant vigilance means I'm ready to adapt, to leap into action at a moment's notice. It also means my shoulders ache from time to time. All that tension, carried with unwavering stoicism.

I try to let myself unravel just a little, even though I know there's a lot more on my shoulders this time around. This mission involves the most precious cargo I've ever carried, and I'm not used to this... *enormity* of emotion. I'm angry, first of all. There's a fading ember of frustration that Jewel tried to run from me today, risking her life in the process. But more than anything, I am furious at Brusilov for coercing me into this and flipping the switch. His order to 'eliminate' Jewel festers in my mind. The one thing I absolutely cannot do. And he knows it.

Killing Jewel was never supposed to be part of the plan. Kidnap the spoiled daughter to extort the despicable father. It was simple-- I should have noticed it as deceptively simple. For one, Jewel is clearly not spoiled. Nor does she embody her father's cruelty and malice. As for extorting the father, the more I learn about Freddie Albany, the less likely it seems the man would lift a finger to save his own kin. I should have been prepared for the worst when I was assigned this mission, not that I would have had any option to decline it either way. That realization ignites that same anger in me again.

My hands clench at my sides to think about how they set me up. The bosses found my weakness and decided to poke it with a hot iron... for what? To teach me a lesson. To burn me into obedience. To break my spirit and destroy what's left of my moral compass. In Brusilov's eyes, this is the ultimate test of my loyalty and strength. If he can force me to kill Jewel, he can force me to do anything. I would go from a liability to a mindless assassin overnight.

But there are too many flaws in his plan. He didn't account for my moral calling to outweigh my pledge to loyalty and, to be frank, my fear for my own life. He assumed I would bend to his will and do the deed. He bet wrong. I would rather risk life and limb to protect this woman. If I have to kill her to stay in the brotherhood's good graces, then consider me out of grace. They wanted to use her like a pawn. Like fodder in a battle that doesn't even involve her. As though Jewel Albany is expendable. But she's a human being with thoughts and dreams and a sparkling personality. She has a life. She's becoming a lawyer, presumably so she can help people. I don't know as much about her yet as I would like to, but I can tell she has a good heart, even if she is the child of an evil man.

Being brought up by the Bratva, I am used to the idea that evil begets and nurtures evil. After all, I was raised by brutal, powerful men to become a brutal, powerful man in my own right, so it makes sense. However, Jewel is the exception to the rule.

I reach up and brush my fingers through my short, thick hair, lightly scratching my scalp. Hot water licks my shoulders and rolls down my back, giving me a tingle along my spine. My brain reminds me with a jolt that Jewel, the girl at the center of all my muddled thoughts, is just outside. Handcuffed to a bed and utterly helpless. Putty in my hands. If any of my so-called brothers were guarding her tonight instead of me, she might be in peril. I shudder to think about that. It makes my blood boil.

But I want to keep her safe. Not just because it's what's right, I genuinely like the girl. I'm impressed by her resilience and her ability to advocate for herself. I smile wryly. I suppose that would make her a good lawyer. On top of that, she's resourceful, clever, even funny. My mind replays the last warm moments that passed between us, before I got that fateful call from Brusilov that made her bolt. We were in the bedroom at the safehouse. I was sitting on the couch, guarding her while she did pilates on the floor. I think about her body, bending and arching into flexible shapes. Her perky breasts barely peeking under her shirt when it rides up. Her bare thighs and her round, juicy ass in the air when she bends over. Watching her body in action made mine respond. I couldn't help it.

I've wanted her since the moment I watched morning light dance across her ample curves, and no matter what I do to squash my desire, it only grows. Even throughout today, our hardest day yet, I found moments to get lost in her beauty. It was damn near impossible to keep my eyes trained on the road earlier, when it was so easy, so tempting to gaze at Jewel in the overhead mirror. Her rich dark hair loose around her shoulders, her full lips and milky pale skin glowing in the fading light of the setting sun. If only I could have seen her eyes, but she was blindfolded. I feel another flicker of arousal. Seeing her blindfolded gives me so many ideas, not one of them related to the "mission" at hand. I have so much pent-up frustration with nowhere to direct it. I wish I could pour it all into Jewel.

Even now, my cock is stiffening at the thought of Jewel's flawless form unfolding in front of me. I remember again how close she is. How easily I could walk out of this bathroom and straight to her bed. I could make her feel things she's never felt before. I could show her incredible pleasure. I imagine her slender arms reaching up to pull me down, her fingertips spreading across my broad, powerful back. I would pin her down and listen to her sigh with delight as she gave in to my touch. It drives me wild, knowing she's handcuffed to that bed, just waiting for me like the most beautiful present, all wrapped up for me to tear apart.

I turn to face the hot water. I let my head fall back as I close my eyes. The water hits my chest and runs down, slicking up my stiff cock. I reach down to wrap my hand around the thick, hard shaft. I grit my teeth, imagining what Jewel would look like splayed out on the bed in front of me, those flexible long legs spread wide. Her soft doe eyes watching me with anticipation. Begging for me to pound her tight little hole. What I wouldn't give to fulfill that desire, along with anything else she could dream of.

But the playful mood between us shifted when she broke through that window and took off into the forest. I hunted down my precious doe and captured her again. I led her back to safety. She still doesn't understand the kind of danger she is in. That we're both in, up to our necks. She seems to think I'm the one to fear.

I try to shake off my arousal as my thoughts turn from lust to concern. I noticed a change in Jewel's disposition during that long car ride today. She was so quiet and morose. I couldn't see her eyes, but I could feel her sadness. Despite her lawyer instincts, she gave up so quickly on interrogating me once I rebuffed her questions a couple times.

I feel a pinch of regret.

I should have been kinder to her in that moment. I should have given her something better than silence, if not a real answer. Although I'm somewhat relieved to have her settled down, I'm concerned about her morale. The spark within her that seemed to keep her questioning, bartering, probing all the time-- it's disappeared. I let the water pelt my face as I wonder, did I make her give up?

Did I break her so completely that she doesn't even have the urge to fight anymore?

I never wanted to hurt her. Not physically *or* spiritually.

Beep-beep-beep.

I cut off the water, a little bemused to hear my wristwatch alarm going off. I'm used to living on the road or in rough conditions. Usually, I don't need a full four minutes to my shower. I'm efficient. I keep my mind empty and focus on rinsing off. But this time, it was just so hard not to daydream about Jewel. I can't stop thinking about her. I grab the towel from the bar and tousle my hair dry. I pat myself down and tie the towel around my waist, not even thinking about it twice. I told Jewel I would be back in less than five minutes, and I meant it. I intend to prove my word is true. I want her to trust me.

I push open the bathroom door and step out, wearing just my towel. Immediately, I see a frenzied movement as Jewel jumps in surprise. The creak of the bathroom door must have startled her as she sat there zoned out.

She's pressed back against the headboard of her bed with her brown eyes all wide and fearful. Her free hand grips the blanket for dear life. Her face is paler than a ghost. She looks at me at first like a frightened prey animal before a snarling predator. Then, something different passes over her face as her eyes pan up and down my body. Her adorable, pouty little mouth falls open in a gasp. Her pale cheeks flush deep pink like roses blooming in the sun.

"Oh," Jewel murmurs. Her hand darts up to cover her mouth.

She averts her eyes. I watch her thick lashes tremble as

she forces her attention to the blank gray wall opposite our beds. I can sense her internally struggling. I wish I could tell her how much I struggle, too. How every time I look at her, my body yearns to get closer. To break all our rules and boundaries.

But I hold back. If this is going to work, she *has* to trust me.

"Sorry to startle you," I tell her. She nods slightly but doesn't look my way.

"S'okay. I'm jumpy," she replies.

"Do you need to use the bathroom for anything?" I prompt her.

Her eyes flick over to me for an instant, then back to the wall.

"I'm pretty grimy from being in the woods. I'd like to take a shower," she says.

"Okay. I'll uncuff you," I offer.

I grab the key from my pants on the bed and walk over to her. She stiffens up as I get closer, and I see her chest rise and fall rapidly. She's transfixed by my bare chest and shoulders. When I lean over her to unlock her handcuff, I can feel her holding her breath. Is she afraid? Is she aroused? I can't tell. Do I want to know the answer?

"Come on," I urge her, taking her by the arm.

She slides off the bed, wobbly on her legs at first.

"You okay?" I ask.

"I'm fine," she replies curtly.

"There's a clean towel on the rack. I'll bring you something clean to sleep in," I instruct her. She looks back at me as she walks into the bathroom.

"I won't look at you. I promise," I add.

She doesn't say anything, but closes the door part of

the way like I did. I listen for the rustle of the curtain, then the change in timbre of the water falling. Once I'm sure she's in the shower, I open my go bag on the bed. I change into a clean black t-shirt and comfortable black pants. I put on socks and shoes, just in case. I'll be sleeping on top of the sheets tonight. I won't let my guard slip again with Jewel in my custody. She's too important.

I grab my largest oversized t-shirt and a pair of boxers she can fold over at the waistband to make fit around her narrow middle, and bring the items into the bathroom.

"Stefan?" Jewel whispers.

"I'm leaving," I assure her.

I set the clothes on the counter and back away, closing the door halfway. I pace back and forth in the cramped room. I try not to imagine her naked in the shower. The water pouring down her shoulders, slicking over those full breasts and perky nipples. I picture her hand dipping between her wet thighs to stroke her sensitive clit, just like she did at the safehouse. I want to kneel between those thighs and taste her flower. I want to flick that tender little bud of nerves with my wet tongue and lap up her sweet juices.

"Fuck," I grumble to myself. I shake my head, as if I can physically shake off the persistent desire burning inside of me.

I hear the shower water cut off. I stand guard by my bed, arms crossed, while I listen to Jewel getting dressed. The soft rustle of fabric pulling over her curves. I lick my lips.

She pushes the door open and steps out, looking good enough to eat. She smells fresh, her skin is glowing, and her dark hair falls in damp waves around her pretty face.

But I sense immediately that her shower did little to assuage her fears. She looks so sad, and it aches to think I helped make her feel that way.

"Do you feel better?" I ask her anyway.

She shrugs. Then, she gives a charitable nod. "A little bit."

"A hot shower is good for the body," I reply.

Suddenly, we both are starkly aware that despite my attempts to give her a completely non-sexualized ensemble to sleep in, the oversized t-shirt still hugs her beautiful curves in all the right places, and falls just low enough to cover down to her mid-thigh. Her cheeks start to turn pink again and she fiddles with her hair, clearly flustered.

"Can we just skip to the part where you cuff me to the bed again?" she mutters.

"Whatever you want," I answer.

I lead her back to the bed and handcuff her like before. She curls up around her bound wrist, nuzzling into the pillow. Her hair fans out behind her and she looks like a resting angel. I can see a tear shimmering in the corner of her eye. I decide to give her space.

I go back to my bed and switch on the ancient television at the foot of our beds. I flip through the channels-- there aren't many, and there's a fair amount of static. But I choose a relatively clear black and white movie from decades ago, lower the volume, and the two of us idly watch it in quiet. After an hour or so, I hear Jewel breathing rhythmically. Her beautiful eyes are shut. She looks almost peaceful.

I wonder what she's dreaming about.

I spend most of the night awake, watching Jewel sleep.

She doesn't make a move except for the occasional toss and turn. But by the next morning, something still doesn't feel quite right. Jewel is so soft-spoken, she might as well be a ghost. I give her an orange from my bag as breakfast while she sits on the bed and I pack up. She picks at it, eating a few segments. Once I'm ready to roll, she lets me blindfold her again.

"Time to go," I say.

I grab her arm and lead her out into the brisk, sunny morning. She doesn't say a single word, not when I load her into the car, not when we pull away onto the back roads. I look back at her, listless in the backseat. We roll along the winding country roads for hours, and she doesn't make a peep. Finally, I decide to prod her a little.

"So, do you have any questions?" I ask.

She shrugs and turns her face away even though she can't see me.

"For a lawyer, you seem ready to concede," I joke gently.

But Jewel doesn't laugh. She just stares off blindly. I don't mess with her anymore. She's not in the mood to play, and I respect her enough to back down. Although, I am worried about her. Especially when, hours later and closer to our next destination, I notice tears dripping down her face from under the blindfold. Still, no sound. Just silent weeping.

My heart twinges for her in a way I'm not used to feeling. I'm supposed to be so tough. I've looked death in the face, and delivered death for many others. But this woman, this beautiful, innocent creature, has my mind all twisted up.

It's after dark by the time we arrive at our next motel.

It's drizzling, with distant rolls of thunder. I park the car right outside our room for the night. I grab my go back and swing out to retrieve Jewel from the back. I click the door open and find her looking right at me, as though she could see me through the blindfold somehow. I can't read her expression, but something about her demeanor stops me in my tracks. Her pretty lips part open.

Softly, she asks me, "How many more nights do I have to sleep alone, waiting for the inevitable to happen?"

I'm momentarily stunned by her question. There are so many implications to her words, and I'm not entirely sure what she means. But I quickly assure her, "You don't have to sleep alone. Not anymore."

I basically lift her out of the car. She leans on me a little when I lead her to the room. I walk her straight to the queen-sized bed. I had planned on sleeping on the pull-out sofa, but I might be due for a change in plans. But first, I need to procure dinner for my captive. I cuff her to the headboard like always and slip off her blindfold. She blinks in the dim light.

"I'll be back in a minute with something to eat. Don't go anywhere," I add, as if she could possibly escape.

"I'll be here," she answers, the closest thing to a joke I've heard from her in ages.

I smile faintly and head down the hallway to the vending machine. I get her a couple packs of peanut butter crackers and a big bottle of water to go with an apple from my go bag. I go back to the room and lay out her rations.

"Limited menu tonight," I tell her.

"I'm not very hungry," she mumbles.

"You need your strength," I counter.

She looks pale at that suggestion for some reason, but I

leave her to it. She picks over the food throughout the tense, quiet evening. When it's close to midnight and I can no longer reasonably keep away from her, I slide into the queen-sized bed beside her. I feel her tighten up, but I make absolute sure not to encroach on her space. Even though my hulking frame could easily sprawl out on a king-sized mattress, I stay rigid and close to the edge, facing away from her toward the nightstand. I can feel the enticing heat of her body and smell her intoxicating scent, but I stay back. She's handcuffed, but she could reach me if she wanted to with her free hand. I don't sleep at all, not even when I'm convinced Jewel has drifted off.

I lie in the dark, burning up inside at how close we are, yet impossibly far. It would break every rule to reach across that tiny space between us. But that doesn't keep my mind from running wild with the potential. I'm adrift in my own thoughts when suddenly, I sense movement from the other side of the bed. She's moving closer. I stay totally still as she pulls herself up almost to a sitting posi-tion. Then she slowly reaches over me. She strains as far as her arm will go-- toward my cell phone on the nightstand.

"Damn it, Jewel!" I snap, grabbing her arm in a flash.

She yelps with panic as I flip her over and pin her underneath me. Her arm is still held above her head in the cuff, while her other arm shields her face. She expects me to hit her.

I take her free wrist and pin it down instead. Her brown eyes are wide with fear.

"Please don't!" Jewel squeaks.

"Don't what? Why are you reaching for my phone?" I demand to know.

Tears sparkle in her eyes. "To call for help! To-to get away from here!" she admits breathlessly.

"You're not safe out there," I growl.

"I'm not safe *here*," she cries. "You're just toying with me. I know you're going to kill me, Stefan!"

I frown at her in the darkness, surprised to be having this conversation in the middle of the night, in bed together. I groan with frustration.

"Jewel, I didn't bring you here to kill you," I assert. "I'm going rogue with you."

"What?" she hisses. "What the hell does that mean?"

"You were right. The man I answer to-- he ordered me to kill you. But I'm not going to do that. You don't deserve to die, *malyshka*. I know that, but the people I work for don't see it that way," I explain. "So fuck their orders."

Jewel's eyes search my face for truth. She desperately wants to trust me.

"You're trying to trick me," she mutters.

"No, I'm not," I insist.

"I don't believe you!" she replies passionately.

"Listen," I snarl, leaning in close. "If I wanted to kill you, you would be dead already."

"Then what the hell *do* you want?" Jewel hurls back at me, like a challenge.

Our faces are so close now. I can feel her warm breath. Her lips are mere millimeters from mine. She licks her lips. Swallows hard. I swear I can hear her heart thumping. And then, just like that, I decide to show her exactly what it is I want.

I close the space between us and capture her soft lips in a forceful kiss.

CHAPTER 8

JEWEL

My eyes go wide as Stefan's lips press against mine. I'm startled for a split second, but my body catches up quickly. I feel warm and tingly from my head to my toes. Emotions burst like fireworks in my mind. Fear, anger, confusion, and potent arousal flood through me. It's a wild concoction. All the electrical signals that keep me sane and stable are firing out of control. There's only one thing I know for sure: the world before this kiss and the world that comes after are not the same. But there's no turning back now.

I push up into the kiss and part my lips as his tongue presses in.

Everything but the two of us fades to a dull hum in the background, while every movement of Stefan's body is vividly magnified. His hand curls around my wrist on the sheets beside my head and I feel his thumb rolling slow circles into the soft pad of my palm. His free hand cups my cheek and trails down to my jawline as his teeth graze my bottom lip.

I gasp when he gently bites down. I don't feel any pain, just a heady rush. My adrenaline is pumping. My heart is pounding like I'm about to leap off a cliff. My nipples tingle and stiffen. I feel them prick against the t-shirt, and every tiny rustle of the fabric gives me a ticklish shiver. Stefan takes my chin delicately in his fingers and tilts my head back. His lips trail down along my jawline toward my ear. His hand slides loosely around my neck as he breathes in my ear. I shudder at the overwhelmingly pleasurable sensation rolling up and down my spine. It tickles like crazy, but it's the most delicious torture.

He growls into my ear, "I want you, Jewel."

"Then take me," I whisper fiercely.

Stefan's hand smooths down my throat and over my collarbone. He kisses and nips at my skin on my exposed neck. Goosebumps prickle up and down my body. When his hand gropes my breast over my t-shirt, I suck in a tight breath. I'm getting so wet between my legs. My juices drip down my thighs underneath these folded-over boxers. I wonder if he can tell, if he can smell my desire in the air. I arch my pelvis up against him in a wordless plea for more. For everything.

He reaches down between us and I feel a giddy rush when his knuckles barely glance across my sensitive mound. He grabs the hem of the oversized t-shirt at my thigh and shoves it up, pushing up my shirt to reveal my taut stomach and pert, plump tits. My lips fall open and my heart pounds faster than ever to be exposed like this. But instead of shame, I just feel desired. Beautiful. So irresistible that this restrained, well-trained man can't help himself. He's desperate to touch me, to taste me, to explore my body. And I am chained here to the very bed we share, helpless under his powerful hands.

Stefan lets out a low growl of lust. His huge hand gropes my breast and I feel his rough, worker's palms against my over sensitized nipples. I moan with pleasure, my head tilting back as my eyes fall shut. I arch into his hand and his fingers work my nipple, tweaking and pinching lightly. I shiver and twitch with every teasing sensation. He dips down to suck my other nipple between his lips. He flicks the tip of his tongue over the stiff peak, then envelops it in his warm, wet mouth. He suckles and softly bites my nipple while his hand squeezes my other breast. There's a ferocity to the way he manhandles me. Like he's been holding back for so long, and now he's snapping forward like a stretched arrow.

"Nnngh, yes," I murmur.

Stefan kisses his way back up to my neck. His hand works down my body, feeling up my tight stomach and narrow waist. He traces softly along the slope of my hips and around to grab my ass. His lips kiss my neck-- the feeling is soft and tickly at first, but then he starts to suck on my skin. I whimper as he sucks a bruising kiss under my flesh. It feels so tender when he leaves it, his lips traveling back up to mine.

"I can't hold back with you," Stefan groans against my lips.

I part them and kiss him hard on his open mouth. I arch my back and press my bare tits against his chest. He pulls back from me long enough to pull his shirt off and toss it aside. I nearly salivate at the sight of his strong, muscular chest. His bulging shoulders and thick biceps.

Before I get a chance to really explore his body, he starts moving down. His lips move between my full breasts and along the line of my stomach. My heart beats faster and faster as he gets closer to my pelvis. He looks up at me and his dark eyes are fiery.

I give him the softest nod.

He grabs the folded waistband of the boxer shorts and pulls them down my legs. I kick them off and Stefan gropes my thighs in both hands. He spreads my legs wider apart on the bed and moves in between them. He dips down to inhale deeply, looking like he's ready to devour me. I stare in amazement as Stefan leans in and flicks his tongue over my swollen mound.

"Oh!" I cry out.

Stefan groans with pleasure as he suckles my clit into his mouth. My eyes roll back in my head and I rock up against his face. His tongue rolls up and down my clit and between my juicy lips. My whole body is on fire, with spirals of pleasure fanning out from every roll of my clit in Stefan's magical mouth. His lips nibble and suck at the tender bud of nerve endings until I'm undulating my hips and trembling all over. He circles my clit rhythmically, then licks down the center, repeating the pattern over and over again.

It feels so unbelievably good I can hardly remember to breathe. My whole body is totally tensed up. My free hand twists and grips the bedsheets. Stefan breaks the pattern to suddenly suckle my clit into his mouth, and the onslaught of unbridled pleasure he elicits from deep inside me is dizzying. I climax against his lips, my honey slicking up his face. Stefan licks his lips and eagerly laps up every slippery drop of my juices. I shiver and moan through the comedown and every residual flicker. I'm in shock, unable to even move yet.

"Nobody has ever-- I've never felt so good before," I murmur. My voice is slightly slurred. Stefan's tongue is truly intoxicating.

He glances up at me, licking his lips.

"I can show you so much more," he replies in a rough voice.

He starts moving up, grabbing my wrist and pinning it down again.

I'm still slick with come from my first orgasm when I gaze right into his eyes and purr in my most daring, challenging tone, "Then show me. Now."

Stefan tightens his grip on my wrist. I can feel his cock stiff against my thigh. I rut against him. I spread my legs wide and wrap them around his waist. I inhale sharply at the feeling of his hard shaft straining through his pants into my sticky mound.

"Careful, *malyshka*," he warns gruffly.

I can't stop the words that come dripping from my mouth.

"I want you to fuck me, Stefan. Fuck my tight little pussy," I tease. "I know you want to."

He leans down to growl against my ear, "I'll uncuff you."

I glance over to see the keys on the counter. Way over there. I look back at him.

"Leave it on," I whisper. "Don't waste any more time."

"Jewel," he growls.

"I need you *now*," I pout. "Go rogue with me."

Stefan doesn't waste another second. With a grunt, he yanks down his pants and kicks them back. He grabs my thighs and pushes them up, hooking my legs over his shoulders. He leans over me, spreading my pussy wide open. The length of his stiff cock rubs deliciously against my slick, pink lips. I feel my cunny pulse around him as he gently slides back and forth. His hands move down to grope my tits as he presses the thick, swollen head of his gigantic shaft at my aching hole. I whimper when he starts to push inside. His fingers tweak and pull my nipples while his shaft spears me open. My pussy convulses around his thickness, and every inch feels better than the last.

Stefan groans and rocks his hips back slightly. His cock slides out, almost completely but not quite. My pussy is twitching, begging for him to come back and fill me up again.

"Stefan," I gasp.

He shoves back into me harder, sheathing himself down to his balls. I whimper and moan at the sensation of perfect fullness. My cunny envelops him so well, like he was meant to be inside me. When he rolls forward, I yelp at the unbelievable shock of deep pleasure. The head of his cock brushes against someplace so deep within me, so impossible to reach with my own small, dainty fingers.

"Oh, right there!" I pant.

Stefan pulls back out again and slides back in again, with more force this time. He pounds into my g-spot and he holds it there, his cock buried so deep inside me. I'm dizzy with pleasure as he slides back, only to slam back into my twitching cunny again. He rocks back and forth when he's deep inside me, and the swollen head of his shaft massages my g-spot. I tense up as I feel a rush of urgency, like something inside of me is about to explode. Stefan's cock pummels my hole harder and faster. He can sense how close I am. Every muscle in my body tightens up, but his cock rolling hard and steady against my g-spot forces me to release.

He pulls out just as a small fountain of come spurts out of my convulsing pussy. I cry out in ecstasy as I drench his shaft in my slick honey. It's the most cathartic, incredible orgasm I've ever had. Like something I've been holding onto for so long has finally just broken free. Before I can even fully process what happened, Stefan swings his cock back inside me. He starts fucking me hard, forcefully now. He can't get enough.

"Fuck, you're so sexy," Stefan snarls.

"Oh--oh my god," I whisper breathlessly. "Stefan!"

His cock pounds deep into me again and again, my legs still over his shoulders. A twinge of pain shooting down my arm reminds me that I'm still cuffed to the bed. Stefan pins my other arm down beside me again. A feeling of pleasure edged with panic crosses over me as I realize yet again just how helpless I am. I'm completely vulnerable to this massive, powerful beast of a man. His gigantic cock is inside of me, pounding my tight cunny until I'm gushing all over his shaft. I have no control over anything. Stefan alone holds my fate. I'm chained here like a sex object, just waiting with stiff nipples and a wet pussy for him to destroy.

There's a bizarre, freeing delight in knowing I'm at his mercy. I couldn't escape, and why would I want to? I'm forced into submission to this brutal master, and I've never felt such pleasure in my life. He could do anything to me.

He could hurt me; he could kill me. But instead, he chooses to give me this erotic bliss.

Stefan's cock slides in and out of me faster and harder now, all slicked up with my juices. My honey runs down my thighs and ass. It drips onto the sheets in a puddle, and still Stefan pounds into me. He pounds into my g-spot hard, pushing me up the bed with the force of his thrusts. His balls slap against my ass as he works me open. My cunny tightens around his thickness again as another orgasm hurtles toward me in the dizzying dark. Stefan slides out and then shoves back in with such force it makes my eyes water.

"Oh, Stefan!" I gasp.

My pussy squirts sticky come all over his cock, making his thrusts extra slippery as he pounds into me again and again. He doesn't let up for a second. He fucks me through every resounding pulse of my climax. I fall almost limp as his cock destroys my cunny, his body tensing up for release. He smacks my ass hard and grits his teeth, his dark eyes locking with mine in an intense stare. His hips snap back and forth faster and more erratically as he loses control. With a few more thrusts, Stefan grabs my legs and leans in, his cock buried as deep inside me as possible as he empties his precious seed into my pussy. I'm still twitching with my own climax and our juices mingle as they drip down my legs and over my stomach.

We breathe together raggedly for a few beats in the silence. We're sticky and stuck together, his cock still inside my spent cunny. He gently withdraws and I fall slack on the bed. He lets my legs drop down. They've been pinned over his shoulders for so long they're almost numb, but the come still leaking out of my pussy reminds me it was worth it.

I watch Stefan stand up and walk across the room. He grabs a clean towel and the handcuff key. He comes back and frees my aching wrist. I immediately clutch it to my chest, rubbing the sore, bruised skin gingerly. To my surprise, Stefan uses the towel to clean me up with as much care and detail as a real lover. As though he actually cares about me.

He leads me to the bathroom, then back to bed. He climbs in beside me in the dark. I wait for him to cuff me again, but he doesn't.

I'm so exhausted and overwhelmed, but I can't help but question, "You trust me enough to take the cuffs off now?"

There's a moment, and then he replies in a rough whisper, "You trusted me enough to leave them on."

Somehow, that's a good enough answer for now. I leave it at that. My eyelids are so heavy, and the dark is so tempting and deep. Stefan's steady heartbeat thumps against my back, lulling me off to sleep.

THE NEXT MORNING, I wake up with a shiver on my spine. I feel cold. I realize there's not a warm, muscular man's body pressed up behind me. I'm alone in the bed.

And uncuffed.

I hear the shower running, the occasional shift of weight on the tile floor. Stefan's in the shower. The bathroom door is halfway closed, the fluorescent light spilling out in a perfect shaft. I glance over at the door to the outside. I'm positioned between the bathroom and the door. Stefan won't be away for longer than five minutes. I know that. What I don't know is how many of those minutes already counted down while I was still asleep. Basically, Stefan could be back any second.

If I want to run, if I want to escape, this is my one moment. Uncuffed and unsupervised-- when will that happen again? But I don't feel the impetus to run. I feel paralyzed. I lie in bed, shivering and torn between two doors. I could break free, but where would I run to? Who would take me? I also have to confront the fact that I might not want to escape Stefan. After everything we've been through, after how many times he could have easily killed me if he wanted to, I wonder if maybe I *can* trust him.

And that's not even accounting for what happened last night.

It doesn't make sense on paper. It doesn't make sense in any logical format. It's all so out of character for me. I'm cautious. I'm slow to affection, slow to open up. I'm always in control, and I never let a silly thing like lust cloud my judgement. Yet, what happened between Stefan and me last night in this very bed doesn't feel wrong. There's no denying what my body feels about him, either. I've never been so turned on. I've never felt such exquisite pleasure. My body opened up and bloomed for him, and he gave me everything I never knew I was missing.

Maybe my primal side knows better than my logical side. Or maybe it's just some amped-up version of Stockholm Syndrome. I'm identifying with my captor so intensely that I desire him. But are these feelings even real? Or just a product of my environment?

Hell, I've been asking similar questions my whole life.

Am I myself, or am I just a reflection of who raised me? Perhaps even a reaction against him?

Before I can follow those thoughts any deeper, Stefan emerges from the bathroom looking delicious and clean. He has a towel around his waist and beads of water still dripping down his shoulders and back. He smiles at the sight of me twisting around in bed to look at him.

Like he's genuinely pleased to see I'm still here.

"You're awake," Stefan says. "I'm finished in there. Bathroom is all yours."

"Oh. Right. Thank you," I answer.

It feels odd to just slide out of bed and walk across the room after being cuffed for so long. I step past him and shuffle into the bathroom, closing the door behind me all the way. To my relief, he doesn't fight it at all. I relax for a moment and take a second to look in the mirror while the shower heats up. It's still foggy from Stefan's shower, but I can see my face all flushed, my lips chapped, and that love bite bruising beautifully on my neck. It gives me a little thrill.

I take a shower, using the slightly dubious hotel soap to rinse off the remnants of last night's forbidden tryst. The warm water washes the tension from my bones. I'm a little sore all over, but it feels good. I step out of the shower feeling refreshed. Stefan lays out a new t-shirt and boxers for me to put on while I towel-dry my hair.

"My uniform," I remark playfully.

"We'll update your wardrobe when we get a second to breathe," Stefan replies.

He zips up his bag and slugs it over his shoulder. "Come on. We have to keep moving."

"Where are we going?" I ask as I follow him out of the motel room.

"The opposite direction we came from," he answers.

Stefan loads me up into the car, this time letting me sit in the front seat. He slides behind the wheel and I shoot him a bemused glance.

"So, what, we sleep together and I get promoted to passenger seat?" I tease.

He fires up the engine and starts backing out of the parking lot.

"You stopped trying to run away. That makes you a companion rather than a captive," he reasons. "Why, would you rather sit in the back?"

I shake my head. "Oh no. Definitely not. The view is way better through the windshield."

He frowns at me suspiciously for a second and I realize how it sounds.

"Not that I'm, like, trying to memorize our location. It's just really pretty countryside out here. Wherever we are," I explain.

"It is beautiful country. If only we could slow down and enjoy it. But we have to move fast because they move faster," Stefan says grimly.

I lean back in my seat and look out the window at the rolling countryside. The immediate threat seems neutralized. For now. Stefan doesn't seem to want to talk about what happened, but I still don't know if I can trust him. I can't resist the urge to ask questions. The lawyer side of me is desperate for answers.

"Stefan, who exactly do you work for?" I ask.

He glowers but doesn't say a word. I keep pressing.

"Who all is involved with this?"

Stefan sighs heavily.

"Who is your boss, Stefan? Who do you answer to when that phone rings?" I push him.

I know he doesn't want to go there, but I need to know more so I can figure out what's right and wrong anymore in this messed-up situation. I need to know if I really can trust Stefan.

"He ordered you to kill me. I at least deserve to know the bastard's name," I murmur.

Stefan looks over at me with pain in his eyes.

"His name is Brusilov," he says. "At least, that is the name I know him by."

"Brusilov," I repeat softly. "I want a face to the name."

"Jewel," he warns.

"I'm serious. If we're really in this together, I need to be on the same page. I want to know what he looks like so I'll recognize him if he… shows up," I explain.

Stefan thinks it over for a minute. Then he deftly unlocks his phone, clicks a few buttons, and pulls up a somewhat blurry photo of a man with dark hair streaked with white, and a patchy beard. He's smiling, but the smile doesn't reach his black eyes. He makes my blood run cold.

And then it dawns on me. He doesn't just look frightening, he looks familiar.

"Wait, I recognize him," I blurt out.

"Brusilov?" Stefan replies dubiously.

"Yeah, I'm wracking my brain to figure out where I know him from," I mutter, closing my eyes. A memory swims to the surface, but it's blurry like his photo. Still, I remember those cold, black eyes.

"He's standing in the stairwell that leads up to my

father's office. It must have been years ago. Two or three. Four, maybe. Before law school," I count back.

"My father is in the stairwell, too. I see them down the spiral, but I'm frozen still because I'm scared. I don't want them to look up and see me. They're talking about something in hushed voices. I can't understand what they're saying," I recount, digging deep to remember.

"What happened next?" Stefan prompts me.

"I guess after a while I got up the courage to step back from the railing and tiptoe down the hallway back to the lobby to wait for Dad. My memory fades after that," I sigh.

"Very interesting," Stefan says.

"Maybe I *am* more connected to all this mess than I thought," I murmur. "Stefan, what the hell is going on here?"

"I wish I had all the answers, Jewel, but I'm surprised, too," he admits.

Suddenly, the quiet air is split with the roaring whine of an engine as a motorcycle comes whirring up behind us. I glance in the rear-view mirror to see the guy approaching-- fast. He's speeding right up to the bumper, and swerving all over the lane from left to right.

"Uh, Stefan," I point out.

"I see him," he grunts.

His dark eyes are narrowed and his brow knitted together as we watch the motorcyclist widen his swerves into the other lane and slightly off the road on the other side. He begins zooming up on our sides, like he's going to pass us, only to drop back to right behind us. He's following so closely we can hardly see him.

"What the hell is this idiot doing?" I exclaim.

"He must have tailed us, and now he's trying to run us

off the road," Stefan says, reaching underneath his seat while keeping his eyes on the road.

"What does he want?" I gasp.

"You," Stefan growls.

He pulls out a pistol and rolls down the window.

"Stefan!" I shout.

My eyes flit up to the overhead mirror and my heart thuds when I see the motorcyclist's arm extended, and at the end of it the long dark barrel of a gun.

CHAPTER 9

STEFAN

My focus narrows in as I clock the threat encroaching on us. My analytical mind immediately leaps into calculating risks and tactics. I assess the speed at which the car is hurtling down this lonely back-country highway, and the curve of the road. It's as though time slows down for me alone. A moment splits and crystallizes into split second snapshots. All of my senses are instantly heightened. My finger presses down on the window button and it slowly starts to whir down to the bottom. Jewel's frightened voice pierces the air beside me as she cries out my name. A gust of cold, powerful wind pushes through the open window, bringing with it the scent of dew on grass. My ears pick up birds cawing in the distance and the faint buzz of insects gathering thickly beyond the treeline. It makes an oddly pleasant sound-track for what is sure to be an unpleasant rendezvous with a homicidal stranger. I can nearly hear Jewel's heart racing at the horror zooming up behind us on a motorcycle.

My own heart is certainly pounding a little harder than

its normal steady, even beat. As my senses sharpen, my body responds in kind. Adrenaline flows through my veins, making me feel like a well-oiled machine revving up to life. Fear transforms into exhilaration, panic melts into a tunnel-vision calm. My hand on the steering wheel tightens up. My beaten-up knuckles show almost bone-white through my skin as I clutch for precision. Every muscle in my body is tensed at the ready, poised for action, but not so tight as to hinder my reflexes. This is a fight or flight moment, and I am always prepared to fight.

I grit my teeth as I flick my eyes over to the side rearview mirror. I feel like a predator creeping through the tall grass, about to whip around and pounce on the threat that will become my prey. I size him up-- his blue and silver motorcycle, his dark clothes and lack of a helmet or even sunglasses on this bright, cold day. His brown hair is gathered in a lumpy ponytail, the straggly fly-aways whipping in the wind. On his face is a contorted expression. His eyes are cold, his eyebrows furrowed inward for focus. But his mouth is curved into a wide, toothy smile. Like a crocodile baring his teeth. He isn't even trying to hide his identity or his glee at tracking us down. This man isn't afraid to die, and he certainly isn't afraid to get sent to prison.

I size him up in an instant: he's an early recruit like me, but he's been working the slimy, undesirable muck work for years. He's recently landed a few good missions which have gained him the fleeting attention and favor of the bosses. They know how and when to turn a servant into a soldier. To strike when the iron is hot, as people say. He's caught enough momentum to land him this prestigious and dangerous mission. He has to take back the hostage, which means having to kill me in the process, because there's no other way I'll ever let them have her. He probably thinks he's invincible. He's high off his recent success and praise. But that's the problem: as soon as you prove yourself useful, they find a crueler use for you. The bosses sent him here knowing full well I'm more likely to survive this encounter than he is. He could have enough juice to complete his mission, but if he dies, that's only one fewer weapon in their massive, swollen arsenal.

And if he hurts a hair on Jewel's perfect head, I'll rip him to shreds. He revs his engine and Jewel whimpers, shrinking down in the passenger seat. Fury floods through my body at the sight of my precious captive cowering in fear.

Then, the bastard fires a shot that splits the air and makes Jewel scream and curl up with her arms over her head. I glance back to see his gun pointing straight up at the sky. He fired just to fuck with us. He's mocking me. Provoking me by scaring her.

I feel a powerful lurch of protective instinct for her. I'm a wolf defending my pack, only this time instead of a brotherhood of broken men held together by obligation and fear, it's just one woman. One beautiful, good-hearted woman. This man has put her life in danger. My own life hardly registers in my brain. I don't get attached to living. It's easier to walk somewhat willingly into battle when you've already made friends with death. But Jewel? She deserves to live. She never asked to be plunged into my shadowy world of bullets and betrayals. What may have started out as an assignment has become my own full-fledged responsibility. I took on the commitment of protecting Jewel's life the moment I went off-script. Everything since then has been my own decision-- and the results that follow. We've gone rogue. We're off the grid. We're outside the old plan, improvising by necessity every painstaking step of the way.

Right now, Jewel is helpless. Out of her element. It's up to me to save her. I don't know for sure what the Bratva would do to her if they take her back from me. But I've been a part of their dirty operations long enough for my imagination to cook up terrible, unspeakable punishments. As far as I'm concerned, the stakes have never been higher. I have to retaliate.

But first, I need to find my center. I have to slow my heart rate. I suck in one deep inhale as I turn to angle my body. My shooting arm lifts up and out to the open window while my other arm moves along the top of the steering wheel. I exhale slowly to sedate my heart as I extend my gun out the window. Despite the awkward positioning and the risks surrounding us like a minefield, I feel calm inside.

"Grab the wheel and watch the road," I command Jewel.

"Wh-what? Oh my god, I can't!" she panics.

I let go of the wheel and turn my body to look out the window. I hiss back at her, "Yes, you can. No one else will."

She squeals and grabs the wheel too hard, making the car swerve a little into the other lane. I can hear her starting to hyperventilate. Instead of yelling at her in the urgency of the moment, I calmly soothe her even as I point my gun at the enemy.

"You can do this, Jewel. You've driven a lot of cars. You don't even have to worry about the brake or gas pedal;

leave that to me. You just look at the road and make the steering wheel match up, *malyshka*," I instruct softly.

"What's going on? Who is that guy? Oh god, I'm freaking out," she mutters frantically. Her hands are trembling on the wheel, poor thing. She manages to keep us from swerving again, even though we're still veering a little from side to side.

"What's happening out there? Are you really gonna shoot him?" she asks.

"If he forces me to," I reply gruffly.

"Right here in the open?" she says.

"Thank god there's no one else on the road," I shout over the gust of wind that whips around me poking out the window.

"Stefan, look!" Jewel squeaks.

I spoke too soon. There's a pickup truck in the oncoming lane, coming at us fast. I quickly duck back in the window to avoid getting clipped. The motorcyclist is still behind us, darting around in the other lane like he might zoom up alongside us on the dotted line. Like he doesn't care if he gets smushed by the truck hurtling straight at him.

"Oh my god, he's gonna get hit!" Jewel cries.

"Don't worry about him, just keep driving," I order.

Instead of dropping his speed to safely stay behind us in this lane or taking the hit straight-on like a madman, he takes a different calculated risk. He revs his engine and peels out to the right to cut around us on the passenger side. His bike putters loudly along the edge of the road where the pavement crumbles into gravel and mud. There's several feet of clearance to the right, but there's a steep ravine beyond it that dips before the tree line. One wrong move and he could go spiraling off into the ditch. But he takes the risk anyway, zooming up dangerously close to the side of the car by Jewel's window. She takes her eyes off the road to look at him as he buzzes past and lets out a little yelp of terror.

At the exact same time, the pickup truck flashes by in the other lane. He lays on the horn as he passes, and I note that it's a grumpy looking older man driving. He looks positively bewildered by what he's just seen, but he keeps moving, thankfully.

As the motorcycle swerves out in front of us and zooms ahead a little, I quickly take the wheel back from Jewel. She slumped back into the passenger seat. I glance over to see her looking pale as a ghost.

"Jewel, are you okay?" I ask her.

Her doe eyes are round with fear. She murmurs, "He looked me right in the eyes. He laughed at me."

It's not petty hurt that has her so unsettled. It's the manic energy of this assailant. She's picking up on what I noticed earlier: that he doesn't have much self-preservation going on in that helmet-less head of his. Not only that, but now he's gotten a good enough look at Jewel to verify for certain that it's her. He has clearance now that he knows his target is in the car with me. Shit.

"What is he doing?" Jewel asks.

She points to the motorcycle far ahead of us now, but still swerving from side to side like he's lost his damn mind. Then he hits the brakes hard, his tires screaming as he cuts a sharp U-turn and starts barreling straight toward us in the same lane.

"Holy shit!" Jewel shouts.

"I have to call his bluff," I grunt.

"What?" she splutters.

I gently press the gas pedal and lean in as the car hurtles straight toward the maniac on a motorcycle. Jewel collapses down in her seat, screaming and bracing for impact. My heart is thumping in my ears. Every cell in my brain is screeching that this feels so wrong, so counterintuitive to staying alive. He's betting on my weakness— the bosses will have told him all about my shift in loyalty, my choice to save Jewel rather than fall in line. He thinks he can scare me into swerving off the road, if not to protect my own neck, then at least to protect her. But I am not so easily defeated. Instead, I'm accelerating straight into an accident, and I hardly flinch. I'm betting on the fact that this man wouldn't have made it this far in the brotherhood if he was completely idiotic, so he'll have to give in first if he wants to live, much less complete his mission successfully. He's a risk taker, but must still have something to live for, even if it's just the hollow favor of powerful men who would let him die without a second thought. I understand him. I almost pity him.

The motorcyclist gets within less than a hundred yards of us before her grits his teeth and decides to stop playing chicken. He zips around in a tight circle and accelerates hard to get ahead of us again. When the collision doesn't happen and she hears the motorbike putter into the distance, Jewel pops back up in her seat, looking absolutely dumbfounded. Her hands are plastered to her cheeks. She's in shock.

"Oh my god, he's insane!" she gasps.

"No, he's just sane enough," I answer steadily. "And I'm a better driver."

This time, instead of driving right at us, the man takes

another tactic. He drops his speed just enough to come within better sight of us. We watch him twist around in the seat with one gloved hand still on the handlebar. With his free arm he carefully raises his gun to point at our vehicle.

"Stefan! Watch out!" Jewel cries.

I swerve toward the side of the road as the biker lets off a shot. It glances off the top of the car with a sharp *TING!* Before we can fully react, he fires another shot. This one whizzes just millimeters past Jewel's window. She screams and ducks down again, her chest heaving with sobs as tears prickle down her cheeks. Seeing her so frightened makes my heart ache with a pang I've never experienced before. In this instant, I wish I could sweep her away from all this, keep her innocent and happy, untouched by the grim dangers that lurk all around me. My longing to protect her doesn't weaken me. I'm in battle mode, and my urge to protect Jewel only lights a fire under my ass.

I tighten my grip on my pistol and slam on the gas pedal. He's already put himself at a disadvantage by having to shoot backwards. Plus, he knows that a battle between my vehicle and his motorbike is a fight between two different weight classes. He and his bike would be toast. If I can keep him moving, he won't be able to aim properly. As for me, I've found my center. It's right here beside me in the car. My beating heart. My reason for going rogue and throwing everything into the wind.

I realize I would do anything to save her.

"I'm so scared," Jewel whimpers.

"Even if I have to drive him off the road, I won't let them take you, Jewel. I promise you that," I growl at her.

I lean out the window and level my pistol. My finger rests on the trigger as my eyes narrow in. With one hand still keeping the steering wheel steady, I line up a shot and fire. The force sends a jolt through my body but I don't budge. The bullet grazes the biker's arm close enough to produce a spray of obscene red blood. There's an audible bellow of agony and the motorcycle jerks to the oncoming lane. He's gripping his injured arm with his free hand, driving with his elbow. Definitely not a good idea. The bike sways in wide angles from side to side as he fights to regain balance. He puts his good arm back to work guiding the handlebar. But I won't grant him that luxury. Not while I already have him disadvantaged and in my sights.

I cock the pistol and fire another shot. This time I get another little spurt of blood and a garbled scream from the biker as the bullet hits his hand on the bar. He's completely overwhelmed with pain and confusion at this point. The motorcycle's speed drops dramatically in the blink of an eye and starts spinning out toward the side of the road. He cuts frighteningly close to the front bumper of our vehicle in the process.

"Brake!" Jewel howls.

For a split second I think he's about to get pulverized under the car, but I slam on the brakes just in time to miss him. The bike goes skidding off the road in a hail of kicked-up mud, dirt, rocks, and dust. I curve us around the cloud of muck. We both look over in time to see the rider manage to propel himself off the bike at the last second. The motorcycle, wheels spinning frantically, goes careening down the steep ravine. The rider rolls along the muddy gravel several times before coming to a stop. I skid the brakes and whip around to the side of the road, intending to check the carnage. I look back and see him lying in a muddy, bloody heap, his limbs all spread eagled on the ground.

"What are you doing?" Jewel gasps.

The car comes to a full, screeching stop and I instantly pop my seatbelt off. I reach to open the door, my gun right in my hand.

"Don't open the door! Wait!" she cries out.

I don't reply.

My killer instinct is kicking in. Years and years of conditioning with the brotherhood. The predator in me knows that my prey is wounded and vulnerable. It would only be too easy to eliminate him as a threat.

But as soon as the thought crosses my mind, I get hung up on the word "eliminate." It is exactly what I was ordered to do to Jewel. Something stays my hand.

It dawns on me that she's shouting.

"Stefan! Please! Let's just get out of here, I'm begging you. Let's go!" Jewel pleads with me.

Her sweet, broken voice snaps me back to reality. I don't need to kill this man. Not yet anyway. If I leave him like this, I can send a message to the Bratva. A warning about what I'm capable of, and what I'm willing to do. Plus, if I let him live right now, then Jewel doesn't have to watch me commit homicide. I want to protect her as much as I can— even from myself. I have to shield her from my cruel tendencies, my dark side she's only caught flickers of so far. She's seen enough suffering for one day.

So I close the door, fasten my seatbelt, and rev up the engine again. I hit the gas pedal and we zoom off down the dusty road. I look in the overhead mirror to watch the biker and his mangled motorcycle shrink away into noth-ingness behind us. I feel confident now that this was the right choice. I've successfully neutralized the threat for the time being. He won't be getting back on that bike anytime soon. Cell service is nonexistent out here so he can't call for help. Other vehicles come by this stretch of road only seldom this time of year. What's the likelihood of someone stopping to aid a scary-looking, bloody, maniacal Bratva assassin? And then the time it would take to hitch a ride into town, find a way to call the bosses and report his failed mission, and accept whatever brutal punishment he'll receive in return… He could be out of the picture permanently. Or a couple days at the very least. As we abandon the scene, I look over at Jewel. The tears have dried, and now she's staring at me.

"What the hell was that?" she demands to know.

"That was a consequence of going rogue," I answer gravely. "The bosses know I've veered off the map. They're sending soldiers to stop me."

"Just because of me?" she asks quietly.

"It's not your fault," I assure her. "You didn't ask for any of this to happen."

"But if you had followed instructions there wouldn't be a crazed biker trying to shoot us on the road," she points out.

I frown at her. "Jewel, if I had followed instructions, you'd be dead."

"I know. But you didn't. You changed everything to save me, and now you have a bounty on your head," she sighs.

"Worth it," I reply.

"You could've killed that guy. I know you know how. But you didn't," she repeats. "I saw the way you got him in the arm and the hand. Your aim wasn't off— you hit exactly what you needed to hit. Just enough to fell the guy but not enough to execute him. I don't know if that was for you or for me but, either way… thank you."

She smiles at me faintly. "He may be a crazy assassin but he still deserves a fair trial, you know," Jewel insists.

"There's my little lawyer," I tease back.

"And the way you fought for me… Stefan, I owe you an apology for being so resistant to trust you. I see now that you're truly protecting me. I'd be a goner without you," she says, passion choking her up.

I reach over to pat her on the knee. It's meant to be an innocent reassuring gesture, but there's no mistaking the flash of hot lust that burns between us for the split second my fingertips are touching her. I quickly put my hand back on the wheel and Jewel clears her voice.

"So, um, I'm kind of afraid to ask this, but where are we going?" Jewel changes the topic.

"Well, we need to lay low, especially with guys like that on the road," I explain. "Unfortunately, most of the safehouses I know in this area are by the main road, which we can't risk. Besides, if they've already caught on enough to send a guy after us—"

"They'll be watching all the safehouses," she finishes for me with a groan.

"We're kind of in limbo out here. Not many places to stop in the backcountry. Not without being too easily tracked," I go on. "But I have my own spot in mind. Not the most luxurious digs, but it'll serve us fine as a temporary resting spot to recoup for a few hours."

"As long as I'm with you, I can handle it," Jewel remarks. My heart soars.

I just hope she's right. She isn't spoiled, but she's definitely accustomed to modern conveniences. Updated interiors. Working appliances. This next place will be a roof over our heads, but it's not much more than that. We drive down increasingly darker winding roads. The trees pack in denser and denser until we're on a narrow dirt path. We're quickly losing sunlight overhead. We roll along until finally a rudimentary sheet metal and wooden shed the size of a one-person camping cabin comes into view. It looks beaten up and overgrown, as nature patiently creeps back to consume it.

We roll to a stop.

"Is that it?" Jewel asks.

I nod.

She nods, too. Then, her face twists up and she bursts into tears.

I put a hand on her shoulder and tell her, "We'll be in much more... normal accommodations by tomorrow night, I promise."

Jewel looks at my hand on her shoulder, then up to my face. Her beautiful brown eyes are sparkling with tears. She shakes her head and points at the shed.

"*That's* not the problem. I can deal with *that*. What I can't deal with is knowing that we're clearly in big trouble, and my presence in your world only makes it more dangerous," she sniffles. She wipes furiously at her eyes, as though she's ashamed to be tearful right now.

Jewel wants so badly to appear strong, even though she already is.

"That is not how it works. You have it backwards," I tell her.

"No, I'm right and you know it. You said it yourself,

Stefan. They don't want you. They're after me!" she cries, her voice cracking.

She turns and pushes open her door. She hops out of the car and starts storming through the overgrown weeds and leaping grasshoppers toward the shed on her own. In her bare feet, it's taking her an almost comically long time to make forward progress. I grab the go bag and my travel bundle from the back, then lock up the vehicle and go after Jewel.

In my boots, I'm able to gain on her quickly just walking at a steady pace. She glances back at me over her shoulder and gasps, startled to see me already so close on her heels.

"You trust me, and you're still afraid of me," I point out, "so imagine how much my enemies fear me. I can keep you safe, Jewel."

She glares up at me as I undo the combination lock on the shed door.

"A combination lock? That's your security system?" she mutters.

"Who's trying to break into *this* shed, Jewel?" I say, gesturing around the very modest interior as the door creaks open and light spills in. "Who could even find this shed in the first place other than me?"

"I don't care about the shed, Stefan," she sighs.

"Great. You have nothing to fear. I will keep you safe, Jewel. If they want you, they have to go through me first," I comfort her.

She does not look comforted.

"That's exactly what I'm afraid of!" she says.

I unzip my travel bundle and two tightly-packed sleeping bags unfurl on the ground, taking up most of the foot space as I close the door. I take out a lighter to ignite two tall white candles situated on the single square foot of what could be called 'counter space.' The tiny shed is illuminated with dancing firelight. I locate the tiny wood stove and the neat but dwindling stack of logs to start heating the place up for the dropping temperatures tonight.

"I don't want you to get hurt because you made an exception for me," she

"Nothing would hurt me more than to lose you," I answer her honestly. I stoke the wood stove fire and close the creaky door. "There. Should warm up in here soon."

"Ugh! You're so goddamn *chivalrous!*" Jewel snaps. She stomps her foot, which makes virtually no sound on the padded sleeping bags. "You show me nothing but patience and kindness and pleasure--"

I raise an eyebrow and get to my feet. I tower over her. I swear I can feel her heart thumping. Her cheeks are blooming rosy pink, her lips fumble to find words. Her lashes flutter as she looks away to finish her thought. I give her time.

"You risk your life to save mine, and I've been wracking my brain trying to figure out how the hell I'm supposed to repay that," Jewel blurts out.

Her eyes are wild. She moves closer to me. I feel the heat coming off of her body in waves. I'm already getting hard, just smelling her scent and feeling her heat. She reaches up with both hands to touch my face, my jaw, my lips.

"But I have some ideas," Jewel whispers.

Her hands trail down my chest and tug at my shirt. I pull it off and toss it aside. Her eyes go wide as her fingers explore the ridges of my chest and stomach. She's never been able to touch me quite like this.

For the first time, we are both unbound.

Her hands are free. And now that I've broken from the brotherhood, so are mine. We've gone rogue together, and wherever we go from here is our own decision. Judging by the lust burning in her eyes, we're going to the same place. Right now.

Jewel peels her t-shirt up and off in one smooth movement while I hastily tug down my pants and boxers. She dives in to kiss me while she pulls down her rolled-up shorts and kicks them off. Her mouth collides hard with mine, but the pinch of pain is worth the way she moans. I grab her around the waist and scoop her up. When she instinctively wraps her legs around me, I kneel down and set her on the sleeping bags.

I catch her face in my hands and pull her back in for another passionate, adrenaline-soaked kiss. We are both completely naked, grasping at one another like two sloppy teenagers on the soft floor of our warm little shelter. She interlaces her fingers with mine and scoots in to straddle me. I lean slowly backward as she moans and ruts against my stiffening cock. Her pussy is already soaking wet, and her juices slick up and down my shaft. But then, she does something that surprises me.

She unlaces our fingers and moves backward on her knees. I brace myself up on my elbows to watch her in motion. Jewel licks her lips as her brown eyes flash. She's blushing, but she isn't shy. When she leans in to wrap her dainty hand around my thick shaft, a warmth rolls up and down my whole body. I groan and tilt my head back, giving her the go-ahead.

Tucking her hair behind her ears, she dips down to flick her tongue over the tip of my cock. I can see a strand of shiny saliva leaving her mouth as she pulls back. Her eyelids are heavy, her jaw slack. I see the way her hand slips between her legs instinctively because she's so turned on. Jewel leans back in to suck the head of my cock into her perfect, wet mouth. Her soft lips and flicking tongue give me full-body goosebumps. When her brown eyes look up at me again, I see how badly she wants this.

Maybe I'm a bad influence on her. But if this is what going rogue feels like, I sure as hell don't regret a thing.

Chapter 10

Jewel

My god, it feels so fucking good. I circle the tip of my tongue around the swollen, thick head of Stefan's cock. He groans and bucks his hips ever so slightly, and it gives me a thrill to know my mouth has that kind of power over him. I moan softly to send little ticklish vibrations down through his shaft and root. I bat my long lashes up at him, making intense eye contact while his cock is stuffed in my mouth. His dick looks even bigger when I pull back and compare his thickness to my delicate little hand wrapped around his shaft. I slowly slide my hand down to the base of his cock, then swivel back up. I take care to run along the sensitive underside and sweep around the head with a little flourish.

His skin is hot and silky-smooth under my palm and fingers. His cock is stiff as a rail, and I can't help but smile mischievously when I see a sparkly bead of pre-come glistening at the tip. I lean in to flick my tongue over the spot and collect it in my mouth. He tastes salty and a little bitter, and I find myself salivating for more. Everything about Stefan turns me on. Everything he does makes me want him even more. He grits his teeth and groans with pleasure when I take the pink, velvety head of his dick in my mouth. I press down slowly to take him deeper into my mouth. Inch by inch, his cock slides over my tongue and stretches out my cheeks. Every inch I take makes me wetter between my thighs. It feels amazing to be so full, so stuffed with his glorious cock. I take him down to the very bottom, his cock pushing further into the back of my mouth to tickle my throat. I feel a deep, urgent need to cough at first, but I quickly regain my composure.

Or at the least, the most composure one *can* possess while throat-deep in cock. Stefan's hand drops to caress the back of my head. His fingers weave idly through my thick, dark hair as I move back up. His cock pops free of my lips for a moment and I let out a little sigh of satisfaction. But I can't leave him be for long. I dive back in and suck the head of his shaft into my mouth, tonguing the tip while my hand wraps around the bottom of his shaft. I massage slowly upward to meet my bobbing mouth, then back down. I smooth my dainty hand down over his balls. I gently cradle them in my hand while I suck his cock. The combination of sensations has Stefan's intense, dark eyes rolling back in his head.

"Fuck, yes," he grunts between gritted teeth.

"Mmmm," I moan in response, watching the pleasure dance across his facial features.

Even while I bob up and down on is cock, I keep getting distracted by his face, his body, his everything. His perfect cheekbones angled in the soft flickering candlelight. My eyes follow the cut of his powerful jaw and the straight slope of his neck, down to his bare chest. My fingers itch to wander, and I feel up the ridges of his abs while I take more of him into my mouth. His body is so hard all over, it's incredible to touch and behold. It feels like Stefan could be carved from marble, like a jaw-dropping statue in some gilded museum. He's something to marvel at, and even his rough hands and battle scars from years of living a hard, cruel life are beautiful to me. I want to worship him. I want to make him feel every bit as good as he makes me feel safe.

I lean back and a trail of saliva connects my pouty bottom lip to the tip of his cock. I click my lips and give Stefan a soft, devious smile. That fire of lust burns brighter in his eyes. He wants me just as much as I want him. We're like two magnets drawn together. We can't hold back, not for long. He's all I have in the world, but right now, what else do I need?

I take him in deeper, sucking him hard down to the root before swiveling back up to let go with a wet pop. I sigh and wrap both hands around his shaft. I pump him up and down while I catch my breath.

"You like sucking that cock, *malyshka*?" Stefan growls.

"Mhmm," I reply, looking up at him.

His hand at the back of my head starts to gently push, like he's guiding me back to his cock. I eagerly take the direction. I wiggle down closer to suck the head back between my lips. Stefan's hand presses down a little more forcefully this time and I take him down to his balls. He pushes my head down, holding me there for a moment. His rod is jamming down my throat, but instead of feeling panicked, I just feel exhilarated. When he rocks his hips to fuck my mouth, my pussy gets so wet I can't resist any longer. With my nose shoved down in his dark pubic hair and his cock choking my throat, I reach down between my thighs to play with my clit. I moan around his thickness as pleasure ripples out from my cunny. I feel warm all over, even as the goosebumps prickle up on my arms and legs.

"That's right, *printsessa*, touch that wet little pussy for me," Stefan rumbles.

I rub my clit in a circular motion while he releases some of the pressure at the back of my head. I slurp my way up his stiff rod and bob up and down with gusto. His pre-come mingles with my spit as it dribbles down my chin. Everything is slippery and sloppy, and every time Stefan groans with pleasure I feel it right between my legs. I grope my breasts with my free hand as I suck his cock with enthusiasm. I slurp and moan, feeling like I'm on cloud nine. Like I'm drunk on dick. I never want it to stop. Hearing his groans of bliss, feeling the tension pull in his muscles as he tries to hold back, and the pressure of his hand on my head. Both hands are gently toying with my hair now while I suck his cock eagerly. I love it when he uses both hands to push down. He bucks his hips, thrusting up into my mouth hard enough to jam his cock in the back of my throat again and again. Every time, I make a euphoric gagging sound, and it's all I can do to keep my eyes from rolling with delight. It feels so good, his cock pummeling my achy throat while my cheeks stretch to accommodate his girth.

I feel Stefan gather my hair in one hand. He gives it a gentle tug, and it's like an instantaneous shock of pleasure to my pussy. When he pulls my hair, there's a primal, almost violent lust that burns inside of me. I want him to show me no mercy. I want him to fuck me hard and make me see stars. I need his cock to fill me up however he can--

whether it's my pussy or my mouth. He wraps my hair around his fist tightly to gain control, as though he's holding the reins. Stefan pushes down to hold me in place and pounds into my throat a few times, getting me dangerously, deliciously close to running out of air before he lets go. Stefan knows exactly what he's doing-- he chokes me with his glorious cock just long enough to make me feel starry-eyed without actually hurting me at all. As always, Stefan tempers his own wild, voracious desires to keep me safe and happy. He wants to push me to my edges, test my boundaries, show me exactly what I'm capable of. But he always does it in a way that makes me feel empowered, even when he's in full control. I've always been a bit of a control freak, admittedly, but I naturally trust him. He seems to know my body better than I know it myself. He knows what I can handle, and he pushes me to the very limit.

I slurp and spit on his cock before I suck in a deep breath and let him hold my head down again. His cock twitches in my mouth as he gets closer and closer to coming. I groan and gag at the intrusion of his swollen member in my throat. I feel a rush of warm, wet slickness from my cunny. My hand sweeps down to spread my natural lubricant around. I slick up my clit and run smooth, delightful circles around the tight bud of nerves until I'm rutting against my own hand. I bounce up and down on Stefan's cock while I play with my tits and pussy, and before long I can feel him tensing up.

His fingers comb gently through my soft hair as he groans his pleasure. I suck him eagerly, excited to make him explode in my mouth. I'm desperate to taste his come, feel it choke down my throat. I'm salivating and wet for it, ready to take whatever he can give me. But just as I'm about to get him to the edge, Stefan carefully pushes me back. His cock slips out of my mouth with a slippery squelch and I rock back on my knees, pouting at him in confusion.

"Why did you stop?" I ask, my face shiny and sloppy as he leans forward.

He tilts my face up for a second, just admiring my features in the candle glow.

"God, you're so beautiful," he murmurs. "Come here."

I think he wants me to come in for a kiss, but to my surprise, Stefan grabs my hips. I relinquish all control to him instinctively, eager to see what he has in store for me next. At this point, I'm wrapped around his finger. As far as I'm concerned, Stefan can have anything he wants of me. Any part of me. Any time. So, I relax and let him spin me around in the soft sleeping bag pile we made on the floor. I turn around to face the opposite direction of him. I let out a little startled, "Oh!" as he grabs me around the waist and easily lifts me, pulling me back. He positions his face underneath my pussy, with my thighs spread wide on either side of him. I look back at him with wide, questioning eyes. I've never done this before.

But as soon as Stefan's tongue starts flicking against my over sensitized clit, I understand perfectly what I'm supposed to do. I cry out with pleasure, starting to roll my hips as Stefan devours my pussy. I lean forward slowly and dip down to pull his cock into my warm, wet, waiting mouth. He groans and suckles my clit, making me twitch and moan around his thick cock. He grabs my hips with both hands and his fingertips gently dig into my soft flesh as he holds me in place. He moves his face back and forth, round and round, his perfect tongue slipping between my swollen lips and around my clit. He tongues my aching, eager little hole, then sweeps back up to my hood. All the while, I have his shaft pressing hard into my throat. I bob up and down while I wiggle my hips, unable to restrain myself from riding his face. Stefan thrusts up into my mouth to meet my slurping tongue. He pounds into my throat while I grind on his face. It feels so fucking good, like the most incredible soft, slippery friction. I slide up and down and hope to God Stefan isn't utterly crushed under my gushing juices and puffy lips. But something tells me he can handle himself. He can *certainly* handle me.

"Nnngh, oh my god," I whimper as my cunny twinges around his tongue.

He licks up and down while I rock back and forth, and after a few seconds the pleasure is so intense I can't focus anymore. His cock slips out of my mouth and my eyes roll back in my head as my whole body tingles with anticipation. Stefan runs his hand up my back and gently scratches down, adding another delicious edge of sensation to the already-overwhelming bliss of my pussy on his lips.

"I'm so close," I gasp.

"Mmhm," he groans, and the thrum of his deep voice through my twitching cunny is enough to send me spilling over the edge.

"Ohh, Stefan!" I squeal.

My pussy bursts in orgasm, gushing honey all over his handsome face. He grunts his approval as he eagerly laps it all up. I shiver like crazy, going almost limp from the intense waves of spasming pleasure. Before I can even come back to reality, Stefan effortlessly lifts me and scoots me over a little. He sets me down on my knees on the slick sleeping bags, my cunny leaking juices while I lie here waiting.

"Stay right there for me, Jewel," he commands.

He moves behind me, kissing my neck and sweeping my hair out of the way. He kisses his way down my spine while I tingle and tremble under his touch. When he lays his huge palm flat against the small of my back and pushes down, I obediently lean down, my ass lifted up in the air. Stefan sucks in a tight breath as he runs his fingers over my juicy, thick ass. He gives it a resounding, stinging smack that makes me cry out and shiver. I twist around to peer back at him. I watch him stroking his long, hard cock in his hand. He gently spanks my ass with his shaft. I wiggle back against him, silently begging him to give me more. To fill me up and take me hard.

He lines up the head of his cock at my slick pussy lips. To show him just how ready I am, I spread my legs even wider, rocking back into him. The swollen tip of his member presses into me, gently at first, then harder. I'm so fucking wet, he's able to push his thick, hard shaft into me easily. He slides down to the hilt, filling me up with every glorious inch.

"Mm, yes," I whisper breathlessly. "It's so big."

"You like that, little Jewel? You like my hard cock inside your tight little pussy?" Stefan growls at me. I nod earnestly and bite my lip as he grabs my ass with both hands.

He rears back, his cock slipping almost completely out of my cunny before he shoves back in, harder than before. I see stars for a second as his cock pounds into my g-spot deep inside. Somehow, this position gives me a slightly different, new kind of pleasure. From behind, Stefan is able to strike an intense, deep angle. He rocks against the fleshy, soft wall of my g-spot again and again. My hands curl around the cool, slick fabric of the sleeping bags while Stefan pounds my pussy from behind. I feel so filled up, perfectly stuffed full with his incredible cock. My juices slick up every pounding, deep thrust so he can fuck me hard and fast. He grunts with every rutting movement, his balls slapping against my ass.

He reaches down to wrap his hand in my silky hair again. He pulls back just enough to tilt my head back. I love the way he takes control and forces me into a new position. He's always showing me just how strong he is, how dainty and helpless I am compared with his enormous power. Stefan could crush me in an instant. He could easily cause me great pain. But instead, he uses just the right measure of personal restraint to keep from destroying me. Instead, he just fucks me hard. So hard, in fact, that every thrust makes a deep, satisfying thudding sound. My pussy aches and twinges with mingled pain and pleasure. His cock reaches parts of me no one can touch. He shows me pleasure I never thought possible. I think of myself as a person with restraint-- someone who doesn't too easily get swept up in the moment. But I can fully admit that I'm out of control here. I'm not the one guiding the reins-- Stefan is. He could do whatever the hell he wanted to me, and I would gladly let him. In a few short days, this incredible, sexy man has transformed me from a prudish wallflower too nervous to even talk to a boy into a cock-starved sex kitten begging to be pounded.

"Nnngh, yes! Stefan, it feels-- it feels so good," I whisper fiercely.

He fucks me harder, his fingertips digging into my skin as he loses control bit by bit.

"*Da, malyshka*, just like that," Stefan growls.

Tears burn in my eyes as the pleasure mounts higher and higher. I'm losing control now, turning to putty in this man's more than capable hands. He slaps my ass hard while he pounds into me. The tension tightens up more and more until I can't hold back any longer. My cunny squelches and squirts as an orgasm shakes my whole body once again.

"Oh my god, I'm coming," I whimper.

My voice turns to trembly whines while Stefan pumps his cock into my pussy. My come only makes my slick lips more slippery, even easier for Stefan to destroy my cunny with his powerful rod. He fucks me hard and fast, smacking my ass until it tingles numbly. I can hardly wait to see the pink handprint left on my milky pale skin, proof that Stefan owns me, that I belong completely and solely to him.

"Good girl, so good for your master," he rumbles, as though he can read my mind.

"I'm all yours, only yours," I gasp out between force-ful, earth-shaking thrusts.

"That's right. You belong to me, little Jewel," Stefan grunts. "And I'm going to pump your tight little cunt full of my come."

"Yes, oh yes, please," I pant eagerly.

Stefan grasps my waist with both hands and ruts into me hard and fast, his hips snapping back and forth as he loses restraint. I look back at him and we lock eyes as he grits his teeth and releases a thick, plush stream of come deep inside my fertile womb. I buck against him while he empties himself inside of me with a few short, violent pumps.

His hands start to caress me all over as we come down together. Satisfied that he's filled me up completely with his precious seed, Stefan slowly pulls out of me. I whimper at the sudden emptiness inside me, but I don't have long to pout about it.

Stefan tugs me into his arms and cradles me against his chest in the soft sleeping bag pile. I nuzzle against him and listen to the soft thud of his heart beat, feeling so safe and protected in his embrace. He strokes my hair as we listen to the pitter-patter of raindrops hitting the roof of the shed. We watch the drizzle out the window, and the dancing shadows on the dusty walls. I finally take a moment to really look around the tiny shelter. It's not much to look at, and the wooden walls aren't sealed well enough to keep the draft from leaking in, but it feels much cozier with my protector holding me close. Stefan lets go of me just long enough to unzip one big sleeping bag. He scoots into it, pulling me along with him as he zips back up. We're pressed up against each other, bare skin on bare skin, soaking in one another's heat. I smile up at him in the dim light. I can feel his come and mine still slowly dripping down my thighs, making me sticky and messy in the best way. I generally like to stay perfectly clean, but there's something so primal about being soaked in my lover's seed. It's natural. It's just right.

"Thank you," I murmur.

Stefan kisses the top of my head. "For what?"

"I don't know. For everything. Showing me kindness when you didn't have to. Saving my life when it immediately puts yours at risk," I list off. "Not to mention making me feel really, really insanely good."

Stefan chuckles softly and hugs me tight. "I can't imagine it any other way," he says.

His words ring like a melody in my mind. I feel giddy and free, even though there's every reason in the world to be scared right now. The fear can't reach me right now. It can't find me way out here in the middle of the dark, rainy forest, with only my dark-eyed guardian to keep me safe. The world feels a million miles away. For the first time in days, there's a peace inside of me. It's crazy how quickly things can change.

When I first met Stefan, I fought my attraction to him because I assumed he was evil. An enemy to be feared. Just another oppressive figure looming over me, taking away what little freedom I had. Then, he became a neutral presence. A protector as much as a captor. Every moment I spend with him, he shows me a little more of his true self. The kindness beneath his cruelty. The softness lurking behind his rough exterior. And every little detail that gets revealed only makes me long for more. I want to under-stand Stefan from head to toe. I want to feel every inch of his glorious, strong body. I want to kiss him in every part of the world. I long to know the depths of his soul, what makes him tick, what makes him weak. As though there could ever be a weak spot to a man like Stefan.

But if there are... I plan to find them and kiss them anew. I will fill all the cracks in his armor with shining, resilient tenderness until nothing can hurt him. He wants to protect me, but I want to protect him, too. There's no denying the feelings between us as we slowly drift off together in the candlelight. We listen to the rhythmic rainfall and soak in each other's warmth. I listen to his calm, steady breathing and let it lull me to peacefulness.

The last thought on my mind as I drift off to sleep is that I only wish we had more time. Time to learn each other, to slow down and really love every tiny detail. I feel like I could spend an eternity watching Stefan, learning every little thing about him. The more I learn about him, the more my feelings grow.

WHEN WE WAKE up the next morning, I'm still wrapped up in his arms. Stefan gently kisses me awake. The rain has stopped falling, and the candles have burned out. The cabin is still dark, but I can see the pale, early glow of sunrise out the window. Birds twitter and flit from tree to tree. The world outside is coming back to life, and we must be moving along, too.

"Come on, Jewel," Stefan murmurs against my ear. "Time to go."

He kisses my cheek. Delightful shivers run down my spine.

"I'm awake," I grumble, my voice all rough with sleep.

Stefan unzips the sleeping bag and we both climb out, stretching and yawning. I'm achy all over from our primal lovemaking last night, and I'm groggy as I watch Stefan pack up. He gathers our stuff together, then grabs my hand to pull me up. I'm still wobbly on my feet as I follow him out into the brisk, refreshing dawn. We crunch across the leaves to the car. I look back at the shed almost wistfully before I slide into the passenger seat.

"I wish we could stay longer," I admit.

"This place is off the beaten track, but it's still too close for comfort," Stefan explains gently. "Besides, you deserve more than a sleeping bag on the floor."

I smile at him as he fires up the engine.

"No complaints about last night from me," I remark.

He smirks back and reaches over to tuck a loose lock of hair behind my ear before he reverses the car back to the rough-hewn trail.

"It'll be a long day of driving, but I promise tonight will be an even better place to rest," he tells me.

I wish I could tell him the location hardly matters-- as long as I'm with him, I'm good. But instead, we both let the easy, comfortable silence fill between us. The sun is rising over the wooded landscape, casting the forest in shafts of filtered golden light. We wind around the curving back roads, windows rolled down to let the fresh, piney air filter in.

After we ride along for a while, we come around a corner to see a vast, beautiful valley sweeping out in front of us. We're both stunned at the sudden beauty of our world. At the exact same time, we both reach out over the center console and our hands meet. His hand envelops my much smaller one, and my heart swells with affection. I know we're still being followed. I know we're still in danger. But right now, for this moment, all is right with the world.

CHAPTER 11

STEFAN

S oft country music from the seventies croons and twangs from the speakers as the car rolls along the winding roads of the New England backcountry. The music wraps around us and whirs out the window, mingling with the cool breeze and getting lost in the air. The invigorating smell of pine and fir trees waft through the window and excite my senses. It's like the collective perfume of the deep forest, condensed into one pungent, bright aroma. It's one of my favorite scents in the world, as it always reminds me of the power of nature. In my world, I have always dealt with a lot of powerful men with forceful ideas and desires. Men who would crush a flower under his boot or fell an entire forest of trees just to track down their next unfortunate human target. They care little for the big picture. They get stuck in the muck of tiny, gritty details. They want money, they want prestige, they want to constantly climb on the heads of their inferiors to get higher up on the ladder. In that world, a man with a gun and nothing to live for is the top of the food chain.

Nothing can shake an assassin who's made peace with his own death. It's easy to feel enormous, too powerful.

But being surrounded by the majesty of nature reminds me that I am only a small piece of the larger tapestry. I may be an apex predator, but I'm not the only one. If I were to stop this car and walk straight into the forest, there's little doubt I would encounter another beast, stalking me through the trees with even more expertise than I have. I can shoot a man dead, step over his bleeding corpse, and move on. But a grizzly bear? Or a tree that decides to fall and crush me? Those are enemies I can't match. Instead of making me afraid, though, that realization gives me peace. It's good to know there are things greater than the capricious ins and outs of life under the brotherhood's thumb. There's a world that exists out here so far away from the world I know, so detached from my deep-seated concerns. Out here, I can almost blend in with the trees. I'm almost a regular man, on a drive with the woman of my dreams.

We encounter very, very few other vehicles on our hours-long journey. One time, we pass a family of four in their station wagon. As they drive past, I catch a split-second glimpse into their tiny, separate universe. The father is behind the wheel, singing along to the music on the radio. The mom in the front passenger seat is turned around to talk to the kids in the back. A boy and a girl, both of indiscriminate age. The little girl catches my eye as they roll on by. She looks out the window and blows me a kiss. She can't be more than four or five. I give her a smile in return, and they disappear around the bend. An hour or so later, we see a big Winnebago rumbling up the road toward us. This time, it's an older couple, clearly enjoying their golden years by traveling the country together. They both wave at us with big, happy grins. I give them a nod in response. It feels strange to interact with these normal, happy people this way. As though I'm one of them. As if I could ever fit into their world. I wish I could only be so lucky.

I have my left hand relaxed on the steering wheel, holding on just tight enough to guide the car around hairpin turns and wobbly cliffside curves. My right hand is draped over the center console of the car, my fingers wrapped around my sweet captive's dainty hand. One thing I've noticed from spending lots of time with Jewel is how cold she always is. Not personality-wise, of course. In that regard, she's a crackling fireplace at Christmastime. Warm enough to make me smile, warm enough to melt the icy fortress that's been guarding my heart for decades.

But physically, her little hands and feet seem to get cold so easily. Last night, as we lay snuggled up in the sleeping bag together, she was shivering in her sleep. Even with my own blazing body heat pressed up against her, the low temperatures outside seeped through the thin wooden walls to chill her. That comes with the territory of spending the night in a shed up on a mountain. But I did what I always do, what my instinct tells me to do: I protect her. I remember waking up to the sensation of Jewel trembling against my chest. I remember fondly how it felt to pull her in closer, tighter to my body. I wrapped my strong arms around her soft, curvy frame and gave her all my heat until she finally stopped shivering. I recall the little smile on her lips when she warmed up. Seeing her smile in her sleep made something powerful and possessive rise up inside me. I want to preserve that smile. I want to keep her safe and warm and so happy all the time. All of this trouble, all the danger and risk and betrayal of the closest thing to family I've ever known-- it's all worth it a hundred times over when I see her smile in her sleep. I would stay up all night if it meant keeping her warm and protected.

Right now, I use my thumb to trace comforting circles on the soft palm of her hand as we drive along the country roads. Her fingertips are getting chilly, so I fold my hand tighter over hers. I feel the tension in her arm loosen up. When she gives my hand a squeeze back, a silent thank you, it makes my heart soar. It's still strange to me how the tiniest gesture from Jewel hits me so intensely. I consider myself a hard, stoic man. My focus is unmatched. My capacity for brutality is only barely restrained. But Jewel does something to me I've never felt before. Even though she makes me harder than a rock, she keeps my feelings soft. It's hard to feel angry and hateful with her sweet, inquisitive self around. She distracts me in the best way.

For example, I've been keeping my eyes trained on the road to make sure we don't encounter any surprises, like a seasonal detour, a wild animal, or worse-- a human enemy. But every now and then, I treat myself with a momentary glance over at the most beautiful woman in the world. Every look is rewarding. Every time, I notice something different. Maybe it's the way the golden sunshine hits her cheekbones or the way she licks her lips. Or perhaps her lashes gently fluttering and catching the light as she looks out the window. Even the way her hair falls around her angelic face makes me wish I could pull over and kiss her right here and now.

"It's beautiful out there," Jewel murmurs. "Look at how tall the trees are."

"Plenty of unspoiled natural beauty out here to take in," I remark, although my eyes aren't watching the scenery roll by outside the window; I'm looking at Jewel. As gorgeous as the forests and mountains are, they can never compare to her.

It's so peaceful, I can almost pretend like we're a regular couple on a road trip, rather than two fugitives from different worlds. I wish I could pretend we're just riding out to our vacation home in the mountains for some much-needed rest and relaxation. Not that I've ever been close to that kind of life. I used to tell myself I wouldn't want it anyway. That I would be bored or feel trapped in the mundane details of every day as a civilian, like I would miss the blood and bruises. The Bratva trained me well, and part of that training is drilling it into my head that I'm different from 'normal' people. I could never live among them. I'm too dangerous. I'm all sharp edges, how would I fit into the rest of the world? The brotherhood taught me to rely on nobody but myself, and to pour all my heart and soul into the organization. I let my missions be my objective, just jumping from one bloody encounter to the next. I learned to be comfortable, if not ever happy, in that world. Until now. Until Jewel.

I steal another glance at her as we glide around a corner. The breeze picks up through her rolled-down window and lifts her hair like a puff of magic. It floats around her beautiful face for a moment, and it makes her smile. She closes her soft brown eyes and beams into the wind. If I didn't have to focus on the road to keep us from careening off the mountain, I would have gazed at her as long as possible. The wind dies down as we turn onto a tree-lined section of the road, and Jewel turns to me looking rosy-cheeked and hopeful.

"So, where are we going? Am I allowed to know?" she asks brightly.

I nod. "We're heading to another safehouse," I tell her.

She tilts her head to one side, curious. "But I thought we were staying off the beaten track so your people won't find us?" she presses.

"Nobody knows about this one," I reply. "Hell, I hardly know about it."

"What do you mean?" Jewel prompts.

"I bought it sight unseen when I first moved to America years ago," I explain. "Paid for it outright, all cash. It's a cabin on a lake in Maine. I've never touched the place."

"Wait. Hold on, rewind. You have a cabin on a lake in Maine that you've never even used?" Jewel clarifies.

"Correct," I answer.

"Okay, I have a million questions," she says. "First of all, why?"

Instantly, I'm hit with the memory of arriving in America. Still nursing just a faint flicker of optimism, hope for the future. Back then, I could still force myself to believe that, one day, if I paid all my dues and followed my assignments to the letter, I could escape. It seems so ridiculous to me now, I struggle to explain it to Jewel in a way that makes sense.

"The same reason a lot of people buy property: as an investment," I begin.

"So, you plan to sell it? You're gonna play the real estate market?" she teases.

"Not to sell it. It's an investment for my own future. *This* future, apparently," I point out. "It's going to come in handy while we're hiding out."

"Okay, so it's meant to be a secret place," she says. "But if you hadn't met me, if we didn't have to go on the run, what would've happened to your cabin? What's it been doing this whole time?"

"Just waiting for me, I suppose," I answer with a shrug. "Hopefully no one has broken in or squatted there while I've been away all these years."

"Stefan, I've been wondering-- why me?" she asks suddenly.

"What?" I ask, frowning.

"You know what I mean. You said yourself you've been living the same way for years. Doing the same dirty work. Criminal stuff," Jewel lists off. "But now, we're totally off-script. You say you've never touched this cabin, so why now?"

I sigh heavily. "I was a fool back then. I convinced myself I could have an illustrious career with the Bratva and then retire to that remote lakeside cabin and simply disappear. Time passed by. I took on more assignments. I carried out orders. I worked my ass off, and I sacrificed everything for it."

"But the opportunity to leave never came," she fills in softly.

I nod. "Exactly. The longer I worked for Brusilov, for the brotherhood, the more I let go of that cabin. It repre-sented everything I could never have: peace, security, a simple life. This cabin is a reminder of everything I gave up when they took me under their wing."

"Sounds like you're not asking for much," she points out.

"And yet, it's a tall order for the Bratva," I remind her. "A life in service to the brotherhood is a lonely one. I accepted that a long time ago. Besides, I came to realize over the years that there's no point to being surrounded by all that beauty and peace when you have no one to share it with."

She squeezes my hand. "Well, now you do," Jewel asserts.

I lift her hand to my lips and kiss it gently. She smiles and blushes.

"That's why I'm going there now," I agree. "I finally have something to fight for. *Someone* to fight for."

"I'm going to fight, too. You saved my life, Stefan. We're in this together now, whatever happens," she assures me.

Her words are a healing balm on my soul. It's so easy to let myself sink into her kindness, soak up her optimism. She still has so much hope inside of her, despite all the horrors she's seen. Despite everything I've put her through. Nobody in the brotherhood has that kind of idealism left. It's been beaten and ripped out of us, systematically, until we no longer feel the urge for normal, human happiness. Her hope is intoxicating, but I have to stay vigilant. I can't let my heart run off into the sunset with her, not while Brusilov and his cruel connections are chasing us up and down the east coast.

"Stefan, what did they do to you?" she asks out of nowhere.

I freeze up a little at her question. It's so direct, so

pointed. She's a true lawyer, always managing to stab the point like a harpoon.

"It's more of what they made me do," I admit.

"Like what? How did all this start?" she keeps pushing.

It's strange. At first, I took her questioning as annoying, but now I understand-- she just wants to get it. To get *me*. Nobody ever takes the time to try and peel back my layers and see the true self underneath. Nobody in my life has ever cared to know, but Jewel does. She cares so much it puts her life in danger.

"Where I come from, there aren't many other options for a man like me," I begin carefully. I don't want to reveal too much, partly for her own sake, and partly for mine.

Jewel trusts me, even likes me. I worry that if she finds out too much about my past and the evil I've done, she'll change her mind. It'll shatter her image of me, whatever it is.

"And where's that?" she asks.

"Volgograd. Russia," I reply.

Her eyes go wide. "So that explains the accent. What's it like there?"

A million images go racing through my mind. The floating church. The yellow river. The wail of the train engine chugging into the station. The bombastic buildings looming stark and oppressive over the city streets. I remember the fish market, the people selling wares on street corners. I remember the harsh cold of winter, and how it made my bones ache underneath my threadbare hand-me-down coat.

"Cold," I answer shortly. "The weather and the people."

"What about your family?" Jewel pipes up.

A dark, sarcastic chuckle falls from my lips. "I have only a few blurry, confusing memories of my mother. She was a quiet, fearful woman. I was still a child when I realized that she needed my protection, not the other way around. She couldn't save me, not from the cruel winter or the slums or the Bratva. I grew up surrounded by their culture. I was entrenched in that world from the moment I was born," I begin.

"The slums?" she repeats sadly. "You never had a chance, did you?"

"That's up to perspective. Some would say it's my fault. I should have resisted longer. I should have died rather than submit to the Bratva. But I was a child then, and I wanted to belong. The bosses promised me a life of wealth and lawless freedom. I was liberated from my poverty-- so long as I did what I was told," I explain.

"What did they make you do?" she questions.

"I was always big and strong for my age, and with only my frail mother to protect me, the Bratva wasted no time in recruiting me. In the beginning, I took on guard duties. Protection or prevention orders," I go on. "I followed the rules. I was smart. I knew how to pick my battles and stand my ground when it was needed."

"So… they became your new family?" Jewel assumes.

I shake my head. "Not in any way that you'd understand," I tell her.

She scoffs, looking sad. "Well, if they're anything like my father, I kind of do."

"You're right. There are similarities. We were both brought up in a culture of cruelty and greed. I was taught to put the brotherhood first, then myself. There was no room for anything or anybody else," I recall bitterly.

"How did you end up here? I mean, America," she adds.

"I was smart enough to rise through the ranks, but obedient enough not to raise any eyebrows. The Bratva recognized early on that I was an asset, especially when I was harsh on my subordinates," I explain. "They thought I showed promise because I was brutal. But they didn't understand why I punished those men in particular."

"Why?" she presses eagerly.

"Let's just say we did not see eye to eye on how we should treat the innocents among us. Women, especially. Most of them, my brothers if you could call them that, were all too eager to harm a woman if she was in the way. Some of them even went out of their way to prey on women and the weak. Easy prey for heartless predators. I disagreed with that sentiment," I say.

"I bet that got you in trouble," Jewel remarks. "Like I did."

I give her a reassuring glance. "You are not to blame for any of this, malyshka. Never forget that. I don't blame you for anything," I tell her firmly. "Anyway, to make a long story very short, I took on a mission that no one else wanted. It was high-risk, high-reward. I took the risk, I was successful, and I got the reward."

"What was it?" she prompts.

"A chance at a different life," I answer. "Early release and a ticket to America."

"Wow," she murmurs. "But what did you have to do?"

I stiffen up. I don't want to tell her outright that I killed a man in prison. He was a terrible man who deserved to die, but I don't want to break the tremulous trust established between us. I don't want her to fear me. I need her to trust me.

"That's a story for another time," I answer grimly. "When I arrived in America, I had money for the first time in my life. I was hopeful that I could escape the Bratva, finally live a life I had never even let myself dream of. I even bought that cabin."

"What stopped you?" she asks.

"The brotherhood does not let go so easily. They were the ones who sent me here, who gave me everything. I should have known that there would be a price tag to their gifts," I growl. "I found work with the Bratva here in America. Little jobs, almost insignificant things. But as usual, the assignments only got darker as I rose through the ranks. I tried to live small, to fly under the radar. But they found me. They knew I was good for more than that. You don't pick and choose, they do. And they weren't going to let me go without using me up first."

"Sounds like an awful way to live," Jewel comments.

I shrug. "I stay busy. I've lived out of a go-bag for years now."

"I'm sorry," she says. And she means it, which only makes my heart ache more.

Changing the topic, I tell her, "At least now I get a chance to see my property."

She brightens up. "How much longer 'til we get there?"

"Just another hour," I inform her with a smile.

The remainder of the drive is peaceful. We listen to music, watch the incredible scenery pass by our windows. Maine is resplendent this time of year. The cool air turns colder as we wind up the mountainside. We start to see snow on the trees, weighing down the branches. The world is so quiet out here. We don't pass another vehicle for the rest of our drive. We might as well be the only souls out here.

When we pull up to the property, I'm relieved to see the cabin still standing, looking almost exactly like it did when I bought it from a listing. The afternoon light shimmers across the partially frozen lake. Snow blankets the ground and the roof of the cabin.

"Wow, it's beautiful," Jewel gasps as I turn off the car.

"Let's hope the inside is as intact," I remark, though I'm admittedly pleased by what I see so far. I grab our stuff, sling it over my shoulder, and then I do the gentlemanly thing and hoist Jewel over my other shoulder.

She giggles as I carry her up to the front door, making sure her poor little bare feet don't have to touch the snowy ground. I set her down on the porch, pull out a key I've never used before, and fit it into the door. We step inside and Jewel looks starry-eyed at the interior. It's a little dusty and it could use a burst of fresh air and some cleaning, but otherwise the place is immaculate. All the furniture and decor in the listing are still here. It's sparsely but warmly furnished with lots of wood, wicker, and stone. There's a small living room with a fireplace and plenty of windows and bookshelves filled with old, musty tomes. From there, we find a full kitchen with an antique-looking stove and a sink big enough to bathe a small dog in. We also check out two bedrooms, one smaller with a twin sized bed, and one larger with a queen and an en suite bathroom. While I inspect the clawfoot tub and dust-covered mirror, Jewel dives into the walk-in closet. I hear a gasp from inside the closet and rush over to make sure she's okay.

"Jewel?" I question, pushing the door open wider.

She whips around to grin at me, holding up a stack of old clothes.

"Women's clothes! And shoes!" she exclaims.

Immediately, she starts stripping off the big t-shirt and boxer shorts I gave her. Right in front of me. By now, I should be somewhat immune to her naked beauty. But instead, I find myself just as transfixed as ever. She doesn't seem at all self-conscious anymore. Jewel stands in the walk-in closet, naked from head to toe, and I can't tear my eyes away. She pulls on a soft-looking floral print sweater and a long, wrinkly skirt. Even though it's not the sexiest outfit, I can't help but feel drawn to her. It hits me that we're alone again, out here in the wilderness. We have all the space and time in the world to really get to know each other, and I have so much pleasure still to show her.

But before I can move closer, we both freeze up. There's a sound outside. We stare at each other while we listen. It's the unmistakable crunch of tires on dirt and gravel. Someone is here. I rush to the bedroom window, pressing myself against the wall as I peer out the edge of the gauzy white curtains.

My adrenaline starts pumping as I watch a police car come rumbling up the drive.

"We have company," I growl.

CHAPTER 12

JEWEL

I stand in the walk-in closet, eyes wide and heart pounding like crazy. I anxiously tug down the hem of the floral sweater I found and try to smooth out the wrinkles in the long skirt while Stefan peers out the window. I find a pair of old boots in a women's size close enough to mine, and pull them on my feet. That way, I'm prepared for anything. To hide, to run, whatever it takes. But who the hell could have possibly found us here? And so quickly?

I quietly ask him, "Business or pleasure?"

"Looks like business to me. It's a police car," he says. His tone is grim.

I'm already nervous, but seeing the shift in Stefan's demeanor definitely puts me into high-alert mode. Just a moment ago, when we were standing in this closet together, I could almost swear I felt that familiar lust picking up again. I could feel his eyes on my nude body, drinking in the curves and slopes he's already shown so much pleasure. He wanted me again. I could feel his desire for me radiating off of his body like heat waves. I had been trying to play it modest, just an innocent young woman glad to find 'girl clothes' to put on after a long stretch of being uncomfortable in Stefan's way oversized hand-me-downs. It's partly true. But there was also part of me, a deeper-buried, more subconscious part that wanted him to see me naked. I wanted to feel his shrewd dark eyes piercing through my body. Sizing me up and fantasizing about me while I innocently get dressed in conservative clothing. For a tense, delicious moment there I thought we might get to jump each other's bones right here in the closet. After all, we are finally alone at last.

Or, well, we were. Until this jackass showed up to ruin everything. And now, Stefan has shifted from lustful lothario to vigilant fugitive. I watch him flat against the wall, his eyes squinting when he slowly tilts around the edge of the window pane. The gauzy white curtain falls around his face when he peers out to check again. From here, I can see him, but not the window. I hastily lace up the boots I put on and crouch down to creep out of the closet. I move just barely to the edge of the en suite bathroom where the pale green tile meets the creaky wood floorboards. Stefan looks over at me from his place by the window, and his eyes are sharp with warning. He gives me just the faintest shake of his head.

"Don't come any closer," he hisses.

He's mutating into that dark version of himself right before my eyes. Gone is the softness in his dark eyes, the true affection in his voice. I can see his body tensing up as all the muscles tighten. He grits his teeth and glares out the edge of the window again. We both hear the sound of a car door opening and slamming shut, followed by the crunching of boots on dirt. The cop must be walking up already.

"Fuck," Stefan swears under his breath.

"What do we do?" I ask him urgently.

"*You* don't do anything," he insists.

"Stefan, don't cut me out," I whisper.

I'm shaking all over, so much that it's hard to keep my voice even. For some reason, I'm just as afraid right now as I was when that motorcycle guy was shooting at us. My heart is racing like crazy. It makes my chest ache with every anxious breath. The adrenaline starts to flow, and I'm itchy to do something, to make a move.

Stefan groans with displeasure when the cop keeps crunching up the driveway with his hands at his sides, under his coat. That alone makes me nervous. What is he guarding? What does he have under that coat?

"Stay put, I'll take care of this," Stefan growls suddenly.

I stand up, wide-eyed and worried. "Wait! Stefan, no."

But he's already striding out of the bedroom with a purpose and his hands clenched into fists. I make a move to run after him at first, but he disappears through the doorway before I can even get close. Besides, what am I going to do? Tackle him? He's got a good foot and a few inches on me, not to mention his massive bulk of muscle versus my willowy, delicate frame. If Stefan sets his mind on something, it would take a damn tidal wave to push him back. He's in possessive, protective mode right now, and I know that's because of me. Plus, I can imagine a lifetime being influenced by the Bratva has made Stefan pretty unforgiving and untrusting when it comes to the police. I don't blame him. I just hope he can restrain his inner grizzly bear well enough to not ignite an already tense showdown.

I listen to Stefan walk across the cabin, open the front door, and go strolling out into the fading afternoon golden glow. The sparkly sunlight glints off the melting snow in the yard as Stefan and the police officer walk toward each other. My heart is about to burst out and fly away, I'm so on edge. I decide I'm not close enough, so I rush to the window to watch the scene unfold. I can hear them, but all the noise is slightly muffled through the window. The cop parked far back from the cabin, and he's walking with some definite caution, like he's half-expecting a fight. That might not bode well for Stefan, who has the sharp dark eyes, hulking size, and commanding, Russian-tinged speaking voice of a movie villain. I wonder if the cop is some kind of city slicker far out of dodge, chasing down a fugitive across state lines. And if Stefan's a fugitive, does that make me an accessory? Or just a victim? I always thought the law was simple enough, black and white enough, to satisfy the whole world's morality. But I see now through the lens of a layperson, of someone entrenched in crime rather than just studying it in a lofty academic library, and it looks different from here. The bad guys aren't always bad, and the good guys definitely aren't always good.

The police office strolls up to stop about ten feet away from Stefan, then he holds up one palm to halt him, too. I can positively sense Stefan bristling at this punk-ass cop telling him what to do. The cop is a tall, gangly man with a slight paunch around his waist. He has thinning reddish hair and a close-trimmed ginger beard. He walks with a sort of swaggering limp, and I almost have to giggle at how ridiculous he looks wearing his sunglasses while the sun is clearly going down. The light isn't anywhere bright enough to require shades at the moment, but I have a feeling the guy thinks he just looks cooler that way. He's wrong.

By comparison, Stefan looks even more like a wolf in sheep's clothing. His enormous size and imposing demeanor make the cop a little nervous.

"Whoa, there," the cop says as he gestures for Stefan to freeze.

Stefan slowly raises his hands in a symbol of truce.

"Evening, Officer. What can I do for you?" he calls out gruffly.

"Stay right where you are, buddy. We can talk just fine from here," the cop insists.

Stefan shrugs. "I'm not going anywhere."

"Well... good," the cop stammers. "Not lookin' for trouble tonight, sir, but I'm the local sheriff around here and it's my job to follow up on things."

"Understood. What are you following up on here?" Stefan asks pointedly.

I wince a little. His vibe is a little aggressive, and his Russian accent is coming through more clearly than usual. I wonder if I just don't usually notice it. But right now, compared to the sheriff's genteel drawl, Stefan sounds like a spy movie assassin. That country cop tilts his head a little and squints, like he's trying to figure Stefan out. Not good.

"Well, I've been patrolling this neck of the woods for about a decade now, and usually nobody comes all the way up here," the sheriff explains, hands on his hips. "People live real spread out around the mountains and down the valley, so there's a lot of land to cover. But I make it my business to know all the uninhabited properties and keep an eye on 'em."

"How close an eye?" Stefan questions sharply.

"Oh, Stefan. No," I mutter to myself.

The sheriff raises one wiry red eyebrow. "Close enough to watch out for squatters and vandals. Opportunists who think they can blow through my district and just set up camp wherever they damn well please," he retorts.

"Who told you anyone was here?" Stefan asks.

My heart sinks. This is not going well. Stefan is too defensive, too intense. The cop is getting more and more suspicious of him by the second.

The cop takes another step closer. "Now, sir, let's get a couple things straight real quick. First off, you don't ask the questions. I do. Second of all, I don't owe you my informants' information. People around here trust me to look after life and land, and that's what I do. I heard there was a car goin' up the mountain to the lake, and I thought it might be hooligans," he says.

"Hooligans?" Stefan repeats, and this time his Russian accent is so clear it makes me go pale. He's been doing his best to hide his true way of speaking, but it slips through, especially when he's angry. Some people still probably wouldn't notice. But this sheriff is obviously used to running a very small, insular community. Everybody knows everybody else, and outsiders are very easy to spot right off the bat.

The cop glares at him suspiciously and his demeanor shifts with his stance. He's got one hand sliding under the bottom hem of his coat, around to the back of his work pants. I swallow hard, realizing he's reaching for his firearm. This simple conversation between two guys is quickly escalating into a dangerous situation. Right now, Stefan is unarmed. The sheriff showed up too suddenly for us to prepare, and now his life is in jeopardy because of a misunderstanding.

All at once, a million different emotions and impulses strike me like a ton of bricks to the face. Time slows down as I try to sort out my thoughts. I'm experiencing a split of conscience.

One option occurs to me from the fog: that this could be my perfect chance for escape. At the start of my captivity, I would have done anything to encounter a police officer. I would have immediately rushed to the other side, let the cop arrest Stefan and take me safely back to my real life. I have that opportunity now, too. It's been several days, but a tiny part of me reminds me that's not very long at all in the grand scheme of things. How could my feelings about Stefan have altered so dramatically in such a short amount of time? Is it right for me to trust him, to want him like I do? Or is it just another side effect of whatever Stockholm Syndrome bullshit is driving my actions? I recall with a twinge of pain what our first encounter felt like. I was so scared of Stefan. I hated him. He ripped me from my life, kidnapped me, and put me in a basement prison cell, chained to a crappy bed. That makes him a bad guy, right?

My father is an ICE agent, a man who taught me that success belongs to the good guys, and the bad guys deserve harsh punishment. He taught me a very black-and-white dichotomy between good and evil: cops and agents like Dad were on the 'good' side, while lifelong criminals like Stefan were on the 'bad' side. Stefan himself has even admitted to doing very bad things for a long time. Sure, he broke his mission to save me, but how many lives did he take before he ever met me? And who's to say for certain he won't eventually kill me, too? I mean, hell, we're already on the run together. How long can that last? And when we're finally backed into a corner-- kind of like this-- what will he do? Will he still defend and protect me? Or will I become just another unfortunate casualty of his lifestyle?

"I hope you're not lookin' for any trouble today, sir," the cop warns Stefan.

"Not looking, but you never know what you will find," Stefan remarks.

Alarm bells are ringing in my head. Some tiny, soft-spoken part of me suggests that I should save myself. I should run out there and throw Stefan under the bus, tell the cop everything, and let him send me back home. I can't ignore the bare-faced facts: Stefan is at best a kidnapper, at worst a murderer. That makes him a 'bad guy' in the simplistic idea of justice Dad taught me growing up. There's not a lot of nuance in the world of law and order.

Then again, if there's anything my time with Stefan has taught me, it's that life is more complicated than that. Things change. People change. But only when they're up against a wall, when they find the one reason worthy of changing for. And people are so much more complex, deeper than I used to think. Even the ones who put up such an impressive, seemingly impenetrable facade, like Stefan. Yes, the first version of him I met was so scary, but now I have come to see him not as a captor, but a protector. Someone on my side. After all, he broke every rule for me. If he was truly selfish, truly evil, he would have 'eliminated' me when he had the chance. And God knows I've given him a thousand opportunities. Instead, he repeatedly puts his own life at risk to save mine.

That's not even to mention the undeniable, irresistible connection growing between us, both physically and emotionally. I could never turn on him even if I wanted to.

Besides, if I were to give up now and go running to that policeman for safety, I would never get the answers I seek. I want to know the truth of my father's connection to all this mess. Clearly, I've been living under a rock this whole time. I didn't even know men like Stefan existed outside of action movies and romance novels. The black and white way of seeing the world I used to hold has changed, and I can never go back. I can't even trust my own father anymore. I'm changed, irrevocably. My investigative instincts won't let me walk away from this any more than my feelings for Stefan will. The lawyer part of me I need answers, and if Stefan gets taken in, the whole thing falls apart.

And the pang of protective worry that comes over me when I imagine that sheriff putting Stefan in handcuffs tells me I can't let that happen. He's protected me against all orders, and it's up to me to return the favor now.

So when I see the cop take another step, and Stefan does the same, I know I can't wait any longer to make my move. This could come to blows and blood any second now. I take a deep breath and comb my fingers quickly through my messy hair to make myself look less like a sleep-deprived captive and more like a happy camper. I smooth down my moth-eaten stolen clothing and speed-walk across the house to the front door. My heart is thumping painfully in my ribcage as I step out onto the porch. Cold, forest-scented air gusts in my face. It's time for me to do a little acting. My role: Stefan's beguiling American girlfriend here to smooth things over and prove we're just here on a little vacay from the city. Nothing to worry about here.

The sheriff and Stefan notice me at the same time. Stefan turns and does a double take, his dark eyes smoldering at the sight of me. I can't quite tell if he's angry or relieved to see me, but either way, I'm here now. The sheriff, on the other hand, looks quite pleased to see me standing here. His pale eyes rove hungrily up and down my willowy, curvy frame. I plaster a big smile on my face and twirl a lock of hair around my finger absentmindedly as I approach them.

Truth be told, I'm used to his type. When I was growing up, Dad used to always bring around his snooty, borderline-pervy good ole boy pals. One of his favorite things to do when they came over was to show me off. He would call me downstairs and make me do little spins and twirls, say my how-do-you-dos to an endless number of middle-aged womanizers who cheated on their wives with women young enough to be their granddaughters. Like me. It suddenly dawns on me how gross it was for Dad to show off his beautiful, virginal, off-limits (wink-wink) daughter to his ghoulish friends, but that's a problem for another time.

Right now, I just have to do whatever it takes to defuse the situation and save Stefan.

"Hi there, Officer!" I call out in my sweetest, peachiest voice.

I give him a big goofy wave as I daintily hop down from the porch. Stefan is frozen in place as I start strolling up next to him. The cop is transfixed on me now, just as I planned. His cheeks are turning pink, and I can tell he feels a little bashful. He probably doesn't get to talk to many pretty young women out here on his daily routes. He was probably expecting some rough-edged old geezer with a rifle and an attitude to come charging out of the cabin. But he seems to melt a little bit for me. His shoulders relax, and he lets the hand on his gun drop to his side. I feel a rush of temporary relief.

"How are you doing tonight?" I ask him cheerily.

"I'm just fine, thank you, Miss. How're you?" the sheriff asks.

"Fantastic, but a little tired. My boyfriend and I have been driving all day long to get here before dark," I tell him.

"Your boyfriend?" he repeats, giving Stefan another dubious glare.

I link arms with Stefan and lean into his shoulder with a smile.

"Mhm. He's a great driver, but boy! These country roads sure make you pay attention, don't they? Especially this time of year," I ramble on.

"So you are from out of town," he clarifies.

"You guessed it. Although, I bet being the sheriff, you probably know just about everybody out here, so you must've known right off the bat," I remark, still smiling.

"Can't be too careful these days," he replies.

"Hey, can't argue with you there," I answer good-naturedly. "Anyway, we're just staying for a little vacation. You know, a getaway from the big city."

"Oh yeah, I get that," he says, grinning. "Way better in the boonies."

"Totally. I told him, I said, 'if we don't get out of this dang city soon, I'm gonna explode' so here we are. It'll be so nice to get fresh air and listen to the birds," I sigh.

"Well, little lady, you sure came to the right spot," the sheriff beams. He's clearly very proud of his neck of the woods, and I'm playing right into that.

"Like my girlfriend says, we're very tired. It's been a long day," Stefan speaks up. He slides an arm around my shoulders, holding me tight.

"Mhm. Yep. We're totally exhausted from all that driving and, uh, bird-watching we did along the way. Can't wait to get a good night's sleep!" I jump in.

The cop looks back and forth between us, thinking it over. Then he simply grins, shrugs, and waves. "Alrighty, then. You kids have a good stay, and remember to respect Mother Nature while you're out here," he says, waggling one finger at us as he wobbles back to his car.

Stefan and I stand here waving, afraid to let our facade drop for a second. We watch the cop car roll away down the drive and disappear into the darkness. As soon as he's gone, Stefan pulls his arm back and whips around to gaze at me with those fiery eyes blazing.

"What do you think you're doing?" he demands.

I blink rapidly in surprise. "Excuse me?"

He pinches the bridge of his nose in frustration. "Jumping in like that? Unplanned?"

"Um, from where I'm standing, it looks like I just saved our asses," I retort.

"It may have worked this time, but we got lucky. You didn't even consider the risks involved in bursting out the door like that?" he scolds me.

My cheeks burn with indignation. I put my hands on my hips.

"Of course I considered the risks! Did *you?* Stefan, that cop was packing heat, and you came out here unarmed," I point out.

He leans in closer. "I was handling it," he growls.

"You needed me, Stefan, whether you want to admit it or not," I snap.

"That's not the problem," he quips.

The sun is sinking down all around us. The world is descending into darkness as the forest comes alive with nocturnal noises. Stefan and I are at a stand-off, face to face, breathing out puffs of air in the cold night.

"I'm not just your damsel in distress. I saved our cover. I'm a part of this team," I insist.

"Don't you understand? I'm doing all of this to protect you, Jewel. Nothing is worth the risk of losing you. I would rather show up unarmed to a gunfight than watch you jump in front of a bullet to save me," he snarls, his face almost touching mine.

"And I'd rather take that bullet than watch you die for me," I hurl back.

Stefan looms over me, anger and hurt in his eyes. I glare up at him with the same fierce energy. Neither of us is willing to back down. Again, we're at an impasse. And again, that intense fire between us stokes the mood from fury to lust.

Stefan grabs my face with both hands and kisses me hard. I moan into his mouth, pressing my whole body flush against his. I can already feel his cock filling out, getting hard against my hip. I put my arms around his neck as he kisses me, and his strong hands grab underneath my ass to scoop me up. I wrap my legs around his waist as he carries me back to the porch. He takes the steps in one long, easy stride, and pushes back into the cabin. Warm air rushes over us both, adding to the fire. Stefan walks me to the wall of the living room, pinning me between the wall and his powerful body. He kisses me deeply, his hands roving up and down my body as he holds me up against the wall. Suddenly, I'm desperate to touch him underneath his clothes. I need to feel his skin on mine, and the feeling is mutual.

Stefan hikes up my long skirt while I fumble to tug down his pants and boxers, just enough for his stiff cock to bounce free. I lick my lips and roll my eyes back in my head as Stefan's lips travel down my throat. He pushes up my sweater to flick his tongue over my perky nipples. I moan and shudder in his arms. My pussy is getting so wet already, I can hardly wait for him to fill me up again. I rock against him and claw at his back with my fingernails, lifting up his shirt to get at bare flesh. His cock slides up and down along my dewy flower, bare underneath the long skirt. My slick juices drip down my thighs and soak his cock, which only makes it easier for him to tease my achy hole with the thick head of his shaft.

"Are you ready for me, *printsessa*?" Stefan rumbles.

"Give it to me," I whisper ferociously.

He doesn't hold back. Still bracing me against the wall, he slides his hard cock inside me inch by inch, and I take him all the way down. I cry out as my mind goes bright with wild sensations. Stefan holds me in place while he bucks his hips. I keep my legs tight around his waist as he fucks me deep and hard. My pussy twinges and clenches around his thickness. His lips travel up to my ear. His soft breath gives me goosebumps and makes me shiver.

"Don't you dare put yourself in danger like that again," he hisses in my ear.

"Don't tell me what to do," I bite back.

I know I'm being a brat, but I can't help it. Besides, every time I say something naughty, it makes Stefan fuck me harder. How can I be good when I receive such a delicious reward for being bad? When he leans in to kiss me again, I gently bite his bottom lip. He lets out a low growl and presses his hand to my throat. I lick my lips and moan with delight when he applies gentle pressure to the sides of my neck. He knows just how to tease me, how to make me feel submissive and powerless without scaring me. He holds my throat while his cock pounds deeper into my gushing cunny. I'm so wet, every thrust slides in and out of me with perfect ease. The tip of his cock slams into my g-spot with nearly every other push, and I'm starting to see stars.

"Oh fuck, it feels good," I pant.

"Don't come until I say so," Stefan commands. His hips snap back and forth faster as he fucks me, and he's starting to lose control.

I pout, making a pitiful little choking sound when he presses harder on my throat.

"Please, I'm so close," I whimper.

"Not yet, *malyshka*. You'll come when I allow it," he snarls.

I'm trying so hard to hold back, but it feels so damn good. His cock pounds my g-spot while the friction of his pelvis on my clit makes me tingly all over. Add to that the thrill of being totally dominated, totally owned by this powerful, sexy man, and how can he possibly expect me to have self-control? My pussy is tensing, my clit burning for a release.

"Oh my god," I whine. "Stefan!"

He's stiffening up, too, his pace speeding up until he's railing my cunny. I'm loose and limp in his arms as he pounds into me again and again.

"Come for me, Jewel. Right now. Come all over this cock," he demands.

"Ohhh Stefan!" I cry out.

My cunny is obedient. I come in a hot gush of sweet juices, drenching us both as his cock pummels into me with abandon. While I'm still dripping and twitching from climax, I feel Stefan's cock spurt his seed deep, deep inside of me. He groans through gritted teeth and rocks his hips to empty every last precious drop in my womb. Stefan kisses me and strokes my face as I come down from the rush.

When he finally withdraws, he lets me gently slide down the wall out of his arms. I'm limp and gasping as the weight of the day and our near-miss encounter with the law hits me hard. He has to basically catch me before I crumple to the floor. Luckily, Stefan is strong enough for the both of us. He scoops me up damsel-style and carries me off down the hallway to the bedroom. Stefan deposits me in the big, cozy bed, where I sprawl out like a starfish.

"Stay here," he says.

"Where are you going now?" I ask, popping up.

He gives me a tired smile. "The kitchen, *malyshka*. I'm going to make us some dinner."

"Oh. Well, that's fine, then," I answer, settling down.

He stops in the doorway and looks back at me, smirking. "Mind if I go in there unarmed?" he teases.

I roll my eyes even though I can't fight a smile. "Unless you think the kitchen cutlery might rise up against you, I think you're good," I report to him.

"Good call. Get some rest, I'll bring you dinner shortly," Stefan says.

"Okay. I'll be right here," I sigh as I flop back into the pillows.

The rest of the evening is as peaceful and soft as anything I've dreamed of. I listen to the wind blow, the insects hum, and watch the tiny flurries of snow past the window. Stefan builds a crackling fire in the fireplace, which quickly helps warm up the whole cabin. He whips up some kind of hearty stew using whatever he found in that old pantry, as well as a lucky bottle of unopened red wine. We sit on the bed together and eat, sip wine, and enjoy the first truly quiet moment we've gotten together. We're both exhausted, and it doesn't take long for us to drift off to sleep together.

But my peace is short-lived. In the middle of the night, I wake up from a frantic dream. The details are already fading as I blink in the darkness. I roll over in bed and reach for Stefan, but my heart sinks when my fingers find only a cold, empty place where he once lay.

Where the hell is Stefan?

CHAPTER 13

STEFAN

I look up at the overhead mirror. My eyes squint in the near-darkness as I pull away from our newest home base. The log cabin up on the mountain, along with any semblance of peace and warmth, has slowly shrunk away into nothingness behind me.

I sneaked out not long after the all-encompassing nighttime swept in. I played it cool and waited until after I was certain my precious charge had fallen asleep. Luckily, she was pretty worn out from our intense, vigorous love-making, and I knew she would sleep like the dead. Of course, that didn't make it any easier on my heart to leave her behind. I slid out of bed so quietly and cautiously as to not wake my sleeping princess. I remember exactly how she looked in the soft glow of the moon through the bedroom window. Her lips gently parted to let out soft, rhythmic breaths. Her dainty hands, one folded under her cheek on the pillow, the other draped across the bedsheets. She looked so peaceful with her lashes gently fluttering as her eyes flit behind her lids. She whimpered a little in her sleep when I got out of bed. I wonder what she was dreaming about. I wonder if she dreams about me, and if so, are they good dreams or nightmares? Either way, I knew that if she was awake to see me leave, she would put her foot down and insist on coming with me.

After her stunt last night with the sheriff, I know she's becoming protective of me. Attached to me. Even though she's the captor and I'm the man in charge, Jewel cares about me enough to throw herself in front of a metaphorical bullet. I can't be sure she wouldn't take a literal bullet for me, too. That is an admirable, impressive trait. She's not even from this world, so she has every reason to be afraid. Hell, to be afraid of me, too. She constantly amazes me with her resilience. She's the dead weight I expected when I took on this mission. Jewel isn't a burden. She isn't a cross to bear. But she could definitely be a liability. We may have gotten out of last night's encounter unscathed, but it could've gone very differently. That was too close for comfort, and it proved even more to me that Jewel needs my protection. I can't let my world of shadows and death consume her in all her goodness.

So I had to be deceitful, just to get away. It's my hope that she's stayed asleep long enough for me to get a good head start on the six, seven, maybe eight-hour journey I have in front of me. That's another reason for leaving when I did-- to drive throughout the night. This particular route is full of surprises. There could be traffic further south, not to mention road closures and detours are basically inevitable in the mountains this time of year. I've been winding down in elevation for a while now as I come down from our hideout on the mountain. I have the car heater blasting, but this stolen old car is just now starting to warm up finally. I've been driving with my calloused hands tight on the freezing cold steering wheel, breathing puffs of warm cloud in the frigid air. Every now and then, I have to rub my hands together to bring them tingling back to life. Even under multiple layers of clothing, the chill reaches down to my bones. I'm strong enough not to shiver, but my body aches for some warmth.

If the cold isn't miserable enough, the pitch blackness certainly helps. That sheriff likely wasn't exaggerating when he said nobody but the occasional hoodlum spent much time up on that mountain. It's a dangerous and difficult place to even find. There are no streetlights, and the occasional one you do find is usually burnt out or flickering like a scene from a horror movie. I have only my dimmed headlights to guide me down the winding, narrow, cliffside roads. But the darkness is my friend in this case. I'm heading south under cover of night, in the hopes that it will be a less eventful drive than our daytime mileage lately.

My mind replays our encounter with that maniacal motorcyclist. Swerving around us, firing bullets at the woman I swore to protect. We managed to make it out with our lives, but only barely. Much like our showdown with the sheriff, it could've gone much worse. Especially if anything had happened to my precious Jewel.

My thoughts turn to worry as her beautiful face swims in my head. Those lovely soft brown doe eyes staring up at me defiantly as she clenched her fists and stood her ground. When we first met, I thought she was a brat. But I've come to see her as inquisitive and persistent now. She doesn't cause problems for the hell of it, she solves them. But her investigative nature might lead her-- and me--

down a dangerous path if she goes too far. I left her a handwritten note pinned to the inside of the front door, explaining that I'm going on a supply run. I didn't tell her where I'm going or why or how long I'll be there. I tried to keep it simple, but not so cryptic that it will send her little lawyer brain into hyperdrive trying to 'figure it out.' For once in my life, I have someone besides myself to care about, which I'm learning is a double-edged sword.

On the one hand, I have someone to dote on. Someone to kiss and hold and protect. She cares about me, too, and it feels good. But on the other hand, I have someone to worry about. Now, when I drive away from her, it's like I'm leaving half of my heart behind. I don't know what she will do when she realizes I'm gone. I can't predict her behavior-- even as I get to know her, she finds ways to surprise me. I'm just going to have to trust that between not knowing where I went or what my intentions are, she won't try to escape while I'm gone. When we're together, she doesn't show any signs of wanting to run off. In fact, she seems pretty latched onto me by now. But I can't know for certain there isn't another bid for freedom left in her.

I shift uncomfortably in the driver's seat as I remember that fateful day she climbed out the window at our first safehouse. The incident returns to me in moments of crystallized sensation. My feet crunching through the dead leaves, my breathing hard, my mind racing as I tracked her dainty footsteps through the forest. I was hunting her down, worried that someone or something would find her before I did. Even just the elements alone could've killed her. She was out there scantily clad and barefoot, under-nourished and panicky. I know there are bears in those woods who would've smelled her as a tasty snack from miles away. Not to mention the occasional hunter who might've shot her thinking she was a deer or something, or the Bratva-trained assassins coming after us. That last prospect makes me shudder.

I don't know precisely what the Bratva have in store for us, but I do know they're willing to let at least one of us perish. I don't want to die, but I definitely can't let Jewel die. It was a measured risk, choosing to leave her at the cabin while I take on this 'supply run.' Sure, it scares the hell out of me to leave her behind. Unguarded. Unarmed. She's a sitting duck at that cabin for anyone who actually knows how to find it. But going into the city right now is like waltzing into a lair of sleeping wolves. New York City is crawling with the Bratva's eyes, ears, and bloodied hands. If anyone catches a whiff of my presence in the city, they could surround me and take me down in a heartbeat. Or at least get close enough to try me. I might be able to fend off my attackers on my own, but if my focus is split between the enemy, myself, and Jewel… I become a much less formidable target. She distracts me in a lot of good ways, but there's a downside, too. I know the kind of dangers that might lay ahead on this journey, and I won't willingly expose Jewel to the threat. And if someone were to kill me, she would be instantly vulnerable.

Even this meeting I'm driving to could be an elaborate setup. I think I can still trust the man I'm meeting up with, but who knows? The Bratva has a powerful vice grip on its members, especially the ones who are still tethered to the city. But this man has never steered me wrong before, and I hope to still count on him as an ally.

He's a fellow comrade of the brotherhood, one I've known for a long time now. He goes simply by the name

Lev, and I've never pushed to know much more than that. Our connection goes way back to the beginnings of my time in America. We both came over to New York City from Russia around the same time. Our missions didn't let us intersect too much, but we maintained a low-key friendship in spite of that. We were both young and fiery then, both inspired and disillusioned by our dramatic entrance to America, a land of promise. Or so we thought. Lev and I would meet up at this tiny, grimy hole-in-the-wall bar and restaurant called Solyanka Sonya's that serves traditional Russian cuisine. Dishes we came to think of as comfort food. We would drink vodka and vent about occupational stress, or eat pierogies and reminisce about the motherland. We talked about where we came from and how different everything is here in America. We discussed adjusting to a new life, what we missed and didn't miss about home. We even talked shop sometimes, sharing tactical strategies. Lev is the closest thing to a brother I've ever really had. I've never felt I could trust anyone else in the business.

In fact, I believe it was our known camaraderie that kept the Bratva from ever assigning us a mission together. The organization is hypocritical in that way. They insist all the time, from all angles, that they are a brotherhood. Their whole schtick is that we're one big, complicated, hierarchical crime family. Bratva before blood. Bratva before anything.

But if your interpersonal relationships within the brotherhood start to slightly supersede your devotion to the group as a whole, they will intervene to separate you-- by brute force. It's cruel, but from the Bratva's point of view, any too-close members are a threat to the integrity and continuance of the collective. They prefer their pawns and knights neatly detached from one another, so they can only go through the hierarchical channels of the brotherhood for help or answers, not each other. If the underlings start communicating and forming alliances amongst themselves, the superiors know they couldn't hold us down for very long. But it would take a massive uprising to make real change. The foundational pillars of the Bratva are strong, and its roots run deep. So they encourage us to be independent. Detached. An assassin who cares too much can't focus on the crosshairs, after all. For a long time, I became very good at being alone. Even Lev, the closest thing to family or a close friend I've had in my life, I haven't seen in ages. What's truly grim is that I didn't even miss him. I'm very well-trained.

Although, I think as I drive along the coast, Jewel is changing that about me. She makes me live more in the moment. She makes me look at the world and people around me as living things with thoughts, feelings, and dreams, rather than just obstacles or enemies to fight my way through. Potential friends and allies rather than arbiters and casualties of war. I think back to yesterday's drama. Even though I'm still angry at Jewel for barging in on that encounter with the sheriff, I have to admit she did a great job of defusing the situation. That cop was reaching for his firearm, and I was unarmed. Not that I would've let him get the upper hand; I've showed up to a gunfight with only my fists before and lived to tell the tale. But our exchange could have easily morphed into bloodshed if Jewel hadn't neutralized the threat. Hell, she may have even converted that ginger-haired cop into an ally of sorts.

The more time I spend with Jewel, the more she

astounds me. I just hope I can keep us both alive long enough to enjoy the world together.

The coast turns to country, which turns to suburbs. The night hours tick away and dawn is reaching its sherbet-hued fingers across the sky as I roll across state borders into New York. The world gets bigger and more imposing the farther I go. The great sparkling city plunged into smog rises like a behemoth before me. I feel a swirling conflict of emotions. I have a lot of memories here in the city, both positive and terrible. In a way, it's where my story began. It's a strange kind of homecoming. As I drive across the Brooklyn Bridge, I'm stunned by the shiny metal facades and skyscrapers ascending into the clouds, the endless scaffolding to rebuild these monuments to greed. I roll into Manhattan surrounded by traffic, just taking in the sights and sounds. Concrete monstrosities rise above packed sidewalks, filled with every type and walk of life. The cars creep along in deep traffic. I roll down my window for a dose of unfettered New York City sounds. Honking horns, yelling, laughter, loud music and bass pumping from a car stereo, jackhammer noises from around the corner.

I park in a big, nondescript concrete parking garage a few blocks from my actual destination. I smell the city as I step out of my car into the brisk mid-morning air. The cold air and sunshine hit my face as I begin the walk to our meeting place. We knew we had to choose a spot that was low-key, under the radar. Public, but still discreet. Solyanka Sonya's is our old favorite, and I'm pleased to see it looks the same as I approach on foot. The building itself is a retail joint with a bunch of shops packed into its brick interior. But down a side alley, if you know where to look, there's a steep little staircase down from the street to the front entrance of Sonya's. I take the steps down and knock on the door. Moments later, a bleary-eyed man holding a glass of what smells like pure vodka opens the door to let me in. He waddles off to his own table without a word to me. Perfect.

Once inside, I soak in the familiar interior. It's comfortingly dark and cave-like, lit by reddish lights along the walls and flickering tea candles on the few tables. Russian radio hits warble from the stereo behind the bar counter. An old man with pale blue, sad eyes is mopping up the counter and humming to himself. Behind him in the tiny, cramped kitchen, is his wife-- Sonya herself. She's back there churning out traditional Russian dishes like she's been doing for longer than I've been alive. I'm relieved to see the old couple still in business, like nothing ever changed. As far as I know, it's still one of the best places in the city to find Medovukha, a traditional Russian honey mead. It may not be well-known, but Solyanka Sonya's is an institution for the community.

I look around for my contact and see Lev posted up in a corner booth in the back. He's nursing a vodka martini and looking characteristically intense, with his black eyes and hair. I stroll over to the table and he finally brightens up a little to see me. He stands up to shake my hand. I usually tower over everyone I meet, but Lev is tall enough to look me in the eye.

"Stefan," he says, his voice still deeply accented.

"Lev, my friend," I reply.

"Let's sit. We have much to talk about," Lev says.

We sit down and immediately the bartender brings me

a vodka martini, too, before wobbling back behind the counter. Lev peers at me with those shrewd dark eyes.

"It has been a long time, comrade," he growls.

"Too long," I agree.

"You look the same," he remarks. "Maybe a little older."

"Same to you," I reply.

The niceties completed, Lev leans in and lowers his voice.

"*Tovarishch*, is it true what they've been whispering about? That you've gone rogue?"

I nod slowly. "*Da*, my friend. But it's for a good reason."

He raises one heavy dark eyebrow. "A woman, I hear."

I bristle slightly, wondering what all the Bratva have been saying about Jewel.

"She's more than worth it," I insist gruffly.

Lev lifts his drink. "I trust your judgement, Stefan. But you know what they've been saying about you for years."

"I'm too soft on women. I let the innocents go. I'm well-aware of my reputation," I sigh.

"You are dealing now with a different kind of beast," Lev says. "This goes beyond the brotherhood. Freddie Albany is involved. You have his only daughter in your possession. Are you certain she is safe?"

I frown at him. "Safer than she would be here in the city with me. I needed supplies, and I need to talk to you."

Lev nods. "Of course. You know what's best, *tovarishch*. But you have to understand that this Albany man is not what he claims to be. He is not a man of the law. In fact, he is more corrupt than the organization itself."

"Tell me what you know, Lev. For the girl's sake," I demand.

He downs his drink and sets down the glass with a clink. In a conspiratorial tone, he says, "The member Freddie Albany has in prison is no innocent collateral damage. He's a suspected rat. An informant."

"But for which side?" I question.

Lev opens his mouth to reply, but we hear an ear-splitting screech instead. We whip around to see that Sonya has come out of the kitchen, brandishing a wooden spoon and, more worryingly, a meat cleaver. She's rushing toward the entrance and shouting in rapid, ferocious Russian at a couple of hooligans who have entered the restaurant. It takes me a second, but then I recognize both young men as Bratva members I knew from back in the day.

"Shit," Lev hisses.

We both duck down instantly to somewhat hide under the table, although it's not an easy feat for two gigantic hulking men. The few scattered patrons do the same, hiding in their booths and tables to keep out of dodge. Sonya brandishes her meat cleaver at them valiantly, but the two men push her aside. One of them looks around the room, no doubt scanning for signs of me, while the other points a gun at Sonya's husband behind the bar. He puts his hands up.

"Tell me where is Stefan, and nobody has to die today," the gunslinger announces.

Shit, indeed. Lev and I exchange fierce looks and get our respective guns at the ready, still crouched under the table in our corner booth.

Lev whispers to me, "Look, Stefan. You have someone

else to go home to. Let me handle this situation. The city is not your turf anymore."

"I promise I will return the favor one day," I whisper back.

Lev just smiles. There's a wildness in his black eyes.

"Go, Stefan. Run," he insists.

As I scurry out from underneath the table and start booking it for the back exit through the kitchen, Lev jumps to his feet and points his gun at the two newcomers. He starts firing at the gunmen before anyone can get hurt, though Sonya is screaming at all three of them the whole time, begging them to stop. I hear her rattle off one line in accented English.

"Get out of my restaurant with your macho mafia bullshit!"

As I duck through the kitchen and burst out the back door, I say a silent prayer for Sonya. She's a community pillar, and she's seen her share of turf wars. I just hope she makes it out of this one alive, too. I stumble out onto the back alley, but before I can fully catch my breath, I hear the impending footsteps of a man chasing after me from the other end of the alley. He must have been waiting for me, letting the other two flush me out. I don't even take time to look at him before I take off running. The man pursues me on foot, but he's not quite as athletic or reckless as I am. I stay off the main sidewalks to protect innocent passersby, but in the alleys and back ways, I'm a pro. I essentially became a man running amok in these neighborhoods, and I remember them like the back of my hand. I'm able to shake off my assailant by turning sharp corners, scrambling up wire fences, hiding behind dumpsters, and keeping to the shadows. I manage to make a big, wide loop around back to the parking garage.

With my heart pounding like mad, I race to the elevator. My pursuant bellows with anger when he sees me going up, and I estimate he's running for the stairs to cut me off. But I have the upper hand, and I return to my vehicle before he even reaches the right floor. I fling open the driver's side door and leap inside. I fire up the engine and peel out, narrowly avoiding collisions with parked cars as I speed-demon my way out. I leave my assailants behind in the dust as I drive across Manhattan northbound. I do need to get supplies, but I decide to stop at a small town closer to the Maine cabin instead of risking it in the city. I put the pedal to the metal and rack up miles and miles in my wake.

The sun is shining high overhead now. I'm in daylight, with no cover and a possible Bratva tail forming far behind me. I weave my way along the coast, constantly looking in my rearview mirror, until finally I'm states away. I start to relax a little, but never let my guard down. I roll into a quiet, quaint rural town along the route to get supplies for our stay, and then I'm quickly on my way again. My mind is racing as fast as the vehicle. I'm putting two and two together while I blaze down the backcountry highway. I'm pushing the speed limit as much as I can without drawing the attention of the police. I'm hurtling as fast as I can back up to our mountain, to our cabin. To Jewel.

I only hope she will still be there safe and sound when I get home, because I've finally figured it out. I know what's going on now.

Chapter 14

Jewel

I feel like a ghost as I wander listlessly through the log cabin. My bare feet pad across the creaky wooden floorboards in almost perfect silence. The blaze in the fireplace has burned down to a low crackle, and that's pretty much the only consistent sound I've heard through the house today. It feels so strange to float around and just soak in the sensations of being alone. As though without someone else to talk to and contrast myself against, I might as well not even exist. It's been a long time since I last felt comfortable by myself, which is weird. I used to be the kind of girl who guarded her alone time fiercely.

My friends-- or rather, the convenient acquaintances I made at college were always begging me to go out to bars and clubs. I would agonize over finding the perfect excuse to get out of social events, just so I could go sit by myself at home instead. It's not that I don't like people, but between being on campus surrounded by other students or at parties surrounded by drunk strangers, it got overwhelming sometimes. Those rare nights curled up with a good book or hunkered over a journal writing my heart out in messy cursive felt like luxurious staycations to me back then. I constantly turned down offers for dates, hang-outs, even study sessions that could've really benefited me, if I already had an alone-time date planned with myself. I needed an escape from the madness. I needed to hear nothing but the wind blowing around in my own head for a while before jumping back into the real world. Being alone felt free. Liberating me from the expectations of others, like my so-called friends and professors and, worst of all, my perennially-disappointed father.

But today I've been alone since I woke up that way in the middle of the night. Instead of feeling rejuvenated by my time alone, I'm anxious. I jump at every little sound outside. Every twig that snaps or animal that rustles through the bushes sends my nerves into a tizzy. I don't want to be separated from Stefan. I miss him. I need him here to feel complete. I've never been that girl before, but something has changed deep inside of me, and I know who to blame.

"What did you do to me, Stefan?" I whisper, shaking my head.

I stand at the window watching the gravel and dirt driveway that winds into the darkening forest. I stare at it so hard my eyes start to blur, and I can almost envision that familiar vehicle emerging from the void. If I close my eyes, it's not hard to pretend the crackling fire is the sound of car tires on crunchy gravel. I can almost hear the key turning in the door, the thump of footsteps, the pleasant rumble of Stefan's voice through the empty house. But it's all just pretend, because the day is winding down, and he still isn't back from... wherever he went.

I look down at the note clenched in my hand. I unfold my palm and the paper crinkles out to reveal Stefan's flat, neat handwriting in black pen. I've been carrying the damn note around all day since I found it pinned to the door. My eyes scan over the words for the umpteenth time.

Jewel, I'm out on a supply run. Don't leave the house, don't answer the door for any person or any reason. I'll be back as soon as possible. - Stefan

I've read over it so many times, scrutinized every syllable, wrung the meaning out of every single word until it's bone-dry. Nothing more to decipher. No hidden meanings for me to break down. But as straightforward as it reads, I can't help but agonize over it. After all, it's not like I've had anything else to do today. There's no cable, no internet. I don't know where my phone is, and it wouldn't be useful out here on top of the lonely mountain anyway. There's an old radio Stefan found under the kitchen sink, but I don't have the technical skills to make the damn thing work, much less play music. So I've just been haunting the log cabin like a sad ghoul, meandering in and out of different rooms in my oversized sweater and long, warm skirt. I've kept Stefan's note either in my hand or my skirt pocket all day, like a talisman. Like if I can just keep the note close, it's almost like keeping him by my side.

I tuck the note back into my pocket and wrap my long, heavy sleeves around myself as I stare out into the late afternoon haze. Last night's snow has more or less melted to expose the browning grass underneath. A powerful wind whips up and rustles around the property. The old cabin creaks. The trees sway and bend at the edge of the woods. The loose window pane in the living room rattles and lets a little draft filter through. I think about how easy it would be for someone to break in if they found me here. This place is not a typical safehouse, I can tell. We're working with what we have. I thought I was isolated at the first safehouse, but compared to this, that was downright city living. The only soul I've met up here was that sheriff, and that didn't go as well as one might hope.

My heart sinks when I remember how things went down. How I was proud of myself for stepping in to defuse the situation until Stefan got so angry at me. I didn't expect it-- I thought he would be thankful or at least appreciative, but instead he was mad. When we fell asleep last night, I thought all was mended, but what if I'm wrong? What if all my incessant questions and intervening got to him, and my stunt with the sheriff was the final straw? What if Stefan didn't really go on a supply run, he just needed an excuse to get out of here and abandon me?

I mean, it would make sense. There's no doubt he can travel much faster without me slowing him down. I'm a liability. Another wave of panic seizes me as I gaze out the window, and I imagine Stefan in that car, speeding like a bat out of hell in the opposite direction of here. What if all this trust-building is for nothing?

I reach into my pocket and give his note a squeeze. The crinkly paper calms me a little. I remind myself that Stefan has already done so much for me. To save me and preserve that safety, he's sacrificed a lot. Maybe more than he even lets on. He deserves the benefit of the doubt from me, at the very least. I have to believe that he'll come back for me. I just have to.

I close my eyes and imagine him driving back to me, and it makes my heart swell with affection. My strong, powerful, stoic Prince Charming rushing back through whatever land and weather to return to me. He could come bursting through that door smelling like pine and adventure any moment now. Infuriatingly, he didn't give me a projected hour of arrival or anything to go by. The minutes melt into hours and hours of waiting and wasting away alone in this big empty house.

I'm so vulnerable here without him, but it's not just that. I miss him. Not only as my guardian who makes me feel safe even in the wildest of circumstances, but as a person in his own right. I miss his masculine scent that washes over me when he pulls me close to his chest at night. I miss his looming presence, his massive height and size that ward away other predators-- Stefan is the apex, the top of the food chain. When I'm with him, I'm protected prey. A dainty fawn under the possessive watch of a grizzly bear. I even miss his way of remaining stoic and calm in the face of chaos. No matter what happens, he maintains that quiet peace that stills the tremble in my soul. I miss his growly voice and his dark sense of humor. I really, really miss the way my body feels when he touches me. Those calloused, magical hands moving over my curves and bending me to his will. Willingly.

I shiver, getting goosebumps all over. I rub my upper arms. I've been feeling chilly all day without Stefan to keep me warm. That fireplace is no replacement for his delicious body heat. But the sunshine is fading out now, and the air is only going to get colder from here on out. I decide to take matters into my own hands and run myself a nice, hot bath to warm up in.

I traipse across the cabin with my skirt dragging the floor. I don't know who owned this cabin before it came into Stefan's hands, but they certainly weren't minimalists. I've pretty much spent the day poking my nose into closets, under sinks and into cupboards, looking for what's been left behind by the tenants years and years ago. Everything is coated in a layer of dust, but there's a lot of useful stuff lying around. When I get into the bathroom, I start rifling through the cabinets for anything bath-related.

"Ah, jackpot," I mutter as I open up the cupboard under the bathroom sink.

I pull out a big glass canister of what looks like Epsom salts. I unscrew the lid and draw in a deep whiff, pleased to find that it's scented like lavender. I decide to keep digging, and I find another glass jar full of little crumply dried flower petals and leaves. It looks very homemade, and seems to have been sealed up for a long time. The lid takes some coaxing, but when it pops off, I get another lovely waft of floral scent. I pick out yellow, pink, and purple blooms dried to shriveled bits on my palm. I lift them to my nose and breathe in, closing my eyes. It's like walking through a garden, and it brings a smile to my lips. In a burlap bag twisted and tied shut, there are a few bars of fragrant but rustic bars of soap. I also find a stash of clearly-handmade white taper candles stacked in the back of the cupboard with a tiny matchbox. There are only two matches left, but I only need one. I light the first candle and set it in the dusty, rusting candelabra on the bathroom counter, then use the first flame to light a few more. The soft bronze light of late afternoon ripples across the bathroom walls through the window.

I start the water in the clawfoot tub. It sputters a little at first, then spurts out cold water. I turn the knob and wait for it to start steaming. I grab the jars of bath supplies and start adding bits here and there. A handful of lavender Epsom soaking salt, a sprinkle of dried flowers, and a bar of soap on the ceramic edge of the tub waiting for me. I stretch and shrug out of my sweater and skirt, folding them on the counter. I sweep my dark hair back into a messy bun, which I secure with a small length of twine I found in the kitchen. I leave a soft white towel out for afterward. Chills erupt on my bare skin as I dip my toe in the tub. The hot water beckons to me. I lower myself down into the warm, wet bath with a sigh of satisfaction.

"Oh yes," I murmur to myself.

The perfumed, flowery water surrounds me. Steam rises and crowds around my face to open up my pores. The humidity makes the baby hairs around my forehead and temple curl up into tight pinscrews. The hot water soothes my tensed-up muscles. The chill in my bones slowly ebbs away under the warmth. Dried bits of flowers and leaves float around in the pink-tinged water. A petal drifts over to land on my nipple bobbing just above the water's surface. I lean my head back and sigh as my troublesome thoughts come leaking back in. Not even a relaxing soak can fully wash away my nerves. I am, after all, on the run.

My mind wanders as I think about what I'm running from. It's hard to know exactly. My departure from real life happened in a total whirlwind, and there are a lot of factors I still don't understand. As usual, my thoughts circle back to the one person who has always been able to make me feel small and afraid: my father. I feel a twinge of guilt thinking about him. I never expected to have to make such a choice, but I realize now that early on, I made the decision to choose Stefan over my own dad. As far as Dad knows, I could've just run off without saying goodbye. I wonder, what if everything Stefan's been saying is a lie? What if he doesn't even realize it's a lie? How can we trust the Bratva's intel on my father when we can't even trust them in the first place? If Dad ended up just being an innocent bystander in this whole thing, or even worse, a victim-- how would I feel then? Guilt washes over me and I feel sick to my stomach. My father, the man who raised me and taught me all that I know-- betrayed by his own daughter.

But then again, if what Stefan says is true, then my father is the traitor, not me. I wasn't supposed to have to go on the run. I wasn't supposed to be gone this long. Dad was meant to just pay the ransom, get me back, and we would move on with our lives. I know my father has the money to do whatever he wants. So, if he wanted to save my life, he would have. Right? If he's really choosing money over me, then I shouldn't feel guilty. I mean, what kind of father refuses to pay a ransom to get his only child back from dangerous criminals?

I wince a little at the thought of Stefan as a dangerous criminal. At first, I thought of him that way. He did drug and kidnap me, after all. My dad taught me right and wrong, and I know what Stefan did to me was wrong. But then, I can remember lots of times my father did things wrong, too. And Stefan has been kinder to me than anyone I've ever met, even though he's supposed to be the villain in my story. I should fear him. I should be happy he's not here right now. If I was really smart, maybe I would've spent this rare day of freedom plotting how to actually escape. I could have started walking down the mountain or something, just tried to find someone out there in the wilderness who could save me.

But save me from what? I could run, but where would I go? And when I got there, would I miss Stefan? Would I regret my decision? Something deep inside my heart says yes. If I leave him now, I'll wish I didn't. Besides, Stefan has already proven more than once that he can just track me down and bring me back. Every escape scenario I imagine ends with Stefan catching up and nabbing me again. I tingle all over at the thought of him finding me out in the woods, his dark eyes all blazing with ferocity. I remember the way he threw me over his shoulder and carried me through the woods like I weighed nothing at all. Just a wayward feather he found floating on the wind and decided to take home.

I close my eyes and run my hands down my body. I imagine that it's his rough fingertips instead of my soft touch on my bare skin. I picture his thick, strong forearm pushing under the water to spread my thighs apart. I picture the look of possessive fury on his face if he found me out in the woods again trying to escape. I want him to gather me up in his arms and cradle me to his hard chest. I want him to throw me on the bed and ravish me, punish me for being such a bad girl. Even the idea of Stefan grabbing me in that parking lot and throwing me in the back of the car turns me on now. I don't fear him like I once did-- but there's just enough healthy fear left to make my fantasies oh so exciting. Stefan could have his way with me if he wanted. His muscular body could restrain me without breaking a sweat. I'm just his dainty, flimsy little sex toy, and if I try to run, he'll only drag me back home.

My nipples stiffen, my pussy aching to be filled. My hand slips between my thighs and I gently stroke my clit under the hot water. My cunny is so soft and velvety to the touch. My fingers tweak and pull at my nipples. I bite my lip as my eyes roll back in my head. I picture Stefan's handsome face glaring at me as he leans over me, tall and imposing. I want him to overpower me, to take control and do what he pleases with my body. I rock my hips as the tension inside of me tightens up more and more. My fingertips circle and pet my stimulated clit until I'm on the edge of coming. I back away a little to tease myself, staying just on the precipice without spilling over. Every time I get close, I move my fingers away for a moment. My pussy clenches and aches as I build up my need for release higher and higher. Right as I'm about to finally let myself come, I hear a strange sound from across the house.

My eyes go wide open and I sit up in the bath, looking around in fear. It's the unmistakable thump of footsteps and rattling keys at the front door, sounds I've been waiting to hear all day long!

"Stefan!" I gasp.

I hastily clamber out of the clawfoot tub and wrap the white towel around my dripping curves. Goosebumps pop up on my cool skin as I rush across the cabin toward the front door. I'm unsure of what exactly to expect. Reason tells me it's Stefan, returning to me after a long supply run mission. But what if it's not him? My brain rapidly sifts through the options, and it doesn't look good. If it's not Stefan, it could be the sheriff. He knows I'm up here, and if he watches over this region half as well as he claims to, maybe he'll have noticed that the car is gone somehow. Maybe he's here to check on me-- or get me alone. It could even be one of the 'hooligans' the cop mentioned. Even worse than that, I run through another scenario: that it's someone from the Bratva, here to finish off the job Stefan started.

I stand quivering in a towel as the door bursts open, and my heart soars with joy to see Stefan walk in. He's carrying several bags of stuff, groceries from the looks of it. He looks instantly relieved to see me still here, though he does raise an eyebrow at my towel-clad body.

"You're a sight for sore eyes," he says in that growly tone that makes me melt.

"I was taking a bath," I blurt out. Well, that wasn't the first thing I wanted to say to him upon his return, but oh well. He makes me so flustered sometimes.

He smiles, and his handsome face looks instantly softer for a moment. He sets down his bags on the kitchen table, then turns to me. Stefan reaches out and touches my cheek gently. He looks exhausted and stressed out, but relieved to be back. I lean into his touch, then turn and kiss his palm. He pulls back and starts putting away the groceries. I'm overjoyed to see him, but I can't let my curiosity just fester without answers.

"You were gone for such a long time," I point out.

"Longer than I meant to," he answers. "I'm glad to see you're still here."

I cross my arms over my chest. "Well, where would I have gone? You took the car."

"You would've run off if I left the car?" Stefan teases with a smirk.

I blush. "I mean, no. Probably not."

"Good. It's not safe out there," he says simply.

I heave a sigh. "Are you going to tell me where you went or not?"

"Are you alright?" he asks, frowning at me.

"Yes, I'm fine. Just… bored. And scared. You know, it's really not very nice to get up and leave in the middle of the night like that," I bring up defensively.

"If you had been awake when I left, you would have tried to come with me," he says.

"Of course, I would have!" I pout. "That's the point. You didn't give me a choice."

"Have you eaten yet today?" Stefan inquires.

"I--no. I wasn't hungry," I answer. My stomach chooses this exact moment to growl, and Stefan gives me a bemused look.

"I'll make us dinner," he says.

But when he turns away to put a box of rice in a high-up cabinet, I stare at him. Something is off. He's being oddly cheerful and cryptic, avoiding the subject of where he went and why he was away so long. I push a little more.

"Your note certainly didn't give much away," I complain. "Where did you go?"

"Like I said, on a supply run," he answers. "How do you feel about chicken and rice?"

"Stefan, come on," I groan, tugging on his arm. "I need more than that."

"Chicken, rice, and beans?" he suggests.

I roll my eyes. "Not about dinner. I mean I need more information."

"I met with a friend while I was out," he adds.

"Okay. Who? What friend? What did they say?" I question.

"Am I on the stand right now?" he grumbles.

"You leave in the middle of the night with nothing but

a cryptic-ass note, and you're giving me a hard time?" I snap.

Stefan turns around to face me finally. He looks serious.

"I had a long way to go. It was a brief meetup. I got what I needed and I left. Then, I stopped at a small-town grocery store for supplies," he explains.

"So if you had to go to a small town for groceries, where did you meet the friend?" I ask, trying to read between the lines.

"Jewel, drop the lawyer act," he warns.

"You're hiding things from me! You're the only person I have in this world right now, and you're keeping secrets," I accuse. "I don't get it, Stefan. You want me to trust you, but then you do shit like this. I was so scared when I woke up alone. I thought you'd abandoned me."

"I would never do that," he growls.

"Why did you leave me out? I could've gone with you and helped out," I insist.

He moves closer, leaning over me. "Everything I do is to keep you safe, Jewel. You would not have been helpful to me on this supply run," Stefan says.

I feel hurt. "I've bought groceries before, you know," I scoff.

"Some things I have to do on my own," he grumbles.

I throw up my hands in frustration, only to remember I have to hold my towel up. Blushing and clinging to my towel, I tell him, "You act like we're in this together, but then you keep secrets. You always have to stay a step ahead of me and keep me in the dark. If you want my trust, you have to earn it."

"And you have to learn not to ask questions you don't

want the answer to," Stefan says grimly. I puff myself up and step closer, too.

Leaning right up into his face on my tiptoes, I reply, "Don't assume what I can and cannot handle. I can decide that for myself."

"Is that so, *malyshka*?" he snarls.

He grabs me and pulls me in close, his lips colliding hard with mine. I reach up to put my arms around him and my towel drops to the floor. Stefan kisses me harder as his hands rove up and down my naked body. I tingle under his touch, my body warming up to him instantly. Stefan hurriedly unzips his trousers and pulls out his cock. My mouth is salivating for him as he puts his hands on my waist and easily lifts me up. He whirls around to hoist me on the kitchen counter, shoving groceries out of the way to make room.

He leans in to kiss me again, both of us groping and pawing at each other in a frenzy. The tension between us is so palpable I could cut it with a butter knife. We've been apart for almost a whole day, and we can't bear it. We need each other desperately, no matter how bitterly we argue. His body knows mine, and vice versa. We don't even need words right now.

Stefan lines up the thick head of his shaft with my slick opening and pushes inside. I wrap my legs around him as he rears back and slides all the way back in again. He pumps into me again and again, his cock slamming against my g-spot as he fucks me on the counter.

"Fuck, I missed you," I gasp.

"I thought about you every second," he hisses through gritted teeth.

"Don't you ever leave me again," I whisper between sighs of pleasure.

He thrusts hard, his balls smacking my ass as he pounds my pussy. We are both so fired up with frustration-- the angry kind and the sexy kind. It all muddles together like a cocktail in my head, intoxicating me with every thrust of his hips.

"I'm trying to protect you," he grunts. He emphasizes every word with a powerful plunge into my cunny. I tingle and moan around him.

"I'm not fragile, Stefan," I whisper. "You don't have to be gentle with me."

His dark eyes flash and he fucks me deeper and harder, just like I wanted. His shaft shoves in and out of my tight pussy, the swollen tip notching into my g-spot over and over until I'm nearly frantic with pleasure. He caught me on the very edge earlier, and now I'm desperate for a release. Stefan pounds my cunny like he's angry at me, and I love it. I drag my fingernails down his strong, broad back while he pounds me.

"I need this," I gasp out. "I need *you*."

"You have me, Jewel. And I have you," he murmurs.

"I belong to you," I agree breathlessly. "I'm all yours, Stefan. I've just been waiting all day long for you to come home and fuck me right."

"Sorry to keep you waiting," he growls.

He picks up the pace, pummeling my cunny until I have tears in my eyes. My body is thrumming from head to toe. I feel him tightening up, too. He's so close, and I am eager to get him there. I clench my pussy tighter around him and he groans with bliss. I rock my hips to match his thrusts. His dark eyes lock with mine and we stare into each other's souls as we tip over the edge together.

"Fuck, I'm coming," Stefan growls.

"Nnngh, yes," I whimper.

He seizes up and releases his thick, precious seed deep inside me while my cunny spasms around his thickness. My pussy gushes all over his cock, both of us panting and clinging to one another as the endorphins whirl around us. I feel his shaft twitching as he empties out every last drop inside my fertile womb, and I hold him here until we're both sated.

Once we finally catch our breath, Stefan slips out of me. He shrugs off his jacket and drapes it around my shoulders to keep me warm and modest. I slide off the counter onto my jelly, wobbly legs. Stefan kisses me slowly, deeply. He brushes the hair out of my face.

"I'm going to start on dinner," he says softly. "Do you want to help?"

I smile up at him and nod. "Let me go put on something… normal. I'll be back."

"Good idea," he says, patting me on the ass.

I get dressed in comfortable clothes and jump into helping Stefan cook dinner. The evening is winding down. The wine comes out and my stress level goes down as we spend time together. Stefan manages to get that old radio working, and we listen to golden oldies while we enjoy our first real dinner together in the living room. The fireplace crackles as the last log gets consumed by flame. I'm getting so sleepy from wine and good sex, nodding off on the sofa. My eyelids are getting heavy. Sleep calls to me like a seductive lover. Curled up under a blanket, I watch Stefan get up to put more logs into the fire.

I sleepily ask him, "Now can you tell me what's going on?"

He comes over and kisses me on the forehead. My eyes shutter closed. I'm so tired.

"I'll tell you tomorrow, Jewel. Get some rest," he says.

"You'll be there when I wake up?" I yawn.

He snuggles up next to me on the sofa and pulls me in close.

"I'll be here. I promise this time," he says.

I have so many questions, but I'm too tired to make words happen. Warm and content in my protector's arms, I finally drift off to uncomplicated sleep.

Chapter 15

Stefan

The next morning, I awaken to the soft chittering of birds in the trees outside. I hear them singing their lovelorn songs to one another, just star-crossed lovers from one branch to the next. I can feel the soft sunlight beaming against my eyelids and the warmth of the sun on my cheeks as I lay facing the window. My eyes slowly open and adjust to the pale light filtering across the bed. I can see tiny particles of dust suspended in the golden light, like magic dotting the air. Everything is so perfectly still inside the house. Distantly, I can make out the soft rustling of the fireplace across the cabin in the living room. That sound reassures me that we will stay warm.

I look down at the beautiful angel resting in my arms. Jewel is fast asleep, with those soft brown eyes tightly shut. Her eyes move faintly under her pale eyelids, and I wonder again what she's dreaming about. There's a little smile on her lips that makes my cold heart melt a little. She must be dreaming of something pleasant. It's a real treat to get to wake up like this and find her immediately right there, already within my reach. I watch her chest softly rise and fall with each rhythmic breath. Her breasts are lightly outlined under the thin bedsheets, even in her oversized sweater. I stare at her mouth, with those perfect rosebud lips, and wish I could lean over to kiss her. Her long, thick lashes flutter on her round, rosy cheeks. My eyes rove across her smooth, milky-white skin. I chart each tiny freckle, every shadow and flick of the light over her gorgeous features. Her dark hair spools out around her head on the pillow, with one lock curling adorably over her forehead.

Careful not to wake her, I gently nudge the lock away from her face. Her perfect button nose twitches a little at my ticklish touch, but then she settles. I can't help but smile while I look down at her in the morning light. Sleeping peacefully like a princess. My precious ward. My treasure. My Jewel.

It feels so good to wake up with her in this quiet, peaceful sanctuary, far away from the world that seeks to drive us apart and destroy us. It's nice to spend the whole night together and find her still wrapped up in my warm embrace in the morning, especially after having to leave her sleeping and vulnerable the night before to go on my supply run. It was one of the most difficult moments of our journey so far, just forcing myself to look at that serene, angelic sleeping figure in the bed and walk away from her. Getting in the car to drive in the opposite direc-tion of the only one I care about, the only place I want to be, felt like an icepick straight to my heart. But last night, I got to curl up around her sleeping figure and stay here, cooped up in our shared body heat. It's magical getting to hold Jewel in my arms and breathe in her sweet, irresistible scent. Snuggling with her sure beats handcuffing her to the bed, and it still lets me make sure she's safe and protected.

I am a notoriously light sleeper, after all. Any considerable movement from Jewel, and I would instantly wake up. So even if she did try to get up and run away or sneak out for whatever reason, I would be able to catch her first. And if something worse happens, like somebody breaking in to attack us or kidnap her back, I would be poised and ready at the first unexpected noise. As it turns out, years upon years of paranoia and always having to look over my own shoulder, sharing space with men I did not trust, and making a long list of powerful enemies does have an effect on my sleep tendencies. I'm used to running on little to no good sleep, and I'm used to waking up at odd hours of the day and night to suit my erratic lifestyle. Sometimes, I needed to be up for days on end while staking out a target. Other times, I had to power-nap in unusual or uncomfortable places just to get enough energy to carry out a mission.

The terrible things I have done used to keep me up at night. When I first got blood on my hands as a young man, it haunted me a little for a while. I had nightmares. I woke up in a cold sweat with my heart pounding and my mind certain that there was an adversary in the room ready to pounce. But I've had a long time to come to terms with danger. Over the years, the nightmares became less frequent. In reality, *I* became the nightmare.

By sharp contrast, the woman curled up and lightly snoring in my arms is a heavy sleeper. And thank God, because there's no way I would've been able to pull off that supply run alone otherwise. If she had woken up, she would have insisted on coming with me, and I'm learning just how powerful her desires are. It's difficult to deny the girl anything, even against my best judgement. I tried to protect her from myself and my own desires, but all she has to do is look at me with those stunning brown doe eyes, and I'm a goner. She even makes my sleep feel better. I slept longer and deeper last night than I ever have, my first full night of rest in over a week. My body is refreshed and strong this morning, and I credit Jewel for that. I like being the big spoon, curled around her delicate, perfect body. It just feels right.

It hits me again how much things have changed. It seems barbaric to me now that I used to keep this girl held captive in a nondescript, hopeless little basement room. Handcuffed to an uncomfortable lumpy bed, wearing the same grimy, inappropriate clothes she'd been wearing the night I kidnapped her. Now, she's lying in my arms, embraced like a lover in a bed I used to daydream about. This place, the cabin on the mountainside, has shimmered like a mirage in my head ever since I bought it years ago. I was losing hope I might ever get a chance to use it. Despite all the trouble that led us here, I'm happy for this one little spot of sunshine I get to share with Jewel. Our calm before the inevitable storm ahead of us. We have to prepare. Today will begin that process.

But for now, I'll let her get as much rest as she needs. I'm sure she expended a lot of energy waiting anxiously for my return yesterday, and then we definitely burned a ton of calories having vigorous sex on the kitchen counter. Plus, there's a physically demanding day ahead of us, so I decide to leave her sleeping in a little longer. But now that I'm wide awake and ready for the bed, there's no reason I can't get a head start. So I slowly start the process of extricating myself from Jewel, sliding my arms out from under and around her. I slide silently out of the bed and stand up to stretch. Jewel wiggles and turns over to face me. She's still asleep as she noses into my pillow. She wraps her arms around it and hugs it tight, like she's holding onto me. I smile over her sleeping form and finally tear myself away to the kitchen.

As I start taking out items to rustle up some breakfast, I think about the changes in myself I've seen in such a short time. Since meeting Jewel, I have learned things about myself I never knew. Rediscovered instincts I assumed would never come back. I used to be cold and hard, definitely not domestic. The brotherhood taught me to become a punisher, not a caretaker. Jewel softens my rough edges and forces me to slow down. I notice details I would usually skip over. I care about things that normally don't matter. She makes me live in the present, like my life belongs to me and what I want to make of it, rather than whatever sharp tool my bosses can fashion me into. For example, I would never have spent much time making a nice breakfast. Just protein and fiber, enough to get by but nothing to write home about. Now I'm whisking eggs, cream, and cinnamon. I'm slicing up bread and dipping them in the batter, making a stack of perfectly crispy, golden French toast. I even take the time to dice up cantaloupe and peel an orange to arrange the fruit on her plate in a ring around her toast. It just feels natural, like something I should do for a person who makes my world so colorful and bright.

At first, I showed her kindness purely for my own end; in general, it's easier to hold someone hostage when they aren't actively trying to escape or fight you at every turn. A certain degree of measured mercy was well within the margins of a normal mission. But it couldn't stay that way with Jewel. Now, I want her to trust me so that she will feel safe in my custody. I want her well-fed and warm and comfortable because she is an incredible human being, and she deserves it. And because it is my sacred responsibility to take care of her. I want Jewel feeling her best, to prepare for whatever we have to do next. Especially because she hasn't yet asked me again about what I learned from Lev. She was too sleepy last night to force an answer out of me, but this girl is persistent. She'll get it out of me eventually, and she needs to be strong and prepared for what the answer is.

I drizzle some real maple syrup over our stacks of French toast on two plates, then start working on the coffee machine. I plan to bring her everything in bed as a sweet gesture, but before I can do that, I hear her soft footsteps padding up the hall. She comes traipsing into the kitchen looking all cute and disheveled. Her dark hair is a messy halo around her face. Her brown eyes are squinting blearily in the sunshine, and she has her sleeves pulled over her dainty little hands for warmth. I play it cool, just drinking in her tousled cuteness and dreading the question I assume will be first on her mind this morning. I denied her an answer last night, and I'm hoping she won't ask, but I'm playing it by ear.

"Morning," I greet her.

Jewel wobbles up to me and leans into my arm. In a froggy little voice, she murmurs, "Is that coffee I smell?"

I nod and kiss her on the top of the head. "Yes. Dark roast."

"Mmm. Just how I like my men: dark and bitter," she jokes sleepily. She turns her face toward the window, blinking in the bright sun. "It's beautiful out there today."

I'm relieved-- she seems to have forgotten last night's topic for now.

"You're right. It's a perfect day to be outside," I agree. I grab the plates and start carrying them toward the door. "Grab the coffee, we can eat on the porch."

She brightens up at that idea. She pours us each a mug of fragrant, steamy coffee. I grab a couple blankets and bundle her up at the little porch table and chairs for breakfast. It is unseasonably warm today, especially for this altitude.

"This is the best French toast I've ever had," Jewel says enthusiastically. "If you ever decide to stop being a hitman, you could always open a brunch restaurant."

"I'm sure I have lots of skills that would translate easily," I joke.

"Skilled with a knife: check. Ability to work long hours: check. Dedication: check," Jewel lists off with a giggle. "See? You're hired."

We continue to joke around and chat through breakfast, while the warm sun beams down on us and the forest comes to life. It feels less like we're two renegades on the run, and more like we're two lovebirds on a honeymoon in the mountains. Of course, I can't let my guard down too much. Danger could be lurking anywhere, around any corner. I won't relax enough to risk our safety. But it's undeniably refreshing to get a breather. We can make believe for a little while that everything is fine... before the world inevitably catches up to us.

As we're cleaning up breakfast, I tell her, "Let me show you the clothes I got for you on my supply run yesterday."

She lights up with excitement. "French toast and new clothes? You spoil me."

"Food and clothing are just the basics," I remark. "If I could show you real luxury, I would. But for now, what I could find in that small town secondhand shop will have to do."

"I love thrifted clothes," she assures me.

"It won't be anything fancy, but hopefully it will fit," I answer.

She chirps, "I'm easy to please."

I bring out the big paper bag of clothes I picked out in a rush after gathering groceries for the foreseeable future. I dump out the clothes onto the bed, and Jewel starts going through the stack, a big smile on her face. She holds up a pair of warm, fleece-lined pants and gasps.

"Oh, this is perfect," she gushes. "I'm going to be so warm."

"Try them on," I instruct her.

Jewel dutifully follows my command. She strips out of her oversized sweater and skirt to reveal her naked, luminous body. My eyes rove up and down those long, shapely legs and her juicy ass. It jiggles ever so slightly with each little movement, making me salivate. She hops up and down while pulling on the fleece pants. Her breasts bounce a little, and I have to fight the urge to grab her right here and now. I watch the rippling soft muscles in her smooth back as she turns and pulls on a long-sleeved, form-fitting white shirt. It's thick enough to keep her warm, but just transparent enough that I can see her pretty pink nipples poking underneath. Every outfit she tries on looks amazing. Somehow, the plainest clothing is transformed on her flawless body. I watch the light and shadows play over her bare skin between outfits. Every flash of milky white flesh awakens that deep, dark desire inside me. Even the way she stands on one foot and hops to pull on her new boots is adorable. I don't know how she manages to be so damn sexy and goofy-cute at the same time.

"Thank you so much for all of this, Stefan. Everything fits perfectly!" Jewel raves.

She does a little spin for me. She's pristine in her thick brown trousers, white long-sleeved shirt, dark brown coat, and boots.

"And wow, does this smell way better than the moth-eaten stuff I was wearing from that closet in the bedroom. Feels great," she laughs. "But the question is: do I look as good as I feel?"

I step closer and loom over her. I stare her up and down.

"You must feel really, *really* good," I tell her honestly. "Because you look…"

I have to bite back that beast inside me that wants to pounce her now. I want to strip all those new clothes off and ravish her perfect body. But I must restrain myself. Instead, I walk over to the dresser and open the top drawer. I pull out two guns and make sure they're loaded, albeit with the safety on. Jewel watches me with wide eyes. I turn around and smile.

"It's a perfect day. We're taking a little hike in the woods," I announce.

"And we need two guns?" she points out nervously.

"You'll see. Come on. Let's make the most of the warmer weather," I instruct.

As usual, she obeys. I can tell she's still on edge as we walk out into the bright, sunny mid-morning. Jewel falls into step beside me. It's a beautiful day. The sun is shining, the birds are singing, and the air tastes fresh and crisp. Our boots crunch over dead leaves, and tiny unseen creatures rustle around the bushes as we pass. I keep my eyes peeled. I'm looking for the ideal location. I need a wide-open space far away from the cabin, from anything resembling civilization. Jewel takes notice of me scouting around.

"You're, um, really playing the long game if you're taking me out here to finally carry out the hit," she jokes somewhat anxiously.

With a gentle laugh, I turn back to her and pull out a pistol. She instantly flinches away, and I swear I can almost hear her heart speeding up. It hits me that even after all this time, she still harbors a little fear for me.

"It would be strange of me to arm you if I planned to kill you," I reveal.

I calmly flip the gun in my hand to face the barrel at myself and hold it out for her. She looks at it, then up to me. She swallows hard, then gingerly takes it from me. The gun hangs limply from her fingers, like it's a bomb that might go off at any second.

"It's not going to bite you," I remark.

Jewel gives me a dubious look. "Yeah, but it might shoot me."

"Only if you pull the trigger," I tell her.

She sighs. "Well, yeah, but I don't know how to use this thing!"

"That's why we're out here. It's time for you to learn," I explain. "Come on. I see a spot for us up ahead."

We trek up a hill to a big, wide clearing. We're deep enough in the woods that the chances of meeting another human being is slim to none. I shift my bag off my shoulder and unzip it, taking out several old tin cans. I set them up on a crest of rocks as targets for us to practice on. Jewel watches, still holding the gun out from her body, as I line up the first shot and fire. She startles at the loud cracking sound, then gasps when the bullet clears straight through the tin can. It rattles but doesn't fall, the shot is so clean.

Jewel is gawking at me. "Holy shit."

"That's how it's done," I say.

"Color me impressed, but there's no way in hell I could ever do that," she replies.

"I can teach you," I tell her. "Come here."

I holster my own gun and come up behind Jewel. I fold around her, my arms on her arms, my hands on her hands. My chin hovers just over her shoulder, and my lips are close enough to give her goosebumps when I whisper in her ear.

"Finger on the trigger. Don't squeeze hard. Try to keep the tension equally spread in your hand. Relax your muscles, but prepare for the recoil. It might jolt you a little, but I've got you. I won't let anything happen to you," I encourage her.

"Okay," she whispers.

"Deep breath in and out," I instruct. She obeys. "Now, we're going to shoot."

I help her successfully press the trigger and fire the pistol. The bullet cracks the still air and the recoil nudges

Jewel back into me with a little yelp. But I keep her steady as the bullet glances off the corner of the tin can and knocks it off the rock. Jewel lets out a peal of surprised, exhilarated laughter and looks up at me with those brown eyes shining.

"Oh my god. I did it!" she enthuses.

I smirk at her, feeling proud. "You did. Now, try again. This time, on your own."

"Okay, okay. Let's see," she mutters.

Pride bubbles up inside me watching this gorgeous girl follow my instructions and line up another shot. She takes a deep breath and fires again, this time hitting a can right in the center. The recoil barely knocks her back, and she fist-pumps the air.

"Yes! Even better!" she laughs. "Stefan, I'm learning."

"Look at you, my little sharpshooter," I tease. "You're a natural."

She lines up and takes another few shots, every time hitting the can. I can see her confidence growing by the second, and her cheeks are rosy with excitement. She looks so damn sexy holding a gun, and judging by the way she keeps biting her lip and ogling me, the feeling is mutual. As I instruct her on how to aim better, we get closer and closer together. Our conversation turns from instructional to flirtatious.

"Not gonna lie, it actually feels amazing," Jewel remarks. "I feel powerful."

"You *are* powerful. And that gun will make you dangerous," I add.

"Good. Maybe now I can be an asset rather than a liability," she says.

"I don't see you as a liability, *malyshka*," I assure her.

"How *do* you see me?" she says, giving me a seductive look. She hands me her gun and puts her hands behind her back. "Remember when you had me all tied up? I bet you never thought you'd be teaching me how to shoot a gun."

I lick my lips as she saunters closer to me. There's mischief in her eyes. I like it.

"It's my job to take care of you," I growl.

"Maybe you should let me take care of you for a change," she tantalizes.

She slowly kneels down in front of me, her doe eyes still peering up at me. I start unzipping my trousers as she opens her mouth wide. I'm already so hard, just looking at her pretty pink tongue all splayed out. I pull out my massive, stiff cock and she groans with anticipation. I feel a lurch of intense pleasure as she pulls my cock into her warm, perfect mouth. Her tongue flicks around the thick head of my shaft while she slowly takes me down to the hilt. Jewel still has her hands behind her back, mimicking handcuffs, only this time it's her choice. She's offering herself up to me, and I can't resist her. I can't hold back.

I reach down and gather her silky dark hair in my hand. I give it a gentle pull to show her I'm in control. She moans around my thick cock in response, and I decide to give her a little more. I press down on the back of her head to force my cock into the back of her throat. Jewel starts to choke a little before I pull back. She gasps for air and licks her lips, happy tears in her eyes. She looks up at me with a wordless plea for more on her pretty face, and I oblige. She wants it hard and fast, and I'm happy to deliver. I grab her hair and give it a light pull, tipping her back so I can see the glistening spit rolling down her neck. I grab my cock and smack her around the lips with it, her tongue darting out to taste me eagerly. She looks so damn stunning, kneeling in the dead leaves with her dainty hands behind her back. Her face is all flushed and she's drooling, keening for more.

I guide her mouth back to my cock and force myself into her mouth. She moans around it, her eyes rolling. I push her head down again, turning her face so that my shaft pokes at her cheek. Jewel grunts and coos with pleasure as I turn her back and start thrusting down her throat. Every pounding motion meets a wet squelch in her throat. Her saliva drips down her chin as I fuck her pretty face hard and forcefully.

"That's my good girl," I grunt between hard, short thrusts.

"Mmmmm," she moans with her mouth stuffed full.

My cock is tightening up, my balls growing heavy and tense as she sucks my cock. I pound her throat hard in the middle of the clearing. Her hot, wet mouth feels like heaven. Every little moan and whimper she makes pushes me closer to coming. I stare down at her, impressed by how she takes my cock. She's eager and willing, a dirty girl made just for me. All I can think about is how I want to pump her throat full of my come, spray across her delicate features.

"Stay right there, *printsessa*," I growl.

I hold her head in place while my hips snap back and forth. My cock pummels her throat hard and fast. My balls tighten up and I clench my teeth. My hand tightens around her dark hair, tugging and pushing her while I fuck her sweet mouth. Finally, I feel that deep pull within me and I groan, pumping hot seed down her throat. She slips back just in time for a spurt of come to dash across her lips and chin. Jewel eagerly laps it up and looks up at me, like a dutiful little girl waiting to be praised. Once I've emptied my come all over her face, I tuck myself away and pull her to her feet. Jewel hastily wipes her mouth as I come in for a kiss. I can taste myself faintly, but I don't care.

I kiss her passionately, my hands smoothing down her tangled hair and stroking her perfect, smooth face. I peer into her face, loving every feature more and more.

"That's enough teaching for one day," I declare. "We can learn more tomorrow."

"Sounds good to me," she agrees.

She grabs my hand as we start the long walk back to the cabin. We walk in happy silence for a while, but slowly I can feel her holding back. I look over at Jewel, and she's already staring at me. She blushes and looks away.

"So, why are you teaching me to shoot a gun anyway? Do you really think I'm gonna need to use that skill?" she pipes up.

I get a sinking feeling. Here it comes. I knew she would need more information soon.

"What happened yesterday, Stefan? What did you find out?" she asks.

I sigh heavily. "I'm starting to understand what's really at play here."

She cocks her head to one side. "What is it? What's going on?"

"You're not going to like this, Jewel," I warn her. "But I think we need to come to terms with reality, no matter how ugly it is."

"You're scaring me, Stefan. Just tell me," she urges.

I stop walking and look at her intently. She stares back, waiting.

Finally, I tell her, "The more I find out, the more likely it appears that your father has a bigger role in this than we thought."

She frowns. "How so?"

"We've been looking at Freddie Albany as a victim in this situation. Like you. But he has more agency in this plot than that. He may be… working alongside the Bratva," I edge in.

Jewel looks nauseated, but she persists, "What are you saying?"

"I'm saying your father may have had a hand in your kidnapping, Jewel," I conclude.

I watch the color drain from her face. Her eyes turn pink at the edges and her chin quivers. She lets go of my hand as hers curl into fists. She stares at the ground for a moment, like she's doing mental equations. Then, she promptly turns on her heel and starts storming back up the trail toward the cabin.

Just like the last time she ran from me, I go after her.

CHAPTER 16

JEWEL

My legs feel heavy as lead as I trek along the trail back to the cabin. The forest looms and lurches around me, the trees stretching out their shadows to spindly lines crossing my path in the glow of afternoon. The sun doesn't stay out long this time of year, and the light is already starting to fade. The wind picks up and howls through the branches. The woods which felt so cozy earlier have twisted into a frightening backdrop for the way I'm feeling. My mind whirls around in a million painful directions. No matter which way I look, there's something horrible waiting for me to unlock. Pieces of a lifelong puzzle notching into place to create a picture so disturbing, it makes me question everything I ever knew.

I lay a cold, trembling hand over my chest to feel my heart beating a mile a minute. My stomach churns with nausea, and I'm so dizzy my head is swimming. The very fabric of my reality is being ripped down in long shreds, and I am helpless to stop it. Dread and denial blare like police sirens in my head. I can hear the muffled crunch-

crunch of Stefan's footsteps a short distance behind me. He's keeping my pace, his footsteps almost matching up with mine. He's close enough to keep an eye on me for safety's sake, but he's far enough back to give me a little space while I spin out of control. He may be brusque sometimes, and things get lost in translation, but even Stefan knows what kind of a bomb he just dropped on my head. He knows to expect some kind of emotional reaction out of me, and he's trying to be tactful about it.

"Ugh!" I groan in frustration, my fingers clawing at my face.

I'm so damn angry at Stefan. First of all, for suggesting that my own father could be the one responsible for all this pain and suffering. For uprooting my life and throwing me to the wolves. For sending Stefan and me down a narrow path to destruction. Stefan just informed me of the one thing I didn't want to consider: that my dad set the order for me to be kidnapped, or worse, killed. I remember the word 'eliminate' and how it frightened me to my core days ago. I blamed Stefan. I blamed his bosses. I thought the problem was the mafia, not my own family. How the hell am I supposed to square this information with the fact that I do love my dad, that I respected and trusted him all these years because what else was I supposed to do?

More than that, though, I'm mad at Stefan because he's so goddamn considerate and gentle with me, I can't even *stay* mad at him. The truth is, I know deep down it's not his fault at all. Stefan is simply the messenger, not the problem itself. I should be thankful to him for giving me an almost straight answer finally. But God, I don't feel gratitude. I feel betrayal. I feel fear.

I emerge from the treeline and storm straight up to the

front porch. I bound up the steps, still spurred on by indignant fury, and burst through the front door. As I step into the cabin, I'm already fighting back hot, bitter tears in my eyes. I bite my lip, trying not to let those tears fall. Stefan is just a few steps behind me. He opens the door and walks in just as I'm storming into the kitchen. He trails after me and stays silent. He's trying to be patient with me, but I'm all out of patience myself. I stand on tiptoe to take down a glass tumbler from a cabinet. I spin on my heel and glare at Stefan. I hold out my glass.

"I need a drink. Now. I know there has to be something alcoholic in this kitchen somewhere," I snap.

"Of course," Stefan says quietly.

He grabs a half-full bottle of whiskey from a high-up cupboard and pours me a glass. He fills it way beyond the standard serving size, which is just what I need. I toss back a big gulp, then push past him back into the living room. I walk over to the fireplace, which is starting to dwindle down to the coals by now. I watch the licks of smoke wafting from the gleaming embers while a battle rages on inside of me. Stefan comes over and dutifully starts adding little logs to the fire. I pace back and forth across the living room while he tends the flame.

I just can't believe it. My own father betrayed me in the harshest way possible.

"Whenever you're ready to talk, I am here," Stefan reminds me in a low, sweet voice.

Something about the kindness in his tone shatters my already-tenuous composure. I burst into tears and a jagged sob rips from my throat. Tears roll down my cheeks as my face flushes pink. I take another swig of whiskey and blanch at the bitter taste.

"I just don't understand it," I sniffle. "I-I don't want to understand it."

"Come on, Jewel. That is not you. We both know you have a drive to understand things-- everything. All the time. It's why you're so curious, why you make such a good lawyer," Stefan reminds me gently.

"But this isn't some random criminal. This isn't an interview with an interesting person. It's family shit. It's betrayal and heartbreak and so much pain," I confess tearfully.

"You're right. I'm sorry, *malyshka*," he says, looking over at me from the fireplace. "I wish I had better news to tell you."

I keep pacing as my mind spins wildly. "I mean, it just… some of it makes sense, but some of it doesn't. He's my father. He's supposed to love me and protect me, right?"

"Yes. That was supposed to be his job," Stefan agrees.

My feelings leap back and forth between wanting to defend him as my father, and wanting to be realistic and decry him as the villain of my own story. But if I don't have him, what do I have?

"All my life, it was just Dad and me. Well, us and a long succession of nannies and tutors," I add bitterly. "I had an aunt, but she died when I was little. I don't even remember her anymore. Dad was the only one around, and he hardly ever was. God, he missed so many of my birthdays I stopped wishing on my candles for him to show up. I was probably nine years old when I finally realized no birthday wish was going to make him *want* to be there. When I was little, I used to think he was just really busy. A man with too many important business deals going on to pay much attention to his daughter."

"That does not sound like a fair relationship," Stefan says.

"You're right. It's not fair. I was always waiting on him to show up, to answer me, to listen, to tell me what I needed so badly to hear. I was willing to do backflips for his attention. He's the only family I really have, Stefan. The only *anything*," I whimper.

Stefan looks pained, as well. I can tell he's feeling my agony secondhand. There's something in the way he looks at me that says he understands. He's willing to listen, and for me, that's something I rarely get in my life. Certainly not from Dad, and barely ever from my friends, either. Nobody ever wants to listen to me. Until Stefan. He stands by the fire, watching me intently and waiting to swoop in when I need him. I feel a rush of affection and appreciation for this strong, charming, kind man who lets me talk things through.

"He always kept me at arm's length," I go on, still pacing. "But at the same time, he wouldn't let anyone else get close to me either. God, he's kept me so isolated my whole life. I grew up in that big empty house with a bunch of strangers taking care of me. They never lasted long. As soon as I would start to bond with somebody, Dad sent them away. He fired my first nanny, the closest thing to a mom I can remember, on my sixth birthday."

"What an awful thing to do," Stefan growls.

I sloppily wipe my eyes on my sleeve. It starts to drizzle outside, the sky going dark.

"He said I was getting too old to need someone the way I needed her. I remember feeling so ashamed for wanting a parent to be around all the time and love me and play with me. Dad made me feel like I was immature, a stupid crybaby," I sniffle.

"You were six," he reminds me gently.

"Yeah. It's crazy how you don't realize how fucked up your childhood is until you're way out of it," I sigh. "I used to spend so much time alone. I must have read a thousand books as a kid. Growing up, it was the closest to friendship I could find. Dad didn't really let me play with other children very often. He said we were better than them. He said it wasn't safe to mingle with our neighbors, even though they lived in the same nice neighborhood as us."

"It sounds like he didn't want any outside influence on you," Stefan notes.

"I tried to ask questions about everything, too. You know how I am," I point out. "I asked about my mother, about what I was like as a baby. I wanted to see an album of baby pictures, like everyone else has. But he rarely answered me. And when he did, he lied. He told me not to trust anyone. He tried to teach me to be tough, but I guess I failed him there. I turned out too soft. I care too much about other people to really be successful."

Stefan frowns. "Is that what he told you?"

I nod sadly. "Yeah. All the time. He was so disappointed in me for going to law school to learn how to defend the defenseless. He said I was wasting my time and his money. He said the only good lawyer is a good liar, but I always wanted the truth. I just couldn't get it right."

"Sounds to me like you had it right all along, Jewel," he assures me.

I stop pacing and stare into the fire. The flames flicker

orange and hot, slowly consuming the wooden logs. I sigh. "You know, if I look deep down, it makes a little sense. My gut tells me it's true. Dad really did orchestrate this whole thing, didn't he?"

Stefan nods. "All signs point to that."

"I tried to stop him, you know. I tried to keep him from becoming a monster. When I was a little girl, I idolized my father. I thought there was no man smarter, stronger, or cooler on the planet. Nobody was tough on crime like Dad. Nobody got shit done like Dad. But I couldn't be tough like him. When he said horrible things, I tried to argue with him, but he wouldn't have any of it. He wouldn't listen to me. He just yelled over me and made me feel worse," I admit. "Deep down I knew he was a bad man, but he was my father, too. I had to make it fit."

"That was all you knew to do," Stefan comforts me. "You tried, Jewel."

He stokes the fire as the rain outside turns to hail. The icy stones pummel the roof, making me jump. It's like the weather is mirroring my emotions as they spiral out of control. My whole world is falling apart at the seams faster than I can pick up the scraps.

"I wonder how long he was planning this," I mutter. "I wonder if he was counting down the days until he could finally be rid of me. God, I was so stupid to ever trust him. I was just a pawn in his game. All my self-worth was tied up in trying to make my father happy. Trying to make him accept me, God forbid actually *love* me. But now I think he might not even be capable of love. I was just a means to an end. Maybe a fun toy to play with until he got bored when I didn't turn out like he planned. When I was useful to him, he used me. Otherwise, he ignored me. I'm alone in the world, and I always was."

Hot tears roll down my cheeks. Stefan walks up to me and takes my whiskey glass. He sets it on a side table and turns back to put his large hands on my slumping shoulders. His dark eyes burn with passion as he looks into mine.

"You aren't alone, Jewel. Not now, and never again. I know we've had our ups and downs. The way we met-- I wish I could change it. But believe me, *malyshka*, you can trust in me. I will never again do anything to hurt you. You say you're alone, but you're not. You don't need a father; you need a guardian. You need someone who will defend and protect you against the whole world. I will guide you. I will take care of you. I promise, Jewel, you will never have to walk alone again," Stefan says fervently.

I crumple under his touch and his beautiful words. The tears course down my face, but I feel different now. The heartrending pain of being betrayed by my own father abates when Stefan gazes into my eyes like this. He pulls me in slowly, enveloping me in his strong arms. He kisses the top of my head, my nose, then finally my lips. I melt into the kiss as my pain turns to ecstasy. Stefan caresses my face while his tongue pushes into my mouth. I moan against his lips.

His hands slide down to my shoulders, then to hold my hands. We rut against each other while our bodies are flush together. I can feel every rippling muscle and swell of his cock. Panic turns to passion as we start peeling off our clothing bit by bit. We kick off our boots and start pulling down our pants. He tears off his coat and shirt, tossing them aside. I do the same.

Goosebumps pop up on my bare arms as he dives in to hold my naked body. His hands explore my ample breasts, my stiffening nipples, my flat stomach. I cling to him with my fingernails digging into his broad, powerful back. He plays with my tits while I reach down to stroke his hard cock between us. I lick my lips at the heat and hardness of his shaft. I wrap my hand around his thickness and start to pump up and down. He feels velvety smooth on my palm, and my pussy aches to be filled next. I need this-- I need him. Right now, more than anything.

"I won't let anyone hurt you ever again," Stefan growls.

"I trust you. I believe you," I pant.

He pulls me in for another intense kiss. His hands smooth down the gentle slope of my back and down to grope my plump ass. He grabs each cheek by the handful and pushes against me. His hard cock slides against my achy mound and I whimper with need.

We slowly fold to the floor. Stefan pushes me flat on my back and climbs on top of me. His hands roll up my arms to interlace his fingers with mine while he leans in to kiss me. His powerful frame keeps me perfectly pinned down as his lips trail from my mouth to my jaw. He kisses a winding line to my ear, where he gently breathes in and out to tease me. I shudder and twinge with ticklish delight at the feeling of his soft breath on my skin. He takes the opportunity to gently graze my neck with his teeth before biting down slightly. I gasp, and he kisses the same spot. He sucks and scrapes with his teeth, bringing blood just under the surface to make a beautiful wine-colored mark. Proof that he's been here. Proof that I belong to him.

Still pinning down my arms, Stefan's lips move down to my chest. He flicks his tongue over my perky pink nipple, which makes me gasp and twitch. I feel the spiraling heat straight down between my legs. I arch my back to push against him while he licks and suckles my nipples. I'm helpless under his strength, but I'm exactly where I want to be.

"I want you. I need you," I whisper.

"I'm yours," Stefan grunts. "All yours."

"Give me what I want. Fill me up, Stefan," I beg him. I rock my hips so that his hard cock brushes over my slick, swollen pussy. I let out a little whine of desire. *"Please."*

"Anything for you, *malyshka*," he growls.

With a grunt, he rubs the head of his cock around my slick hole. The ring of sensitive nerves there go haywire and I buck up into him. Still holding one arm down, he pushes inside of me with one swift, forceful movement. I gasp at the onslaught of sharp pleasure tinged with delicious pain. His thickness stretches my pussy, and I feel myself clenching around him. He slides in deep, knocking against that fleshy, soft spot inside me that makes me dizzy with pleasure. His cock strikes my g-spot over and over, and I revel in the sensation of his hard cock pummeling my insides.

Stefan grabs my thighs in his hands and pushes them out, spreading me wider. His cock is so massive, I feel completely stuffed when he's inside of me. He slides in and out rapidly, fucking me with unbridled passion. Both of us need this so badly, especially after the emotional rollercoaster we've been on for the past hour. My heart is still hurting, but nothing cures my pain like the mind-numbing pleasure Stefan shows me. I feel more love, more honesty in our feverish fucking than I ever have before. He knows how to satisfy my needs before I even know. I give myself completely over to this magnificent beast of a man. I trust him. I respect him.

And as I gaze into those dark, passionate eyes, I realize with a jolt that I'm really falling for him. We aren't just a pairing of convenience or forced proximity anymore. We've crossed into something so much richer, much more genuine. There's no guard up when he looks at me. There's no restraint when he touches me. We are two broken people who have walked winding, scary, painful paths that led us right where we needed to be: here. Together.

"Don't ever leave me," I gasp between forceful thrusts.

"I never will," he grunts.

"I'm so close, Stefan," I whimper.

"Me, too, *printsessa*. I'm going to fill you up. This pussy is mine," he snarls.

"God, yes. I belong to you only," I encourage him breathlessly.

Stefan fucks me harder, his hands caressing me all over while he loses control. His body is tensing up. His flawless muscles tighten and he grits his teeth. The ball of tension inside of me grows bigger and tighter until I can't hold back any longer.

"Ohhh, Stefan!" I cry.

"My Jewel. My precious Jewel," he croons back.

My pussy gushes sweet, hot honey all over his fat cock as he explodes deep inside my cunny. I shudder and clench around him, my fingernails digging into his shoulders. He kisses me hard on the mouth while he pumps into me a few more, ragged, intense times. He empties himself entirely inside my womb, and I cling to him tightly through the waves of afterglow. We gasp and hold each other by the crackling fireplace as the sky pours hail on the cabin.

Slowly, sweetly, we come down from the immeasurable high. We float back down to Earth together, the same as always and yet forever changed. Because now, when he lies down beside me and gazes at my face, something is different. That great question that used to loom up between us is gone. I know now that there is only one man in this world I can truly trust, and he's right beside me. Naked, tangled up, sticky with each other's come, we hold each other close. Stefan strokes my hair lovingly.

"It's going to be hard from here on out, isn't it?" I ask softly.

He nods and kisses my hand. "*Da, malyshka*. Very hard. But now I've taught you how to defend yourself if you must. Either way, *I* will defend you to the death."

"Do you think it will come to that?" I question.

"I don't know, my Jewel. But I know that we are equals now. Partners in everything we do. We went rogue together. We escaped together. And now, we will walk back into the fire together. I won't let you down, *malyshka*. We can do this," he assures me.

"Then let's do it," I agree firmly. "Let's burn the whole thing down."

CHAPTER 17

STEFAN

It's a beautiful clear morning after the hail fell on the roof throughout the night. When I woke up this morning, the birds were singing and the sunshine was basking on Jewel's lovely sleeping face. I didn't want to wake her, but we have a lot to do today. I gently kissed her awake, and the two of us have been preparing for the journey ahead all morning since. We both put on black long-sleeved shirts and dark, fleece-lined pants, along with thick black socks and boots. It's imperative that we look unassuming and feel comfortable, since we will be in the car for at least six or seven hours today. I have to admit, Jewel looks adorable in her soft winter pants. Her round, juicy bottom jiggles as she moves through the kitchen. I'm hard at work making us coffee for the road, but it's hard to stay focused when the most beautiful woman in the world is making sandwiches just a few feet away.

Out of the corner of my eye, I watch her methodically lay out the slices of wheat bread, then perfectly stack two squares of cheese and a few slices of deli turkey on top. Her brows are furrowed and her mind is laser-focused while she cuts up fruit to bring with us as snacks. She's taking her food rationing responsibility very seriously, and it's cute.

"Make sure and pack a few extras," I remark.

She breaks concentration just long enough to look up and nod before returning to her very important task. It's good that she's making a lot of food for the road. We don't know how long we will have to stay out there. I'm planning for a short, to the point trip-- we know generally what we need, and I don't want to be there a second longer than necessary. But I can't say for sure when we'll be back. Or even *if* we will be back. Truth is, a lot of things can go wrong today. We need a lot of luck and skill to do this right. But I don't share my more pessimistic concerns with Jewel just yet. I don't want to scare her.

I pour the freshly-brewed, fragrant coffee into two gigantic travel mugs for the road. Jewel is finishing up the food, and I stop to admire her for a moment. She takes great care to make each sandwich symmetrical and equal with the others. When she cuts up fruit, she does so in perfect little cubes, all the same size. She painstakingly packs and seals every individual item, then tucks them neatly into a big brown bag. It's more like art than packing a lunch. My princess looks so lovely and domestic bent over the kitchen counter in full concentration. For a moment, I imagine what it would be like to have a normal life with her. There's an urge in my heart to just say 'fuck the world' and hide away up here in the mountains indefinitely. Play house with my sweet, beautiful queen, and just let the bloody drama play out in another city. We could just pretend our past won't catch up to us... until it does.

It's only a matter of time, and we're sitting ducks up here. We have been hiding long enough. Now it's time to strike back, find out what we need to know. We are about to walk right back into the mouth of the beast: we're going to Freddie Albany's stately family home in Medford, not far from Harvard where Jewel attended law school. It's the place she called home, as well, until I plucked her out of her life. It's one of the riskiest places we could go, but we have to-- we need to find proof of Freddie's corruption. Not just for tactical reasons, but for closure. Jewel needs undeniable proof that her father deserves whatever dark fate we may have to deliver to him. She deserves the truth about her own family.

"You almost ready, Jewel?" I ask her.

She looks over at me and nods. She hoists the brown bag into her arms.

"I'm ready. Food is packed. Let's go," she says.

With all of our necessities packed up, we head out into the bright, sunny morning. We pile into the old white car and start rolling down the long, winding driveway out to the road. The forest is teeming with wildlife today, putting on a little show for us as we wind down the mountain. Jewel rolls down the window part of the way to breathe in the fresh air. I watch her dark hair billow out around her face. She closes her eyes and tilts back. The sun beams on her round cheeks and full lips. It's almost enough to make me drive off the road, but I stay alert. I tell myself again that no matter what happens today, I have to protect this angelic creature.

"It's gonna be so weird, seeing my house again," she says a little while later.

"The last time I saw the place, I was staking it out to learn your habits," I admit.

She chuckles softly. "Isn't it strange how things change?"

"It is, my Jewel," I agree.

"I wonder how that house will appear to me now, after… all of this," she muses aloud. "It hardly feels like home to me anymore when I think about it. I almost don't want to go back. But I know we have to. There's so much we don't know yet."

"Is there anywhere in the house you think we should start with?" I ask.

She chews on that for a moment, then answers, "The top floor office. My dad spent a lot of time in there, pretty much all his time when he was actually home. He always kept the door locked, too, so I couldn't get in."

I frown. "That's suspicious."

"Yeah," Jewel sighs. "I guess it is. Back then, I just thought it was because it was work stuff. Confidential information or whatever. I never tried very hard to get in there before. I assumed it wasn't my business."

"It sounds like exactly the place where he would hide important information. Things he doesn't want getting out," I add. "We'll find something. I'm sure of it. But we will have to be extremely careful. I'm sure I don't have to tell you how dangerous it is breaking into an ICE agent's personal home."

She winces a little. "Especially one like Dad. He, uh, is known to hold a grudge."

"We'll do it carefully. When we first arrive, we'll stake the place out, see what we are dealing with," I explain. "Then we make our move."

"Oh, we'll have to be careful about the car, too," she pipes up. "Not to bring up sore memories, but this is the car you kidnapped me in, Stefan."

"Right," I grunt.

"It's my friend Gina's car, and she will definitely have reported it missing. The cops will be looking for the car, even if Dad doesn't have them looking for me," she reasons. "Plus, we'll be driving it around in the same vicinity as that club we stole it from."

I notice how she uses 'we' instead of 'you.' It warms my frigid heart. She sees me as a teammate now. A partner, rather than a captor. Things *do* change.

"That's why we're taking the back roads as much as possible," I reply.

"Good. Because Medford is full of nosy busybodies with way too much time and money on their hands. Everybody watches everyone else. Constant scrutiny and gossip," she says.

"That sounds terrible," I comment.

She nods. "Oh yeah. Trust me. It was like growing up in a fishbowl. Of course, Dad did whatever he could to make it even worse, not just for me but for the neighbors, too. He was always calling the HOA on people for their grass being a centimeter too long or their garage doors left open. One time, the old lady down the street painted her mailbox pink, and Dad raised hell so they'd make her change it back," Jewel recounts with disgust.

"He likes the rules as long as they suit him," I reply.

"Exactly," she agrees. "And no matter how awful he was to everybody, no one could fight back. Dad knew how to keep enough leverage with his powerful allies to stay immune. He ran this neighborhood. The whole town, really."

"I believe the word is 'megalomaniac,'" I sound out in my accented pronunciation.

Jewel snorts. "Yeah, pretty much. You know, it would actually make sense if he is involved with the mafia. Dad always loved lording control over people. Ultimate control is his dream. He doesn't just want to rule, he wants to be a tyrant."

We roll along through the scenic, wooded back country, making good time as we avoid all major cities. Surrounded by trees and rarely other vehicles, it feels almost peaceful to ride down the highway with my girl beside me. But as we creep closer to our destination, the scenery starts to change. The area becomes more populated. Houses crop up in greater density. The forest makes way for buildings and parking lots, grocery stores and shopping malls. Still, I stick to the path less traveled.

"The Bratva could have eyes anywhere," I warn her.

"ICE could have eyes out, too, at my father's command," she reminds me grimly.

At the same time, we turn to glance at each other. We reach out and take one another's hand. She gives it a little squeeze, and I squeeze back. I feel instantly recharged with motivation.

"We're in this together, either way," she says.

"Till the very end," I agree.

I feel a flush of intense affection for this strong, brave, surprising girl. I'm impressed that she's so dedicated to truth and justice that she's willing to go to such lengths to prove her own father is a villain. Despite his best attempts to sculpt her in his image, Jewel is truly good at heart, and he could never erase that. She's so good, in fact, that she makes me a better man. She is a moral compass in the palm of my hand, and I will go to any length to protect her.

As we draw nearer to the Albany house, the scenery changes again. Everywhere you look, there's perfectly trimmed hedges and topiary. Marble promenades. Concrete columns and pillars that would look better at an ancient theater than on these oversized houses. I wrinkle my nose at the flawless lawns and gardens, knowing that they were made beautiful by underpaid hired help, not by the people who own the houses. Once again, I'm amazed that a selfless, wonderful woman like Jewel came from a place of such blatant entitlement. It's further proof that not even an evil man like Freddie and all the luxury in the world couldn't corrupt her.

Finally, we pull onto her street. We stop the car in the same spot I used to stake her out, a few houses down. The car is obscured by high hedges, but I still have a good view of the Albany house with my binoculars.

"Let me check the scene," I murmur as I lift the binoculars to my eyes.

"What do you see?" Jewel asks eagerly. "Is he there?"

"His car is gone," I note.

"Oh good. He's probably away on business, then," she says. "So it's unattended?"

"Not entirely. There's a man guarding out front. I recognize him," I relay to her.

"Wait, really? From where?" she asks.

I look over at her, pained. "The brotherhood. We never worked together, but I remember his face. He's usually on security detail because of his size."

"So, he's a big scary guy, basically," she sighs. "Sounds like the type my dad usually hired for security. He's probably been hiring from… those people all along."

I hand her the binoculars. "Stay here. I'm moving in."

"What? Stefan, what if--"

"I'll neutralize the guard. You watch me. When it's done, you come catch up to me, okay? But not until he goes down," I command her.

She gulps and nods. "Okay. Be careful."

"I will," I assure her as I step out of the car.

I keep low to the ground as I move in on the house. I use Freddie's ridiculous topiary shapes against him, hiding behind the carved hedges until I'm within a hundred feet of the guard. He looks like a mean guy, but he also looks bored. A little sleepy, too. He yawns and checks his watch. He's itching for a break.

Well, I can give him a little rest.

When he happens to turn away from me, I go barreling out of the hedges full-tilt. I tackle the big brute to the ground before he can even process what's happening. I put my elbow against his throat, crush him with my full body weight, and give him a swift butt to the head. His eyes roll back and he goes limp. He's knocked out cold, and probably will be for a little while. My own forehead smarts a little, but it's no wound. I search the man's pockets and find a set of keys. Easy enough. I look back toward the car and see, to my relief, Jewel running my way. She looks pale and nervous, but she followed the mission.

"Oh my god. Is he dead?" she whispers, eyes wide.

"Just unconscious," I assure her as I fit the key in the door. It clicks and falls open.

We step inside. I'm instantly struck by the stately decor. Everything is very orderly and classically-styled, with the typical leather and dark wood theme I find in houses like this one. Everywhere you look, there are signs of major wealth. It feels more like a museum than a home. We make our way up the first flight of stairs. Jewel pauses at one room with the door open. She peers inside, looking sad.

"My bedroom," she says. "Weird. It hardly feels like home anymore. I look around and I don't see myself anywhere. Even my own bedroom is designed like the rest of the house. Dad never let me put much say into that stuff."

I put a hand on her shoulder. "Come on. Let's keep moving."

She nods and follows me up the next set of stairs to the top floor. At the end of a long, eerie hallway is a locked door.

"This is the one," Jewel confirms. "Dad's office."

None of the keys on the ring fit this door, but that doesn't matter. I brace myself and bust down the door with one strong bump of my shoulder.

"Well, that works," she says.

We spend a good few minutes snooping around the office, which is just as stately and meticulously organized as the rest of the domicile. Jewel digs through some filing cabinets while I open up the laptop on his desk. It instantly prompts me to enter a six-digit password.

"Jewel, what's your father's birthday?" I ask.

"December 19th, 1963," she answers. "Why?"

"I'm trying his password," I reply.

She abandons the cabinets and comes to look over my shoulder. I type in 12-19-63.

Password denied.

"Your birthday?" I ask.

"April 14th, 1996," she says.

I try that one. No luck again.

"Makes sense. I doubt he even remembers my birthday, much less makes it his password," Jewel admits bitterly. "What's this mean, you think?"

She picks up a tiny yellow sticky note on the side of the desk. There's a recent date on it.

"Might as well try it," I murmur, typing in the date.

To our surprise, the password is accepted. The laptop opens up, and countless folders populate the screen. As I dig through the files, looking for incriminating information, Jewel looks to be doing math in her head. Then she gasps and covers her mouth.

"Oh my god. Stefan. I just realized… if my memory is right, that date he wrote down is the same day I tried to run away from you in the woods," she says.

The weight of her discovery hits me, too.

"The day Victor ordered me to kill you," I growl.

Jewel's soft brown eyes fill with tears. "He was looking forward to it. So much that he made it his password," she mumbles. She leans against the desk, looking deflated. "I knew it was bad, but not this bad. My god, he must have always hated me."

"That's not all, *malyshka*," I tell her cautiously. "These files are filled with email conversations and transcripts. Your father runs a tight ship. He keeps every detail. The wording he uses… it's familiar to me, Jewel."

"What are you saying?" she asks, sniffling.

"The mafia likes to speak in code whenever possible. I

learned that early on. Your father uses the same code throughout these conversations," I explain.

"Well, what is he talking about?" she questions.

"Human trafficking," I break to her. "Sex trafficking, to be specific."

Her jaw drops and she looks ill.

"But he's an ICE agent. He's supposed to follow the rules. He's supposed to protect those people," Jewel murmurs, more to herself than to me. She's coming to terms with a painful truth. She looks at me with deep agony in her eyes.

"My father is an even worse man than we thought, isn't he?" she asks.

"*Da*, my Jewel. Much worse," I agree.

For a second, I think she might completely lose it. Her face crumples and she fights back a sob. Then she wipes her eyes, takes a deep breath, and sets her soft lips in a hard line.

"We don't have to feel bad about taking him down, then," Jewel says fiercely.

"We'll put a stop to this. I promise," I tell her.

Suddenly, we hear a bizarre moaning noise from outside. I look out the window to see the guard starting to slowly stir down on the ground out front.

"Shit. Clock is running out. Let's go," I order her.

We hurry out of the office, locking it behind us. We rush down the two flights of stairs and out to the front steps, where the guard is starting to twitch and groan. While he's still helpless, I feel around his pockets one last time.

"Come on, Stefan, he's waking up," Jewel urges me.

I pull out a cell phone and immediately notice the log

of missed calls on the screen. The name associated with every call… Freddie Albany.

"We have to go. Now," I tell her, thrusting the phone into her hands. "Run!"

Jewel tucks the phone in her pocket and we take off for the car, knowing that the world is about to collapse around us any minute now.

CHAPTER 18

JEWEL

My eyes glaze over as I stare out the window of our stolen getaway vehicle. It seems bizarre to me now to remember this used to be Gina's car. I used to ride around with her from one party to the next, trailing after her like a halfhearted sidekick. This car has driven me to nightclubs, to campus, to pep rallies-- but it's never seen the kind of action we've gotten in the past week or so. After a brief dip back in the familiar Harvard town this car and I used to call home, we're rocketing back up the country back roads toward the place that feels more like home than anywhere else.

It's been a few hours since we finally got out of the vicinity of Medford, but I'm still barely able to relax. My shoulders keep tensing up by my ears, my neck and eyes ache from peering intently out the windows in search of enemies, and I'm exhausted. The whole time we were leaving Medford, my heart was pounding. I kept thinking every dark vehicle we passed was a cop on Dad's payroll or a mafia guy... also on Dad's payroll. Everywhere I looked, I found places where they could hide. I've been nervously watching all the mirrors for signs that we're being followed. The further we get from the suburbs, the calmer I start to feel. The cookie-cutter mansions and trendy shopping plazas turn to rustic country houses and rolling hills. The land becomes far less curated. Nature runs wild. The scenery goes from suburban to overgrown, and my mood goes from paranoid to too-tired-to-be-paranoid.

We have been riding in more or less silence after we made our desperate run to the car from my father's house. At first, we were out of breath. Once we nabbed the cell phone from that mafia guard's pocket, we booked it out of there in a hurry before the guy could fully wake up. Or before any of my nosy-ass neighbors could report our suspicious activity. We were silent as we watched the road for attackers or pursuers. I was nervously flinching at every vehicle that passed, and Stefan was busy scanning the road for trouble. But once we got a little further out, the silence turned contemplative. We have both been lost deep in thought for over an hour or so. After all, there's a lot to think about. So much new, painful information to process.

I look down at the phone in my lap. I poke the screen open and it flashes all those missed calls from Freddie Albany again. My stomach churns. It's more undeniable proof that my dad is, at the very least, involved enough with the mafia to hire one as a guard. But I know his engagement with this whole filthy enterprise goes deeper than home security. I try to think about what we uncovered on Dad's private laptop, but denial keeps rearing its stubborn head. Coming to terms with how evil and uncaring my father is feels like staring into the sun. I know it's there, I can feel it, but God, it's so hard to look at. I feel numb all over, but there's dread lurking just behind that wall of pain I keep avoiding. My denial is starting to wear thin. Doubt and anger are creeping in on me. I gaze out the window and gently bite the inside of my cheek to try and stem the flow of hot, bitter tears in my eyes. I don't want Stefan to see me crying. I don't want him to think I'm weak, or that I'm mourning for my dad. We both know he's a bad man, and I shouldn't waste my feelings on the likes of him. At the same time, he's the only family I know. If I can't find a way to love and forgive him, who can? But then, does he even deserve my love, much less my forgiveness? I feel so betrayed and confused.

My hands curl into fists in my lap. I mutter in an undertone, "I just don't get it."

Stefan looks over at me. It's the first thing either of us have said in hours.

"What is it?" he prompts.

I look at him with tears in my eyes. "How can a father choose to harm his own daughter like this? How could this really be happening?"

"I'm sorry, Jewel," Stefan consoles.

"It doesn't make any sense, but the evidence is damning," I go on. "I mean, all those folders you found on his computer."

"Exactly the kind of paper trail I expected him to leave," he says. "I suspected he would be more cautious about hiding his information, but he's cocky. He's been running this business for so long, he's untouchable. He doesn't think anyone can reach him."

"Well, he's wrong. It only took us a few tries to get into his laptop. And that password… I can't believe he was so enthusiastic about the day he picked for me to die that he made it his fucking passcode. If that doesn't say 'heartless corruption' then I don't know what does," I sigh.

The car pulls onto the winding, narrow road that circuits us back up the mountain. The scenery changes again as the forest grows darker and deeper. The trees lining the road grow taller. They loom and cast long shadows across the road. The sun is starting its sinking descent across the valley below. The sky is tinged with peachy gold and lilac, enchanting me as we ride along the edge of the cliff. Fog is settling in over the higher peaks, and before long we find ourselves driving in a thick, wet haze. Insects hiding in the trees and bushes strike up their nocturnal chorus. The dusty gold clouds part in an indigo sky to let the luminous orb of the moon hang bright and beautiful over the mountain. As we get closer to the cabin, we talk about what comes next in our 'plan.' We talk about the need for stealth as we gather more intel and evidence, enough to damn my father. Stefan talks about setting up particular meetings, weighing our options and who's left to trust. We have to finally confront the evil behind all of our trouble.

The car rumbles up the rocky driveway and putters to a halt. Stefan turns off the engine and glances at me meaningfully.

"It's going to be risky. There's no way around that. But we can't turn back now," he says.

"No going back. Only forward," I agree grimly.

We get out of the car. Stefan grabs all of our stuff and we pile back into the cabin. As I cross the threshold, I feel a rush of relief. It smells, sounds, and feels more like home than anywhere else in the world. Walking into the Medford mansion felt like attending a museum, or walking through the memories of someone else's life. Not my own. I don't recognize the woman I used to be and the life I used to live. It's like an old outfit that shrunk in the wash. None of it fits me anymore. In fact, I wonder if I ever fit into that world anyway. I feel more at home here. I feel more like myself when I'm with Stefan.

We're both shivery cold and achy from our long day of car travel and breaking and entering. Stefan drops our stuff on the table and says, "Come on. I'll run us a hot shower."

"God, yes," I groan with appreciation.

We traipse off to the bathroom. Stefan starts up a hot, steamy shower and lets me get in first. I strip off my tactical clothes and happily step under the comforting spray of hot water. I peek out of the curtain to watch Stefan take off his clothes. I ogle his hard, strong chest, powerful back, and perfect tight ass. I love the chiseled range of his abs and his cock, hanging full and thick between his muscular thighs. I remember not too long ago when he first let me shower in captivity, how I was so afraid he would peek at me naked. Now, I'm impatient waiting for him to get in the shower with me. Naked. He climbs into the stall and we share the hot water as we get lathered up with fresh-smelling soap. At first, we're just cleansing ourselves, but then Stefan wordlessly starts washing my hair. My lips fall open in a soft sigh at the sensation of his fingertips working my scalp. I feel so loved and comforted by this sweet, caring gesture. Nobody has ever taken care of me like this, not even when I was a child.

"Jewel, I want you to know that I'm sorry," he says softly. "I never wanted any of this to affect you. I never wanted to hurt you."

His fingers work carefully through the snarls and knots in my hair while he speaks. I have my eyes closed, letting the water rush over me while this guardian angel of a man washes me.

"I don't blame you for any of this," I assure him. "You didn't do it on your own accord. You were forced into this situation, just like me. And you've shown me so much kindness since then. Stefan, I know this is going to sound weird, but I'm actually glad you kidnapped me."

"I stole you away from everything you knew," Stefan says. He sounds pained.

"What I knew was bullshit," I answer sharply. "What I knew was all lies. You know, I spent my whole life trying to please other people. Especially Dad. I was a ghost in my own life because it's never been what I wanted. My father's shadow ruined everything. Every time."

"You deserve so much better," he murmurs.

"I agree. *Now* I agree," I clarify. "You forced me to see the world differently. I thought I knew what strength was. My dad made me think cruelty and greed were signs of strength. But you're strong in a different way, the real way. You make me feel more powerful than I am alone. With you, I can do anything. Whatever happens, I'm glad I met you, Stefan. And if we die, we do it side by side."

I turn around to face Stefan, looking up into his handsome face. His dark eyes bore into mine. His hands brush my hair back and cup my face. He traces his thumb over my bottom lip.

"I would move heaven and earth before I let harm come to you," he growls.

"I know," I answer breathily. "I trust you, Stefan. I need you."

The tension between us snaps once again. He dives in to capture my mouth in a passionate kiss. His hands slide down my face and neck to smooth over my full, plump breasts. I sigh into his magical, warm touch. His tongue pushes into my mouth and I press against him so our bodies are flush together. I rock my pelvis into his growing, throbbing cock. Stefan's hands fondle my tits, his fingertips sliding over my soapy, slippery nipples. They stiffen into pink peaks under his machinations. Spirals of searing hot pleasure go straight down between my wet thighs.

Suds slide down my back as Stefan grabs my leg and hikes it up around him. Wobbling on one foot, he holds me steady while he slips one hand between my thighs. He swallows my moan with a kiss as his fingers stroke up and down between my swollen, puffy lips. I twinge and burn for him from head to toe. Every time he touches me, it leaves a momentary tingle. When he starts massaging my clit and hood, I have to cling to him for balance. Pleasure washes through my system and makes me feel light-headed. I rest my face against his hard chest while he flicks and rolls that tight bundle of nerves.

The hot water pelts my back and keeps me deliciously warm. My hand wanders to find Stefan's hard cock. His skin is velvety smooth and hot to the touch. He's yearning for me like I ache for him. I wrap my fingers and palm around his thick shaft to slide up and down, using the rivulets of hot soapy water to lubricate each pump. I swoop down to the root, slide around to gently fondle his balls, and then sweep back up. I swivel my hand around the tip and let my thumb rub up and down the sensitive underside.

"Fuck," Stefan grunts.

His cock twitches in my hand. I feel his balls getting heavy as I work his shaft up and down. Stefan strokes my pussy, running two fingers along my quivering lips, then up to circle my clit. It feels so goddamn good, and he's slowly bringing me closer to the edge. He starts to play with the band of muscles and nerves around my tight little hole. I gasp and moan with pleasure as he slowly pushes two thick, long fingers inside of me. His fingers gently hook to stroke that fleshy, soft place deep within my cunny. He tickles my g-spot and awakens some deep tension I didn't even know was there. His thumb rubs my clit while his fingertips press into my g-spot again and again. By now, my pussy is dripping slick juices all over his hand. I feel my honey run down my trembling thighs while I stand here, half held up by this magnificent man. I can hardly maintain a rhythmic pace pumping his cock as my own pleasure spins wildly out of control. I gasp and keen with sensation as Stefan fingerfucks me to oblivion.

"Oh my god," I breathe. "I'm gonna come!"

"Mmmhm. That's right, *malyshka*. Come for me," Stefan commands in a growly voice.

"Nnngh Stefan!" I gasp.

My pussy convulses and hot, slick juices gush down

my legs. My vision swims, my knees buckle, and I nearly collapse. But my perfect, powerful provider is here to catch me. We rinse off together as he holds me up, and then he turns off the shower. I'm still trembling from orgasm as he pats me dry with a towel, then wraps it around me. Stefan scoops me into his strong arms and carries me into the bedroom. He splays me out on the bed, fully naked and all warmed up. I spread my legs wide and bite my lip coquettishly as he takes off his own towel. I lick my lips at the sight of his hard, thick cock stiff and ready for me. He stands at the foot of the bed stroking his enormous length, and I recline coyly on the bed. My hand is between my legs, stroking and teasing my slick pussy. Stefan makes me feel so alive, so filthy in the best way. I entice him to bed with a pout of my lip and the burning desire in my eyes.

"There's never been any sight more beautiful than this," Stefan rumbles.

He gently wraps his hands around my ankles and pulls me to the edge of the bed. I lay back while he hooks my legs up over his shoulders. I'm tingly all over in anticipation of what's to come. When I feel Stefan shove my thighs apart with his hands and dive in to suckle my clit, I immediately come again. I whimper and shiver as my pussy cascades another burst of juices down his chin. Stefan groans his approval and eagerly laps up every last drop. His tongue dives between my lips, licking between every groove. He devours me like a starving man at table, and it feels oh so incredible. His magical tongue flicks and bats my clit while he slurps up my juices. I lift my hips as best I can to rut against his face and beg for more. His lips suckle my clit, then his tongue swathes over my sensitive hood.

He alternates between these different little techniques until I'm so overcome with pleasure all I can do is try and remember to breathe. But even as I squirt another intense orgasm all over his lips, Stefan is preparing to give me more.

He pulls back and wipes his mouth. His dark eyes are determined. He smooths his hands down my legs, massaging my sore muscles as he works his way to my feet. I'm in heaven when he gently rubs my feet. I've never had a lover do this before, and I'm unprepared for how good it feels, especially when he starts sucking on my toes. The ticklish, dirty feeling makes me so wet, I'm creating a puddle on the sheets.

"Oh my god, I can't take it," I gasp.

My hands wander to my chest. I grope my tits and roll my nipples between my fingers while Stefan grabs my legs. He wraps them around himself again and pulls me tight to the end of the bed. He lines up the thick head of his glorious, gigantic cock at my dripping hole. When he pushes inside of me, fireworks burst behind my eyes. I feel so filled up and whole, so complete as I only ever do when we're together. Stefan's shaft prods past that thick circle of muscles at my opening and into my tightness. I twinge and convulse around his girth as he pushes inside inch by heavenly inch. I rock against him, lifting my hips and arching my back.

Stefan groans with pleasure as he sheathes himself entirely inside me. He's so big, it almost aches, but in the best way possible. I bite my lip and toss my head from side to side, unable to control myself as he starts rutting into me hard and fast. His cock pummels my g-spot deep inside. I'm so dripping wet, every thrust is smooth and quick. Stefan grasps my hips and pounds into me vigorously.

"No matter what happens, you are mine and I am yours," he grunts.

"Yes-- oh god, yes," I whimper. "From the very start."

"Till the very end," Stefan adds between gritted teeth.

His dark eyes lock with mine as he pumps into me again and again. My pussy is so gushy wet by now, every thrust makes a slick, wet sound deep inside. My juices dribble down my thighs and ass. I feel it seeping into the bedsheets, but we don't care. My body comes alive for Stefan, and vice versa. The world outside could be on fire, and we wouldn't care. All that matters is his cock inside my pussy, pushing hard into my womb, filling me up with love. I tighten my legs around him and he leans over me. He cradles my lower back with one strong arm while he fucks my tight little cunny. He smacks my ass hard, again and again. I cry out with mingled pain and pleasure, and my pussy gushes wetly with each slap.

"Nobody-- will ever-- take you-- away from me," Stefan grunts between vigorous thrusts.

"They'd die trying," I gasp.

Stefan leans over and grabs my hands with his. He interlaces our fingers as he pins me down. His cock pummels into me again and again, each thrust more erratic than the last. We are losing control together, unraveling in this shared bed. His eyes and mine lock as we hold on for dear life. Stefan is tightening up, his dark eyes flashing. His cock spears into my fertile, gushing pussy until we're both gasping with pleasure.

"Jewel," he growls.

"Stefan," I whisper.

His cock slams into me a few more rapid times and then he pushes hard and deep. He holds still as his cock pumps spurt after spurt of thick, precious come inside me. I lock my legs around him to hold him there until I can squeeze out every drop. My cunny twinges with one last, helpless orgasm. Stefan's come mixes with mine as it slowly drips out of me.

He withdraws and gets into bed beside me. He pulls me close, into his lap. I rest my cheek against his strong chest while we breathe hard and slow, coming down from the incredible high we shared. Stefan strokes my hair and kisses the top of my head.

"I meant what I said," he murmurs. "I won't let anyone take you. Not now, not ever."

"I don't want to be with anyone else," I tell him honestly. "Stefan, I don't know if it's okay for me to say this, and I totally understand if you--"

"I love you, Jewel," Stefan breaks in stoically.

My cheeks flush pink and I look up at him with happy tears in my eyes. I giggle.

"You do? Oh, that's good. Because I love you, too," I ramble

He wipes away my tears and kisses me softly. He gazes into my eyes. He looks serious.

"It's not going to be easy, what we have to do," he says. "But we can do it together."

"I'm not afraid of anything, as long as you're with me," I insist.

We hold each other for a little while longer as the night deepens. I'm exhausted, especially now, and it's hard to keep my eyes open. I start to drift off, feeling satisfied, warm, and loved. I barely register when Stefan finally lets go of me and slides out of bed. As my eyes are falling shut, I hear him murmur something.

"I have to go make a call," he says.

There's an ominous note to his tone, but I'm too sleepy to question him. He walks out of the room and I collapse into deep, unbothered sleep.

CHAPTER 19

STEFAN

It is a dark, gloomy day as the car rumbles across the striking scenic views of the Brooklyn Bridge. The city of New York gleams like dark gems in the pelting rain. The sky is gray and filled with swarming clouds. The streets are packed with people carrying umbrellas of every shade, their faces and bodies shrouded underneath. Cars pack in tightly around us, sardining on the bridge to bottleneck into the city. I look over at Jewel. She's gazing blank-eyed out the windshield, and I can tell she's deep in thought. We left the cabin early, early this morning before dawn so that we could make it to the city by noon. That gives us plenty of time to set up and go where we're needed. As we roll off the bridge and into the zooming metropolis of Manhattan, I calmly captain the vehicle toward a rather nondescript hotel in Harlem.

"Are we almost to the hotel?" Jewel asks, glancing at me.

"Just another twenty minutes or so. It may not be the most luxurious stay, but it has the necessities," I tell her.

"Hopefully I won't be there long enough to need those necessities," she says pointedly.

I reach over and pat her leg gently. "Hopefully we can use them together tonight, once the job is done," I brighten. But she's still reticent.

"What if you don't come back?" she murmurs.

"I'll come back for you, Jewel. Do not worry about that," I affirm.

"Okay," she sighs. "Run it by me one more time. Please."

"You will wait at the hotel. I will go on foot across town to intercept the money exchange meeting between Victor Brusilov and the *pakhan*," I explain.

"Where's the meeting taking place again? Soul-something?" she tries to recall.

"Solyanka Sonya's," I clarify. "It's a hole-in-the-wall restaurant."

She frowns as we turn a corner. "How did you know about this meeting?"

"My personal contact in the brotherhood. Lev. He's an important man to know, because he knows everyone else. He has a good reputation, too. Men respect him. He's honest, but he understands nuance, which makes him the perfect liaison for this mission," I assure her.

"How do you know this guy?" she presses.

I smile. She's in true lawyer mode. "Lev and I have known each other for many years, *malyshka*. He's one of the first allies I made when we moved to America from the motherland. He has a strong relationship with the owners of Solyanka's-- Sonya and Pavel. He has done a lot of good work for them and the neighborhood, so their alliance is firm. Lev is also closely tied with the *pakhan*. He's made a name for himself as a big player who knows how to lay low, and the *pakhan* respects that," I go on. "Lev is the man I met up with on my supply run the other day. He's the one who gave me much-needed information."

Jewel whips around to look at me, both impressed and frustrated. "Well, I wish you had just told me all of this stuff back then, but at least I know now. If you trust this Lev guy, then I trust him, too. I just hope he doesn't betray us in front of the head hauncho. Speaking of which... who is this *pakhan*? What does that mean?" she asks.

"It's complicated, but there's a rigid hierarchy within the Bratva," I explain to her as we pull closer to the hotel. "Lev and I are *avtorityet*, or captains. We answer to Brusilov, who is our local chapter's *obshchak*. You can think of him as a money-holder."

"So he's like the big bad accountant?" Jewel remarks.

I snort. "More like a bookkeeper who protects the treasury by force," I answer. "He's the middleman, but he's also my superior. The *pakhan* is a cold, calculating, but fair man. He cares more for the big picture rather than the details. He's too big to get caught up in the petty corruption Victor and your father are running. He has plenty of subordinates like Brusilov and the *avtorityet* to do his dirty work."

"Well, if there's a strict hierarchy, you answer to Brusilov, and he answers to the *pakhan*, what makes you think he will listen to you against your own superior?" Jewel questions.

I drive up into the concrete parking garage underneath the hotel and start patrolling for a place to park. "The *pakhan* is a fair man. He values loyalty. I have proven myself a loyal servant, driven by competence and morality-- when I can make it fit. He sees all of that. Brusilov may see me as a liability, maybe even a threat. But the *pakhan* knows I am an asset."

I park the car and we step out once I make sure the coast is clear. I grab our bags and Jewel sticks close to my side as we make our way to the elevator. She clings to me while we get her checked into the room. It's a small suite, dimly lit and sparsely furnished in a minimalist style, and it has a view of the city. You can see the Brooklyn Bridge from here. Jewel sits on the edge of the bed looking nervous. I hand her a burner phone.

"Don't answer the phone or the door for anyone, not even room service or cleaning staff," I tell her. "This phone should only ring one time, from this number."

I scribble my burner's number on the hotel notepad on the desk, then turn back to Jewel. She looks so dainty and small and helpless on the edge of the bed, biting her lip and looking downright heartbroken that I'm leaving. I walk over and grab her hand. I pull her to her feet and lead her to the big, wide window overlooking the city. I point at a drab, dark building in the distance, mixed in among the shining towers and apartment high-rises.

"You see that building? That is where I'll be. If you get scared, if you feel alone, just remember I'm not so far away. Even when we're apart, we're together, *malyshka*," I encourage her gently.

Jewel's brown eyes shine with tears as she leans into me. I put an arm around her and kiss the soft crown of her head. "I'm so scared for you, Stefan," she murmurs.

"I know, *printsessa*. But I can do this. Trust me, I have embarked on much more difficult missions than this," I tell her. It's partly true. I've been through a lot, but this mission definitely has a different feel to it. This time, I'm on the right side.

I flash her the thick file of printed documents gleaned from Freddie Albany's computer, once I was able to initially crack the passcode. From there, it was too easy to steal his files and put together a stack of proof. I also carefully show her my concealed weapon, a short-range pistol. Her eyes go wide.

"Once the *pakhan* hears me out, he will side with me," I insist. "And if there's any trouble, I have my weapon ready for a fight."

"I hope it doesn't come to that," Jewel whimpers.

"If it does, I'll be prepared. I can do this, Jewel. I'll take care of this and we can move on to the next part of our plan. We won't have to dash from shadow to shadow anymore. We're getting closer to living in the sun, my love," I conclude.

She stands on tiptoes to kiss me on the lips. I kiss her passionately back. I hand her the car keys and she pockets them.

"If I'm not back within twenty-four hours, you take the car and you drive as far away as you can, okay?" I tell her.

She sniffles and nods. "Please come back."

I pat her cheek. "I will, my Jewel. Stay by the phone. Wait for my call."

I turn to leave and she walks me to the door. "I love you, Stefan!" she cries.

I give her one more kiss as I'm stepping out the door. "And I love you, *malyshka*."

Walking away from her is damn near impossible, but I force my feet to keep moving. I take the elevator down to the lobby and walk out into the drizzling rain. I put up my black hood as I walk to the bus station. My location is blocks and blocks away. I could walk, but I'd rather duck into public transportation for a little cover-- not from the rain, but from prying eyes. Like before, I know that every moment I spend in this city could be monitored. The Bratva has eyes all over New York, maybe even on these buses I ride. But unless the brotherhood is now hiring young single mothers and the elderly, it looks like today's bus crowd is harmless. Still, I keep my eyes peeled and my hand ready to reach for my pistol every step of the way. I take a bus, then walk a few blocks, then take another bus. On the second ride, I give Lev a call.

"*Zdraste*, comrade. Are you en route?" he asks immediately.

"*Da*. Arriving shortly. All in position?" I reply.

"Wolves in the den," Lev says. "Four deep, each pack. Hen is roosting in the back."

"Understood. Thank you, friend," I answer.

"*Udachi*," he says, meaning 'good luck.' He hangs up.

The bus squeals up to the stop. I quietly deboard and walk a couple more blocks, then turn down a familiar narrow alleyway off the main thoroughfare. Instead of taking the steps down to the front entrance, I go around to the brick wall at the back. I tap lightly on a rusty-looking door, and moments later, a grumpy woman's face pokes out. She scrutinizes my appearance for a second, then lets me in.

"Stefan," she mutters.

"Da, Sonya," I answer quietly.

She nods and starts shooing me through the kitchen. She brings me to the double doors that look out into the dimly-lit restaurant. I crouch down and peek through to take stock of the scene. As Lev implied, Brusilov and the *pakhan* are seated at the bar, with barkeep Pavel serving them drinks. There are four other men, seated at other tables in pairs. They look to the untrained eye like an unassociated group of restaurant patrons, but they're all here together. They are the modified, reduced-down entourage for Brusilov and the *pakhan*, respectively. No doubt they're all heavily armed and ready to leap into action.

There's a tenuous balance of power in the room I can almost taste. They're prepared for war, but they're trying to be civil. Lev tipped off the *pakhan* that I would be showing up today. His men will either remain neutral or possibly even come to my aid if needed. But I know Brusilov and his men won't take well to my intrusion. Sonya pokes my arm.

"Don't break anything," she hisses. "I can't afford to replace any more chairs."

I give the old woman a smile. "I will do my very best."

"*Da*. You'd better. No more bullet holes in my tables, either," she scolds as she hobbles off to tend the big bubbling pot of stew on the stove.

She leaves me to my own devices, and I decide it's time to break in and make my move. I take out the thick folder of evidence in one hand, and keep my other poised on my pistol. There's no telling how harsh the backlash will be, but I can't turn back. With one last romantic, aching thought of my precious Jewel, I burst through the double doors with a bang.

Instantly, the dominoes start falling. The *pakhan* and Brusilov look over at me-- the latter doing a double take. The *pakhan*'s face doesn't change at all except to give me the faintest smile and nod. Brusilov, on the other hand, looks downright apoplectic to see me here. He stands up and squares up, his hands balling into fists. His two men stand up at their table, too.

"Stefan, what are you doing here?" Brusilov demands.

"You are surprised to see me, Victor," I growl as I stalk over to the bar. "Perhaps you did not think I would make it this far."

"I don't know what you're talking about, *brat*, but you're interrupting a very important meeting. I have business to discuss with the *pakhan*. My men can show you out," Brusilov says in typical weaselly fashion.

There's no illusion about what he means. His men would not simply 'show me out' but probably capture me, if not just kill me outright. To let them take me would be an act of suicide. I stand strong. The *pakhan* remains seated, his long fingers steepled together in front of him.

"Sit, Victor. Let us hear what our comrade has to say," he commands in a gruff, smoky voice. He waves his hand, and Brusilov sits back down reluctantly.

Favor is tipping in my direction, and I'm going to ride it out. I pull out the thick packet of printed evidence and drop it on the counter in front of the *pakhan*. Brusilov is shooting daggers at me with his eyes as the *pakhan* flips through the papers.

"You bring me evidence. Tell me in your own words," the *pakhan* instructs.

"Evidence of what?" Victor snarls.

I glare at Brusilov as he fumes on his bar stool.

"Our very own Victor Brusilov has involved himself with an ICE agent by the name of Freddie Albany to pursue corruption and destruction within our ranks," I declare. "He and Mr. Albany conspired to embezzle funds, imprison the innocent, and kill anyone who would stand in their way."

"How dare you speak of me like this?" Victor spits furiously.

The *pakhan* raises one hand to quiet him. "Go on, Stefan."

"He put a bounty on my head in what I believe was an unsanctioned order of execution. And he further failed when he lost the captive, Freddie's daughter," I list off.

Brusilov bangs his fist on the counter. "I won't listen to this slander! The girl is not lost. She's dead. By your own bloody hands, Stefan!"

The *pakhan* lifts an eyebrow at me and I shake my head.

"No," I reply with a smirk. "She's alive."

Victor's face falls. He snaps his fingers. "Liar! Honorable *pakhan*, you must stop this man from embarrassing himself and the organization further."

I take out my burner phone and dial a number, putting it on speaker phone as it rings. Everyone listens with rapt attention as I hold up the phone and the line clicks. The sweetest voice fills the air.

"Hello? Stefan?" Jewel says.

"I'm here, Jewel," I answer, still holding up the phone. "Say hello to our friends."

"Oh, um, hi there," she says awkwardly.

"Are you alive?" I ask her, half-joking.

"Well, yeah. Of course. What's going on, Stefan? Are you alright?" she asks.

The *pakhan* smiles broadly and nods.

I say into the phone, "Yes. I'm just fine. Hang tight."

I hang up the phone, knowing Jewel is probably

panicking in her hotel room trying to figure out exactly what happened. But right now, I'm more focused on the *pakhan*. Brusilov is sweating like a pig, his eyes bulging out of his ugly head as he realizes his evil plans are falling apart faster than he can mend them.

"Honorable friend, surely you won't take this-- this pawn's side over mine?" Victor appeals nervously. His two men are slowly standing to their feet. I keep an eye on them and my hand on my pistol.

"Stefan is a loyal servant and a skilled asset to the brotherhood," the *pakhan* announces. "I never sanctioned his execution, nor the execution of the girl. There is enough evidence here to damn you to hell, Victor, but only the devil can take you there."

"You two dare to turn on me?" Brusilov snarls. "I am *obshchak*! I have power here!"

"Go quietly or go to tell, Victor," I growl.

He looks back and forth between us, totally stunned to be caught with his pants down. I give Pavel behind the bar a quick glance, and several things happen all at once. Pavel ducks down behind the bar counter. Victor whips out a knife big enough to decapitate a grown man and lunges for me, causing his two men to take out their guns.

Victor's hand wraps around my throat and the other rears back, lifting the gigantic knife up in the air. I see it gleam in the brassy lighting before he brings it down, swinging right at my chest. In a split second, I knee him in the gut to break his swing, and while he's momentarily winded, I fling my head forward to headbutt him-- hard. Victor yelps in pain and collapses to the floor while his two men pounce after me with their guns pulled. One of them takes partial cover behind the table while he closes one eye and aims his gun at me. The other runs up and tries to pistol-whip me, but I dodge out of the way fast enough. In his hurry to catch up, the guard trips over Brusilov and clatters to the floor beside his boss.

The third man fires one shot that glances over my shoulder and strikes a beer glass hanging to dry. It shatters into a thousand tiny shards. Not one to waste a weapon when it appears, I grab for the broken glass. Even as I feel a sharp edge of it slice my palm, I grip it tightly and swing my arm around just in time to smash the prickly, sharp glass into the first guard's face as he stands up. He bellows in agony and falls to the floor, clutching his bloody face. Brusilov is struggling to get up as I push past them to go after the gunner. He looks petrified to see me coming after him, and he ducks down behind the table again.

By now, the *pakhan*'s entourage have leaped into action to protect him. They surround the *pakhan* and form a human shield, their own guns raised and pointed at the others.

Certain that he's safe, I focus wholly on neutralizing our enemies. When the man with a bloody face staggers to his feet to inaccurately point his gun at me, I can tell he's blinded with blood in his eyes. He tries to fire off another shot, but the gun malfunctions and slips from his wet hands. I hurriedly kick it away behind the bar counter and lunge after the guy. I quickly take care of the problem by putting my hands around the man's throat. I throttle him until he's blue in the face, then I cleanly twist his neck. He drops to the floor and I move on to the first gunner, hiding behind the table. He pops up again to point his gun, but his arm is shaking and the aim is way off. I grab his arm and twist it behind his back, forcing him to drop the gun. I kick it back to the bar with the other one.

"You'll pay for this!" the man shrieks. His free hand smacks at my face. He's feeling around, trying to gouge my eyes out. But I swiftly get control of both arms and summon all my brute strength to fling the man into the far wall. He hits the brick wall hard and falls to the ground in a still heap. I turn around just in time to see Victor, the true villain, eyeing me fiercely.

Brusilov makes another running jab at me, but I jump to block his hit. The big knife slashes my forearm and a spurt of scarlet blood sprays out. But the adrenaline won't let me feel any pain. Instead, I grab Brusilov's arms in mine and overpower him with my superior strength. I curl his arms back over his head until he's screeching for mercy. I push him backward and he stumbles, only to rally and run right back at me with his knife up. In a split second, I decide there's only one way to end it.

As he's running at me, his beady eyes wild with fury, I shove a chair directly at him and he goes tumbling head-first over it. He lets out a spine-chilling scream as he falls face-forward onto his own long, pointed blade. The knife juts right into his abdomen, where it sticks like a dagger. Blood gurgles from his mouth and his eyes bulge from his face as he takes his last shuddering breaths and collapses in a growing pool of his own blood.

Pavel slowly rises up from behind the bar, looking tired and pale. Sonya peeks out from the kitchen, shaking her head with disapproval at the mess. The guards around the *pakhan* ease up, giving me access to the older, distin-guished man.

"Three kills, no gunfire," the *pakhan* notes, sounding

impressed but unbothered by the carnage all around us. He's seen worse.

"Sonya said no more bullet holes," I growl back, tucking my pistol away.

The *pakhan* rises and shakes my hand. "You have done good work, Stefan. I sincerely thank you for exposing Victor's corruption. I owe you a favor."

I nod, wipe the blood off my hands with a napkin, and growl, "You know what I want."

CHAPTER 20

JEWEL

I stand at the big hotel window gazing out across the vast metropolis of New York City. Even though the sky is a velvety dark blue, there's not a star to see. The city below is lit up with a fuzzy halo of neon glow. Signs flash, traffic lights change from green to gold to red. My stomach is twisting into knots. I'm shaky all over thinking about what we're going to do tonight.

Stefan stands just behind me with his strong arms draped around me. His warm breath tickles my neck as he leans in to kiss my cheek.

"You can do this, Jewel," he assures me.

I nod slowly, in a daze. "Sure. Yeah. I can handle it."

"Remember that you are not alone. We're not in the dark anymore. The *pakhan* is on our side, and he has connections your father doesn't even know about. And of course, I will be right there to jump in if anything happens," he says.

"Run it by me one more time?" I ask for the fiftieth time tonight.

Stefan is patient as ever. "I used Victor Brusilov's cell phone to set up a meeting with your father at an abandoned shipping warehouse on the edge of town. He thinks he's meeting Brusilov, and I made him swear he would arrive alone and unarmed. He wants to discuss how to proceed with the prisoner at the black site."

"But instead of Brusilov, he'll meet me," I mumble.

"Exactly. You can confront him, give him one last chance to repent and repair the immeasurable damage he has done before he goes to prison," Stefan explains. "The *pakhan* has payroll cops on standby to sweep in and detain him for arrest at my word. I will secure the scene until they arrive, and then you and I will get out of dodge."

"Okay," I sigh. "Let's go. I want to have time to... get ready."

"You're right. Let's get going," Stefan says. "We'll put an end to this once and for all."

My heart is aching the whole ride across town to the shipping warehouse. I can't believe my tumultuous, unhappy relationship with my dad is going to end this way. It was always just the two of us, and now I'm going to betray him. I try to remind myself that he hurt me far more than I could ever hurt him, and that he tried to do much worse. But it's hard. I still feel the crushing guilt on my shoulders. Stefan senses my anxiety and reaches over to squeeze my hand. I feel my tension ease up just a little. I look out the window and watch the city get smaller and less shiny as we move closer to our destination.

On arrival, I have to admit this is a perfect meeting place. Clearly, nobody has been out here to upkeep the place in a long time. The warehouse is rundown, the shipyard outside a total disaster of old broken machinery, shattered glass, and moldy ropes. Stefan easily breaks the shoddy lock on the door, and we step into the huge, musty old warehouse. There are cobwebs and thick dust lining every surface. I see shelves and shelves of rusted metal pieces, probably tools and hardware for whatever company used to exist here. The place is perfectly dark except for the wide shafts of moonlight beaming in through two huge, high-up windows. Stefan leads me to take my spot just a few feet back from one of the moonlit spotlights, so I'm still hidden. He takes my shoulders in his hands and peers into my eyes.

"How do you feel?" he asks.

"Honestly, like I'm gonna throw up," I answer.

He pulls me in for a tight hug and kisses the top of my head.

"You've got this, Jewel. Confront him. Say what you need to say. You don't have to do anything but talk and keep him distracted while I tip off the backup crew," Stefan recounts. "I'll be right over there out of sight. He won't know I'm here. All he'll see is you. It'll be a surprise for him, but I don't predict that he'll turn violent. Not immediately, at least."

"I thought he was supposed to show up unarmed," I mutter nervously.

Stefan nods. "He told Brusilov-- or who he thought was Brusilov-- that he would abide by that rule. And if he thinks he's meeting an ally, he'll have his guard down."

"What if he does freak out? I mean, he thinks I'm dead," I point out.

"Then I'll be here to protect you. I won't let him touch you, Jewel. I will never allow any man to lay a finger on you without your consent," Stefan promises me fiercely.

I take a deep breath. "Okay," I mumble. "I can do it."

We hear the soft, muffled rev of an engine and the crunch of tires over shattered glass outside. My heart leaps up into my throat. Stefan looks at me hard and mouths, *I love you.*

I mouth the words back to him and he gives me one last hug before he retreats into the deep shadows between shelves, probably twenty feet back and to my left. I'm petrified down to my core, standing here in this dirty building on the outskirts of town, waiting for my own treacherous father to show up. It's scary enough to play bait for a dangerous man, but there's an added level of stress because he raised me. Or at least, he hired a bunch of nannies to raise me. He has spent my whole life finding ways to avoid spending time with me. I'm sure it's a load off his shoulders to think I'm dead. But tonight, finally, he has to confront me. He has to face me. He has to look his own daughter in the eyes and confess his sins.

I only hope I'm strong enough to stand up to him.

The car sounds stop. I hear footsteps approaching, then the creak of the door opening. I swallow hard and stand my ground in the darkness as my father comes strolling into the warehouse. I feel a rush of conflicting emotions. On the one hand, he's wearing a dark blue suit that awakens childhood memories in my head of watching him board a plane from the tarmac. On the other hand, I remind myself how many times I *had* to do that: watch him leave, with little more than a joyless wave goodbye. He's as tall and rotund as I remember, with a perpetually wrinkled nose and downturned mouth. He looks around the warehouse with disgust, taking cautious strides in his shiny patent loafers.

"Victor!" he calls out in his familiar booming, brash voice. "Where the hell are we? You couldn't have picked a nicer meeting place?"

He gets no response. I stand in silence, shrouded in darkness, shaking from head to toe as my father's imposing frame moves closer and closer. He groans with frustration and checks his expensive wristwatch. He throws up his hands and steps into the first shaft of light.

"Come on, man. Don't keep me waiting," Dad calls out. "We have a lot to discuss."

He blinks around in the bright light, getting annoyed at the silence.

"Victor, I don't have all night. If you wanted to make a businessman wait, you should've picked a nice hotel bar or something. This filthy place is beneath men like us," he complains.

"Actually, Dad, I think it's just dirty enough to suit you perfectly," I interject.

"Jesus, fuck!" he swears in shock.

I step out into the second shaft of light and his eyes go wide. His jaw drops and he gapes openly at me. I fold my arms over my chest and feel that long-buried rage bubble up inside of me. Suddenly, my anger overrides my fear.

"What's the matter, Dad? You look like you've seen a ghost," I quip sarcastically. "But that makes sense, considering you thought you had me killed."

He gawks at me, shaking his head slowly like he can't believe his eyes.

"Jewel. My daughter. I-I can't believe you're alive! I've been worried sick since you went missing. I've been looking everywhere for you," he says, waggling his finger at me.

I narrow my eyes at him. "Come on, Dad. I know you don't value me very much, but even you should know I'm not that stupid."

He stands up straight and glares at me, all pretenses of fatherly love gone in an instant. He's terrifying and cold. I feel the same old lurch of nausea I always felt in his presence growing up. I'm a grown woman now, and yet he can still make me feel so small. But I remind myself that I'm not alone-- Stefan is just several yards behind me, hiding in the shelves with his gun aimed at Freddie. One false move, and Stefan will take him down.

I see the cogs turning in my father's cruel mind. He frowns at me in that disapproving, stomach-churning way he always does. He points an accusing finger at me.

"You turned on me! You weren't kidnapped by the mafia, you've been working with them all along, haven't you?" he hurls at me.

"No point lying to me anymore, I know everything," I retort.

"You ungrateful little bitch, scheming to get even more of my hard-earned money. I should've known my sister's weak-minded, stubborn little brat would turn against me one day!" he spits furiously.

I feel my whole body go rigid. His words pierce me like a bevy of needles.

He smirks cruelly at me. "Oh, that's right-- you know everything, hmm? You think you've got it all figured out. You thought you'd trick me, huh? You don't even know yourself, Jewel. I did my best; I tried to raise you right. But your mother's faulty genes must have taken over. You were always too weak, too slow, too soft. I couldn't have that, not in my family. You have to find that weakness in your breeding stock and eliminate it."

There's that word again. *Eliminate.*

"My mother? Your sister?" I repeat, my voice shaking as the truth dawns on me. "I thought my aunt-- my mother-- died in an accident."

"Accidents happen, of course. But sometimes you have to give them a little push," Freddie cackles. "I have the strength of will to make things happen."

I feel so cold and dizzy. I'm speechless. He goes on.

"That's right. You've embarrassed and dishonored me, but at the end of the day, I don't have to claim you as my own. I thought I could teach you to be obedient and strong, but you're too much like your bitch of a mother," he snarls. "Yes, I did order your execution. My only regret is not doing it years ago when it became clear you were going to be worthless to me as an asset."

"You never loved me. You never even liked me," I mutter breathlessly. I bite back tears. I'll be damned if I let this scumbag see me cry at his words.

He takes a few aggressive steps toward me, grinning like a wolf.

"And now I don't have to pretend to anymore," he snaps. "Don't worry, Jewel. You'll be back with your mother very soon."

He pulls a dark item from his waistcoat and it catches the moonlight as he points it in my direction. I realize it's a gun as he closes one eye to take aim. I'm frozen in place, stunned to see the man who raised me ready himself for a kill shot.

The next thing I know, a loud crack splits the air. I scream and duck down, assuming the bullet is coming to me. But instead, I watch as the first shot rips straight through Freddie's extended forearm, forcing him to drop his weapon and clutch his bloody arm to his chest with an agonized cry. He looks up at me with pure hatred in his beady eyes. He puts his head down and barrels toward me like an enraged bull.

I jump back and squeal with fear as two more shots are fired. Freddie crumples to the ground as the bullets strike one knee, then the other. He lets out a horrible bray of pain and fury as he curls into the fetal position on the ground. His one free arm swings out to try and grab his gun, lying just inches from his fingertips. But Stefan comes darting out of the darkness to kick the gun far away into the shadows. He looks down at my former father, writhing and screaming on the ground, with a scathing look on his handsome face.

"Don't kill me! She's a liar! Don't listen to her, I can give you money!" Freddie screeches. Stefan kicks him hard in the ribs, knocking the wind out of him. He spits in Freddie's contorted face.

"I'm not going to kill you tonight, Mr. Albany, but don't count your lucky stars just yet. You will never harm another living soul again. Your days are numbered, you slimy bastard. You and your rat will make great cellmates in prison," Stefan threatens him ferociously.

Only a moment later, the door bursts open and a team of police officers in all-black tactical gear come rushing into the warehouse. They shout instructions and draw their weapons as they close in on Freddie's cowering body. He puts up both blood-soaked hands in surrender as they make quick work of him. Stefan hurries back to wrap his arms around me and hold me tight while the payroll crew drag Freddie out of the warehouse, moaning and screeching.

"Jewel! Don't let them do this to me! Your own father!" he bellows as they pull him away. "Show me some mercy!"

But I hold my tongue. I stand strong and resolute, with Stefan behind me, as I watch my father get arrested and taken into custody. As he disappears out the creaky, rusted warehouse door, I hear his tortured cries get farther away. I turn and bury my face in Stefan's chest. He holds me while I softly weep in his arms. I know that's the last I'll be seeing of my so-called father-- the man who killed my mother and tried to kill me, too. I won't be visiting him in prison, and he won't last long there anyway. The Bratva won't allow the likes of Freddie Albany to ever roam the streets again. He's been exposed for his cruelty and corruption, and it's only a matter of time before they have him killed in a prison yard, along with his informant. Maybe I should feel bad for him. Maybe I should feel pity. But instead, I just feel relieved.

The man who made my life a living hell is gone, soon to be dead.

And the man who brought me back to life is here, still standing, right beside me at this darkest hour. When I look up into his dark eyes, I know I'm right where I need to be. Come what may, we will face it together.

Finally, we are free.

CHAPTER 21

JEWEL

SIX MONTHS LATER

The sun shines warmly on my face as I lie back on the bed. Birds chirp and sing outside in the trees. The trees are showing new green on the branches. Our snow-dried yard is starting to sprout again, and it seems like every day now we find more flowers blooming on our walks through the forest. The optimism of springtime is bright in the air. Our little corner of the mountain is coming back to vivid, colorful life.

Stefan climbs into bed with me, the golden light streaming across his chiseled features. I reach up to pull him down to me and our lips crash together in a passionate, joyful kiss. I smile against his lips as his hands brush back my silky dark hair, now grown out a couple inches past my shoulders. My strong, powerful man straddles me, but he's careful not to crush me. It's not that I can't handle him, but now that I'm four months pregnant with his precious baby, Stefan is extra cautious when it comes to my body.

I always thought it would be so daunting to be pregnant, but Stefan makes it easy. He treats me like a queen, so reverent and respectful of my changing form. He comforts me though every ache and pain. He kisses me and whispers me to sleep when the insomnia kicks in. He brings me healthy breakfast, lunch, dinner, snacks-- in bed or wherever I am. Stefan dotes on me like nobody ever has before. I didn't realize how alone I felt all my life, with only my cruel, uncaring 'father' to keep me company. But Stefan erases a little more of that pain away every single day. I fall asleep listening to his low, growly voice or his rhythmic, steady breathing. I wake up in the morning to his handsome face or a soft kiss on the lips. I have never felt so loved.

Every moment we get to spend together is cherished to the maximum, especially now that my law school classes at Harvard have picked back up. During the week, I attend those classes and focus hard on being the best student I can be. I take notes, I study in the library, I make endless flash cards. After the whole debacle with Gina's car (which we did accidentally steal for over a week), I expected not to have much of a friend group left to speak of. Luckily, Gina's wealthy parents bought her a new, sleek SUV mere days after we disappeared with her old white car. I was worried about the rumor mill on campus, too-- after all, I was sure something of my bizarre story would've made it to the university circles. But the Bratva did a remarkable job of scrubbing the scenes clean. Nobody knows how to clean up after themselves like the mafia. Stefan told me that Lev and the *pakhan* did a lot of behind-the-scenes work to keep my own reputation clean of all the blood and guts we've encountered at the hands of my father and his co-conspirators. Nobody has breathed a word about it to me, and I've been able to blend back in on campus with no problem.

Well, except for my pregnant belly. I've just recently started to show, and everyone is dying to know who the father is. I'll let some of my friends meet Stefan one day, but for now, I enjoy keeping the secret. We don't have to hide any longer, but we love feeling like it's just the two of us in our own little world.

While I'm highlighting and taking notes in the library during the weekdays, Stefan is out here at the cabin in Maine. After risking his life to expose Brusilov and my late 'father' for corruption in the mafia, the *pakhan* put in a good word for Stefan. He was able to do something few people can ever claim: he got to leave the Bratva. He's finished with that life of crime, blood, and paranoia. It's good to know there are still good guys like Lev out there, trying to guide the brotherhood in the right direction, but I'm glad Stefan is a civilian now.

Finally, he gets to enjoy the peace and bliss of a normal life. He supports my career completely, whether I choose to be a stay-at-home-mom (at least for a while) or jump right into the world of practicing law. I could do a lot of good in this world, and Stefan is proud to help me achieve it. But he keeps himself very busy, as well. He spends all his time here now, working on the cabin and around the property to transform it into a functional, nearly self-suffi-cient homestead. It's going to be our family home, the place where we will build beautiful memories together. We will raise our family there, teaching our children how to grow things and take care of the earth and each other.

I can't wait for us to meet our child and find out what she's like. I make myself get all teary-eyed with happiness imagining Stefan and our future toddler wobbling around in the yard out front while I watch from the porch with a cup of tea. Until the baby is born, though, we spend our time together making love and just basking in each other's presence. It's hard to be apart sometimes: me in our Massachusetts apartment and Stefan here at the Maine cabin. But we talk on the phone and video chat constantly when I'm away, only building more excitement and anticipation for the weekend, when we get to be together again.

Today, it's a gorgeous sunny Saturday morning, and we have been making love all night. Stefan and I are so in love, so obsessed with exploring one another's bodies. He discovers new ways to thrill me and make my toes curl every day. It's like my body comes to life when he touches me, and I've never known a feeling like this. I never understood how love could make my heart race and my soul feel calm at the same time, but that's what Stefan does for me. I am so excited for our future together, and for once in my life, I'm not afraid of anything. Law school is tough. Homesteading isn't easy. Raising a child is no walk in the park. But with Stefan as my beloved partner, I can conquer anything.

Stefan kisses me on the forehead and lays a gentle hand on my growing stomach.

"What are we going to do today?" I ask him brightly.

"Well, I'm sure you're still tired after last night," he starts out, and I nod vigorously in agreement. He chuckles, "So I was thinking I would bring you tea and breakfast in bed, then I'll give you a massage and a long, hot bath. After that, we can take a walk through the woods and forage some plants to add to tonight's menu. Then we can just relax, play it by ear, see what happens. I gave you a little taste last night, but I'm not done with you yet, *printsessa.*"

He gives me a seductive look that melts me inside. I grin up at him.

"You spoil me, Stefan," I murmur happily.

"You deserve all the pampering. My Jewel is having a little gem," Stefan croons in that gravelly voice that makes my heart flutter so much.

"I'm so happy to be back here with you. This cabin was our first taste of freedom, and now you're turning it into our dream home," I sigh blissfully. "How could I be so lucky?"

"It's not just luck, *malyshka.* It's fate. We were meant to find each other, and we did. It took the adventure of a lifetime to get here, but I am so happy," he says.

"Me too," I gush.

"When I was a soldier for the Bratva, getting my hands dirty and always looking over my shoulder, I couldn't imagine a life like this. Not for me, only for someone else. But now, I can see that I deserved this all along. And so do you, my Jewel. We fought hard to win our happiness, and nobody will ever take this away from us," he affirms.

"I love you, Stefan," I murmur adoringly.

He holds me tight and whispers in my ear, "I love you, too, *malyshka.*"

Stefan softly rubs my pregnant belly while we listen to the breeze rustle through the windchimes outside. We whisper about the exciting days to come, about all the places we will go and sights we will see. Nothing is off-limits to us anymore; the world is our oyster. It feels so damn good to belong to Stefan, and I am eternally grateful that he is mine. The future looks so bright for us, and there is so much we still have left to do. But for now, there is nothing closer to paradise than lying in the sun with my sweetheart, wrapped up in warm, luminescent love.

294

THANK YOU FOR READING! You may sign up for my newsletter to be notified when I have a new release on the way.

https://alexisabbott.com/newsletter

~Alexis Abbott

Connect with Alexis

Get an EXCLUSIVE book, **FREE** just as a thank you for signing up for my newsletter! Plus you'll never miss a new release, cover reveal, or promotion!

http://alexisabbott.com/newsletter

facebook.com/abbottauthor

twitter.com/abbottauthor

instagram.com/alexisabbottauthor

amazon.com/Alexis-Abbott/e/B013YL5290

bookbub.com/authors/alexis-abbott

pinterest.com/badboyromance

youtube.com/@AlexisAbbott

patreon.com/alexisabbott

ALSO BY ALEXIS ABBOTT

HEARTBREAKERS MC

Breaker

Bones

Ironside

Big Daddy

HITMEN SERIES

Owned by the Hitman

Sold to the Hitman

Captive of the Hitman

Saved by the Hitman

Stolen from the Hitman

Hostage of the Hitman

Taken by the Hitman

The Hitman's Masquerade (Short Story)

HOSTAGES

Trafficked

Stealing Her

The Assassin's Heart

Killing For Her

Abducted

Stolen Jewel

Possessive

THE KILLER TRILOGY

Book 1: Killer for Hire

Book 2: Killer Desire

Book 3: Killer on Fire

KILLERS

Hunter's Baby

I Hired A Hitman

SEALs

Sights on the SEAL

Sweetheart for the SEAL

SIN CITY

Vegas Boss

Betting on Love

STEPBROTHERS

Criminal

Ruthless

OTHER

Rock Hard Bodyguard

Innocence For Sale: Jane

Bound as the World Burns

Redeeming Viktor

About the Author

Alexis Abbott is a Wall Street Journal & USA Today best-selling author who writes about dangerous men and the women who love them. If you can't resist a bad boy who is a good man, you just found your next addiction. With heart-stopping action, mouth watering sex, and passionate romances that will leave you breathless, Alexis Abbott writes romantic thrillers like no one else can.

When she's not writing your next book boyfriend, you'll find her living a real life romance novel with her own bad boy soulmate in Bonavista, NL, Canada.

facebook.com/abbottauthor

twitter.com/abbottauthor

instagram.com/alexisabbottauthor

amazon.com/Alexis-Abbott/e/B013YL5290

bookbub.com/authors/alexis-abbott

pinterest.com/badboyromance

youtube.com/@AlexisAbbott

patreon.com/alexisabbott

Acknowledgments

Thank you to my amazing Patrons. I'm constantly humbled and grateful for your support.

Ramona Cabrera
Melissa Hedrick
Virginia Swanson
Dawn Daughenbaugh
Don Doss
Stacie Currie

If you'd like to join them — and get my ebooks or paperbacks — you can find me here on Patreon.
https://alexisabbott.com/Patreon